**VAL]**

**Kit E**

CW00433377

1

For Marie, with love.

# Chapter 1

The dashboard clock winked over to 02:32.

Max peered through the rain gushing along the windscreen wipers then slowed to a crawl. No one else was on the bypass, but the cab juddered as puddles slapped along the wings and she clenched the steering wheel to keep the car from shuddering. It'd take another twenty minutes to get to the General like this – if she made it at all.

Flashing hazards off towards the nature reserve caught her eye. The cab drifted across to the central reservation as she craned her neck to see into the car park. A fancy interior, lit up like a lighthouse, was glittering while the rain sheeted down. Max strained her eyes until they picked out a figure bent over near the bonnet, coat and hair billowing out in the wind.

Knowing it was a woman back there made her ease off the accelerator when she came to the break in the carriageway a quarter of a mile further up. She squealed around in a U-turn and veered into the nature reserve's car park. The cab crunched over the gravel, stopping in the middle of sodden weeds glistening under the headlights of the two cars. No woman in sight.

Max rolled down the window, rain spraying into her face.

'Hello?' she called.

Nothing. Just the sound of water hammering against metal and the clinking of hazard lights. She clicked her seatbelt loose then tugged her collar up before she lurched out into the downpour. Not that it made a blind bit of difference – rain slithered along her throat and dribbled into her shirt the second her head was exposed.

'Hello? Look, I'm not after anything. I just wanna help, yeah?'

Still nothing.

Maybe it was a trap. Some of the lads had been done over by damsels in distress in the past. Drew had even ended up at the General when some pretty redhead nabbed the takings and shut his hand in the cab door. He'd bleated about it for weeks, yammering on about how it was the worst pain in his life and she ought to try it. Only when she'd threatened to do the same to the other hand had he shut up.

'Hello?' Max shouted again.

She reeled when a stumpy jack handle loomed out of the shadows, jerking out of the way and catching her heel on a lump of something. Her spine cracked against the pebbles and she rolled onto her hip, automatically shielding her face from whatever was coming next.

Then the jack handle clanked to the ground and a hand grappled for hers.

'I'm so sorry.'

Max blinked at the voice, smooth as a pint of Guinness. She gave in to the fingers coiled around her wrist and clambered up to her feet, water slopping into her shirt. The woman didn't let her go, almost drawing her closer, though Max still couldn't see anything apart from her outline. Diluted perfume mingled with the rain and tingled on her tongue as the woman edged into the light and the image sharpened.

Petite, blonde hair drizzling rain into the hollow of her translucent blouse. Max's eyes followed the trim down until words whirled around with the incessant clicking of the hazards.

'Are you all right? I thought you might be a murderer or something. I broke down about an hour ago – I'm on my way back from a meeting – and I dropped my phone in a puddle and I couldn't . . . I'm sorry, did you hit your head?'

Mascara was trickling from her nose, dribbling across her plump lower lip and dripping down her throat. Max was transfixed by it then the question filtered through and jolted her back into the soggy car park. Her jeans were waterlogged, lugging towards her flooded trainers. She shifted and tugged her arm away to shield her eyes against the rain.

'Tyre, is it?' she asked.

'Yes, I can't get the jack to move anything. It just keeps slipping out of my hand.'

'This thing would.' Max crouched to pick it up. 'I've got a proper one in the boot.'

'Thank you, I'd – I'd appreciate that.'

It only took a minute to get it, but it was enough for Max to give up on keeping anything dry. She rolled up her sleeves and bent down to lodge the jack handle over one of the wheel nuts. She strained to the left then growled when it didn't shift. Once she'd tightened her grip, she put her back into it as the woman hovered above.

'What's your name?'

She switched position, pushing instead of pulling. 'Max.'

'Well, I'm Valerie Smythe. You know, I'd say it's good to meet you, but I'm sure you're cursing me right about now.'

'Not really.' Her fingers skimmed along the jack handle and she swore. Then she blew rain from her lips and adjusted her weight. 'Sorry, that wasn't at you.'

'No, I know.' Valerie paused. 'Forgive me, Max, are you all right?'

More pressure and the handle groaned and gave way. Instead of twisting the nut around, she'd crushed it in on itself. She jumped up and kicked the tyre then scrubbed her face with her arm. Before the pain faded from her toes, she booted it again and again.

A hand on her bicep worked like a tranquiliser dart. She stopped with her foot aloft and lowered it to the ground, tasting that perfume again in the rain. She let the hand steer her into the rear seat of the BMW, squinting against the dazzling ceiling lights.

'The car . . .'

'Is due for a valet,' Valerie answered as she slipped in beside her. 'I'm so annoyed with it right this minute, it might end up in the crusher.'

Max tried to smile, but her face wouldn't stretch that way. 'Some white knight I am. Usually, I could change a tyre with my eyes closed.'

'So, what's different?'

She shrugged and water drizzled between her shoulder blades.

'You're a taxi driver,' continued Valerie. 'Were you out on a fare at this time of night?'

'No.' Max sniffed then cleared the rain from her throat. 'You a customer? Feel like I recognise you.'

'Not to my knowledge. You might've seen me in the paper or something. I'm standing for election next year.'

'Really? That's . . . way above my head.'

'I don't believe that.' Valerie stretched slender fingers onto her wrist, warm despite the weather. 'Come on, tell me what's wrong. I tried to decapitate you not ten minutes ago, I think you get a free ear.'

A flush crept onto Max's face, burning more when Valerie's tongue flicked out over her lips. She shivered and clumped her knees together.

'I'm fine,' she said.

'Pardon my saying it, but you don't look fine. Listen, you stopped when you didn't have –'

'And made it worse,' she interrupted then she clenched her jaw. 'Damn it. I haven't even got my phone. I left it on the side before I . . .'

Valerie's palm settled on her bare forearm when she trailed off. 'You're still here, you still tried. I'd be worse off if you hadn't – I'd be alone. So, let me help with whatever's bothering you. Look, I'm exceptional at keeping secrets. I want to be a politician, after all.'

Max's chuckle bubbled up before she could stop it. Once she met Valerie's eye, she couldn't help the words spilling out.

'I shouldn't have stopped. I'm meant to be at the hospital right this minute. My business partner – my mate's – girlfriend lost her baby. Well, I say lost but . . . She was six months gone. They're making her go through it all. Drew called me in bits, asked me to get down there.'

'Now I'm even more grateful you stopped.'

'Don't be,' Max muttered.

Valerie exhaled. 'Oh, I see. Still, there's no shame in wanting to avoid something like that. They don't have a choice but to endure it – you do.'

'Doesn't make it right, me sitting here.'

'Then I'll come with you,' Valerie replied.

'Hang on, you just said –'

'One good turn deserves another. This is either a colossal coincidence or the universe trying to tell us something. I'm in dire need of help and you appear. You need assistance, here I am. It's irresistible as far as I'm concerned. Besides, I was about to cadge a lift to civilisation anyway. What's wrong with extending the journey a little further, hmm?'

Max rubbed her neck with her free hand. 'Are you sure? I wouldn't want –'

'Trust me,' Valerie interrupted. 'I always know what I'm doing.'

The rain wasn't letting up and the further they drove the more Max noticed how her jeans clung to her like leeches. She'd be walking into the hospital like Frankenstein's monster, as dignified as a bloody Jack-in-a-Box. Mind you, she wasn't the only one who looked a state.

She glanced to the passenger side. 'Can I suggest something?'

'By all means.' Valerie shifted, reclining further into the seat. 'Oh, this is wonderful after an hour in that car park, absolute luxury. Suggest anything, I'm completely at your disposal.'

'There's a box of wipes, that's all. In the glovebox. For your face, I mean. You've got a bit of . . .'

'My face?' Valerie yanked down the visor and giggled. 'Well, I'd certainly know if I walked into a hospital looking like this. Thank you.'

Max said nothing, just focused on driving safe while Valerie cleaned herself up as best she could in a damp cab with only streetlight streaks to help her. It wasn't far to the hospital, even though the car sloshed along the side streets once they pulled off the dual carriageway. The car park was swamped, crisp packets bobbing in the puddles like a raft of headless ducks. Max steered through standing water into the nearest space that wasn't doubling as a swimming pool then unbuckled her seatbelt.

'I'll find a payphone when we get inside, call one of the lads to come and get you. Free of charge, yeah?'

Valerie stretched for the door handle. 'Let's see how your friend is first.'

Water slopped around their shoes as they rushed across the saturated tarmac. Max tugged her jacket off and held it above their heads, more over Valerie's than hers.

'Don't suppose you know where the maternity unit is?' she asked.

'Top floor. Carless Wing. This way.'

Max slid over a kerbstone, nearly going headfirst into the verge. 'How the hell do you know that?'

'Three reasons. One, I've been here before for party visits with the Shadow Health Minister. Two, I work in the care sector so appointments aren't exactly uncommon for me.'

'Okay, what about number three?'

Valerie tilted the jacket to cover them both. 'It was on the sign as we came through the gates.'

Max snorted and kept pace with her. They worked their way round the puddles until they reached the gleaming foyer, trampling in enough rain between them to coat the floor with a slick layer of grime. Max scraped the water

10

from her hair and shook her jacket out while Valerie just fluttered her suit sleeves towards the floor.

'We'll need to take the lift,' she said.

They made a few false turns upstairs then hit the maternity ward and a locked door. Valerie jabbed at the buzzer, getting them access into what looked like a chicken coop with cockeyed aqua splodges on the wall. A gaunt nurse was waiting for them, more asleep than not.

'Can I help?' she queried.

'We've been called to attend to a friend,' Valerie replied. 'Her name is . . .'

'Elena Marshall,' Max croaked. 'Her boyfriend, Drew – er, Andrew Wallace – called me as his support.'

The nurse's expression softened. 'Of course. Come sign in for me and I'll let Mr Wallace know you've arrived. It's good of you to come out in weather like this. You look soaked to the skin, the pair of you.'

'Well, I could be persuaded to put my head under a hand dryer,' Valerie said.

'The bathroom's just off to your left when you get through the doors.'

Valerie nodded, meanwhile Max dragged her eyes away and onto the sign-in sheet. She scrawled her name across two boxes then scrubbed it out with her fist. The ink speared through the dividing lines and smeared off the edge of the paper. She stared at it before passing the pen to Valerie who printed, signed, and handed the sheet back with a flourish.

They were buzzed through to the deserted waiting room which stretched from one side of the wing to the other. Porthole windows on the left were just dark, but the floor to ceiling windows on the right were being lashed with rain. All you could see of the town were tower blocks wedged amongst washed out specks of streetlights.

'It's a sight, isn't it?'

Max flinched then thumbed behind her. 'Think the loos are that way.'

11

'You need to clean up yourself, you know,' said Valerie.

'I'm all right, I've warmed through.'

'I understand,' she answered as she stepped away. The scent of her perfume stuck for a bit then dissolved the further away her heels clipped.

A door closed in the distance and Max blew onto her palms until they tingled. Her breath came back at her, laced with the dregs of last night's booze. She screwed up her face and scuffed her palm over her nose, pressing the stench out of her nostrils. Then she tried levelling her hair out with her fingers, but it just curled up more. She'd about given up when a creak spun her around.

Drew shuffled out from a corridor and leaned against the door. It cracked back into its frame when he made it clear then he twisted towards it, confusion etched over his face. He finally started moving again with lumpy steps while Max stared, wondering whether someone had lopped him off at the knees when he'd walked into this place tonight.

'Max . . .' He cringed at the gravel in his voice and staggered over to the nearest chair. 'It's done. The labour, I mean. They're . . . Elena said to come out, said she wanted a minute. I'm off back.'

'How long?' Max sat next to him, watching his legs ripple. 'Drew – how long?'

'They don't know. Might be an hour, might be more.'

'How's Elena coping?'

He dug both thumbs into his eyes. 'She's not. Can't do anything, can I?'

'Yeah, you can get your arse back in there.'

'I will. In a minute, I will.' Tears trickled over his hands, clumping in his beard like rock pools. 'You should see him, Max. So small, like he'd – he'd blow away.'

That caught at her throat, coiling around and strangling her voice. She worked her fist in and out of a ball till the coil loosened itself then she gripped his elbow with her other hand.

12

'Drew, mate, you've got to get back in there, all right? She needs you with them, spend as much time there as you can. Doesn't matter how you get through it, but you will. Think of what it's doing to her. Help her – that's what you want, yeah?'

He raked his heel against the floor. 'Yeah.'

'Okay.' Max glanced at the teddy bear cuckoo clock on the wall. 'You've got thirty seconds.'

They sat in silence until the little hand was at the hour. Even when it twitched past, she didn't have the heart to move him. It wasn't the way they worked, her and him. They were all banter over rugby and roadworks, never anything more serious than what gossip the customers had come up with. She couldn't picture going back to that, not after seeing his knees give way when he tried to stand up. He wobbled back into the chair then threw her a pleading look.

'Go,' she insisted.

Fresh tears clustered in his eyes, but he hauled himself up and swayed towards the door. Only when he was nearly there did she chuck him a bone.

'You'll be all right. You and Elena, you'll be all right.'

His throat quivered then he slipped through into the corridor. She held her chin until the door cracked shut before burying her head into her hands. Damp hair wilted around her fingers and she became aware of every pucker in her clothes, from her stiff collar down to the hem of her jeans scratching at her ankles. The fabric stretched between her thighs was still sodden, along with the insoles of her trainers. Her whole body was numbing through.

A hand rested on her wrist, rubbing circles into the skin. She raised her face enough to see Valerie kneeling in front of her. It was the first time she'd been close enough to notice how blue her eyes were, little baubles of sapphire glistening under the white lights.

Max swallowed. 'You'll do your knees in.'

'I think I'll be lucky not to come down with pneumonia after tonight, actually. You know, you can be as tough as you need to be in front of him, but that's not to say it isn't taking its toll on you.'

'It's not like that.'

Valerie's hand shivered down her arm. 'Are you close to Elena?'

'Not massively. They haven't been together long, the baby wasn't planned or anything like that. But Drew went the whole hog and proposed right off. She's got a lousy family, mad mother and all that. Once she found Drew, they were happy together. Even if he is an idiot most of the time. I don't – I don't know what happens next though.'

'Well, I haven't got any remarkable words of wisdom. I can't imagine what they must be going through or how they'll cope. But you're here, Max. You're supporting them when they need it most. Trust me – that'll be remembered, and it matters, don't you dare think it doesn't.'

She gazed into Valerie eyes until she picked apart the pigments. 'You said you work in care or something?'

'Hospice nurse,' said Valerie with a smile. 'Only part-time these days, what with the election and everything.'

All Max could do was nod then she shuffled to her feet and offered a hand to Valerie. She took it and rose like a swan in a cardboard skirt, clinging onto her fingers with her left hand. Max squeezed as she helped her up, not deliberately, but enough to notice there was no wedding ring on her finger. Just thinking that was a betrayal of Drew and Elena so she set her jaw and let go.

'I'm gonna find a payphone. Call the switchboard, get you a lift home. There must be one downstairs.'

Valerie ran two hands through her unkempt hair. 'That would be wonderful, thank you. I may as well walk out with you.'

They exchanged platitudes with the reception nurse on the way out to the corridor before swerving into a stairwell that led down into the foyer. The rain was still hammering down outside, rattling against the façade and echoing in her skull, right behind her eyes. She'd be hearing it in her sleep.

'Wait a second.'

Max twisted around. 'What? What's up?'

Valerie was two steps above, spearing her fingers together and apart. 'Listen, Max, I've got the European elections coming up. I need to be focused on that, I really do. But, afterwards, perhaps we could . . . I don't know, have dinner or something.'

Every muscle in her body ignited, blasting away the cold for a moment. It faded and left her clammy. She wiped her palms on her jeans then took another step down.

'I only did what any decent human being would've done. Anyway, you came here with me so . . . we're even.'

'You think I'm trying to repay a debt?'

Max shrugged. 'You're grateful. There's no need for it.'

'No.' Valerie tucked her arms behind her back and straightened her shoulders. 'I don't suppose there is. I think I'll call a taxi myself, if it's all the same to you. There's a firm I favour and I obviously don't know your company at all. Excuse me.'

Max stepped aside, groping for the banister to steady herself. It was enough to allow Valerie past then she continued to glide down the stairs without a backward glance.

'Thank you,' Max called.

Valerie hesitated before carrying on her way. 'You're welcome.'

## Chapter 2

The driveway was empty.

Amy pulled her rucksack from her shoulder and fumbled in the front pocket for her keys. They came away tangled in her earphones and it took a minute to tease them free. She managed to open the door then glanced around to check if any of the neighbours were watching. The curtains fell back across at No. 7, but that was only Mr Larkford and no one cared for his gossip.

Nothing was out of place in the hallway. Amy kicked off her shoes against the wall and took her bag through to the kitchen. She let it fall onto the tiled floor then rubbed her eyes to try and ease the pressure scraping inside her head. Her hands fell away as she heard something scuff across the carpet. She jolted back from the angular man in a familiar dressing gown until her spine cracked into the corner of the table.

'Who the hell are you?' he demanded. 'The cleaner?'

She clenched her fist. 'No, I'm the daughter. So, why don't you take off my dead dad's dressing gown and put some clothes on like a good little boy?'

'Daughter? I didn't – I thought –'

'Don't you read those leaflets she makes you deliver? I'm here to make sure she fits into that happy family crap that everyone –'

'That's enough.' Valerie swept into the kitchen with her silk dressing gown trailing behind her. 'Rob, why don't you go get dressed?'

He sidestepped towards the door, almost tripping over the threshold. That left Amy looking around for something to do. There was nothing to move, nothing to clean. She settled for filling the kettle and setting it to boil. The rumble spurred Valerie into speech.

'What are you doing here?'

Amy dug into the cupboard for her otter mug. 'Where's the car? Did you leave it outside a swanky bar because you were too interested in – How old is he, Mum?'

'The car's with the mechanic. A tyre went a few nights ago, left me stranded, and the inspection's thrown up a raft of other issues. What are you doing here, sweetheart? You don't usually come back through the week if you can help it.'

'I needed to pick something up,' she lied.

'Well, you could've called me, I could've brought it to Clarice's later. What is it, a dress or –'

'Hold on a second. You keep whining that I'm not here enough, that it doesn't look good in front of the neighbours. And, when I turn up, you just –'

Valerie held up a hand. 'I didn't mean it that way. It's a trek, that's all, and you don't usually choose to make it.'

'I'll give you notice in future, I'll put it in writing.'

'There's really no need to be like this. It was a surprise, that's all.'

'Oh, I bet. Tell me, Mum, what is it you do? Give out bags of clothes with every shag? That's one way to get rid of –'

'Amy!' Valerie scampered to close the door. 'Will you please keep your voice down? I am an adult, I'm entitled to see who I want. Now, if I'd known you were going to be here –'

'That doesn't excuse it,' she snapped.

'You've made it abundantly clear you don't want to live with me, sweetheart. What is it you expect me to do? Am I meant to be a nun? I'm 35, I can't live that way.'

'It's not about that.' The mug shook in Amy's grasp. 'Come on, how many members of your campaign team have you been screwing or have you lost count? So much for being serious about your new career in politics.'

'I am serious, of course I am. It's – it's simpler, dealing with people that don't expect a relationship. They understand the constraints of what I'm trying to do with

17

my life and it serve its purpose. Unless you're saying . . .' Valerie twitched at her dressing gown and drew it closer to her throat. 'I've deliberately kept myself away from anyone I might well and truly fall for. Do you want me to meet someone, bring them into this house?'

'You don't want that.'

'How do you know? You haven't asked. Without Clarice as a buffer we hardly communicate. I miss your father as much as you do and I need company, sweetheart. Every human being does. Perhaps I'm not going about it in the right way but . . . I'm not sure I know what that is.'

Amy lowered her mug to the counter before it dropped. 'Why would you?'

'Hang on –'

'Do you think he'll be decent up there? Only I'd like to get to the study and I'd rather not bump into a naked man on my dad's staircase, if you don't mind. We'll need to leave for Biddy's no later than six if you haven't got the car.'

Valerie's lips parted then she turned and plucked open the door. 'Just leave Rob alone while you're up there. If word got around –'

'Don't worry, your secret's safe.' Amy grabbed her rucksack on the way past. 'Just like they always are.'

The study was warm with the almond odour of Tim's books.

This smell used to soothe her. She'd sit as she was now, her back pressed against the side panel of the desk, with the leather spines towering over her. Tim would be tapping away at his computer and the sun would lower over the fields stretching away towards the horizon. He only turned on the desk lamp when she grumbled about the words of her comic blending together.

'Are you ready to go, sweetheart?'

Her head jerked forward. The door was open and Valerie was resting her shoulder against the frame. The silk dressing gown was gone, replaced by one of the grey suits that seemed to breed in her new fitted wardrobe.

Amy pulled herself up with the sharp edge of the desk and stowed her books into her bag without making eye contact with Valerie. Then she stepped towards the curtains.

'You can leave those,' said Valerie.

She ignored her and tugged the burgundy material across until the ruffled hem kissed the radiator. She stooped to pick up her bag before edging out of the study, keeping her chin low. The rustle that followed her down the staircase was the sound of Valerie returning the room to normal.

Their walk to the local station was punctuated by businessmen racing home in their Audis and Mercedes. Valerie was an exotic anomaly, plunging on ahead through the pockets of midges with her Ted Baker coat dazzling under the fading sunlight.

The train shrieked as it drew alongside the platform. Glazed commuters spilled out of the doors and trooped towards the car park, leaving a deserted carriage for them to settle into. Amy pulled out her Law textbook and propped it up to block out Valerie's inquisitive gaze. That strategy helped her survive until their stop, although she was startled when flashing lights greeted them at the roadside.

She grabbed Valerie's arm. 'What are you doing dragging her out of the house?'

'She offered. If she'd been having a bad day, she wouldn't have.'

'Yes, she would,' Amy argued before pasting on a smile as the Kia window rolled down and a head popped out. 'Hi, Biddy.'

'Hello, dear. Did you have a good day?'

'Not bad.' She kissed her cheek then slipped into the back, warming her hands between her knees. 'Are you sure you're well enough to be out like this?'

'Oh, shush,' Biddy replied as Valerie installed herself in the passenger seat. 'Put your seatbelts on, girls.'

She veered onto the road with a flourish that had Valerie groping for the dashboard. The image brought a smirk to Amy's face and she closed her eyes to keep hold of it for as long as possible. That allowed her to ignore the chit-chat ricocheting back and forth in the front of the car.

## Chapter 3

'Maybe you'd best go home. I'll tell him the same when he comes in.'

Elena twisted her engagement ring from her finger. 'Then he'll get waylaid on the way back.'

'Yeah, but you won't be stuck here for God knows how long. Besides, if he does turn up now, he'll be –'

'You're right, I know.'

Max cast a glance through the greasy glass that divided the office from the waiting room. Mrs Brinsome had pitched up on one of the benches, straining against her walker to cop an earful. She caught Max looking and shot her a toothy grin before pulling on the loose threads of her magenta cardigan. Max turned back to Elena in time to see the engagement ring slip on again.

'You'd be better at home,' she said in a low voice. 'Walls have ears around this place.'

Elena moved to perch on the edge of the switchboard desk. Her eyes were paler up close, limp balls of stained chocolate rounded off with a hollow shell. She kept her fingers clutched onto her elbows, though the material of her shirt sagged around them.

'I can't take much more of this,' she muttered.

'I know.' Max hesitated and fiddled with the volume on her headset. 'I don't think it's deliberate, I don't think he's planning it.'

'But he knows what he's doing. He does – I've told him. Every time I try and talk to him, he just gets angry and it gets worse. It's been months, Max. Does he think I don't care about Andrew? Does he hate me? Is that it?'

'He loves you. Maybe the more you tell him what a prat he's being, the more he feels like he is one, then it repeats. With Drew, anything's possible. It doesn't mean he hates you.'

Elena mustered a smile. 'I thought he was turning up to work, I thought he was doing that at least. He's stopped answering his phone when he's out. I think he leaves it in the cab while he goes off drinking. He's going to do something stupid, isn't he?'

'I don't think he's that far gone.'

'Not yet.' She paused and exhaled towards the ceiling. 'Anyway, I'll leave you to it. You don't need me prattling on.'

'You're welcome here, you know that. Just wish there was something I could do.'

'Talk to him?' Elena suggested. 'He might take it coming from you. Make it about the business, tell him that he's going to run it into the ground if he doesn't get himself together. At least if he doesn't love me anymore, he'll do it for the business.'

Max bit her lip then nodded. 'I'll see what I can do.'

There was more colour in Elena's eyes as she slipped out of the dividing door then through the main one. It'd hardly closed before Mrs Brinsome shuffled her walker to the window.

'Terrible do that was,' she said.

'Don't know what the hold up for your car is, Mrs Brinsome. I'll chase it up.'

'Your Kevin told me all about it. Terrible do.'

Max gritted her teeth as she radioed through to Raj. 'All right, mate? You back at base yet? I've got Mrs Brinsome waiting.'

'My lucky day,' he answered. 'I'm just pulling round the corner, I'll meet her out front.'

The switch went through an afternoon spurt once she'd got her office back. It tailed off until she managed to get more than two pages of her crumpled Terry Pratchett read at a time. She was just finishing the dregs of a stewed cuppa when Drew staggered in.

He stumbled straight into the shelves that'd been up for three years and scattered empty binders over the carpet, glaring as if they'd jumped out into his way. It took him thirty seconds to work out what'd happened then he giggled and kicked one onto the side of the sofa. Max rose and thumped them back into the shelves one by one, ignoring the stench of the pub spreading through the office.

'Where the hell have you been?' she demanded.

'Forgot work. Here now.'

'You're not fit to work. Go home.'

He groaned and chafed at his beard. 'Can't I go to yours?'

'Not again. I've already had Elena in here chewing my ear off because you didn't have the bloody decency to go home last night. What are you trying to do?'

His eyes locked on hers, sizzling until the fire sputtered out and she was staring into the same numb expression Elena had been wearing when she'd walked in earlier. He lowered his head and slumped into the switchboard chair, wiping his mouth with the back of his hand.

'Drew, mate . . .'

She trailed off when the words wouldn't come. The switch rang again and he grabbed the headset before she could, slurring his way through the beginnings of a call. Max leaned against the dividing glass, biting the tip of her thumb as he mispronounced the name "Gardener" five times in a row.

The bell jangled behind her, announcing a customer. She swivelled then blinked to clear her vision when she assumed she was imagining things through the window.

'Please say you remember me,' Valerie murmured.

Max blew out her breath. 'Erm . . . yeah. Course I remember. Just wasn't expecting to see you, that's all.'

'Well, I'm hoping it's a nice surprise.'

She opened her mouth then closed it again. Valerie's sapphire eyes – the ones that she couldn't get to calling just plain blue – matched her coat. There was nothing accidental about the way she put herself together. Max glanced down at her own mottled shirt and crusty jeans and cleared her throat.

23

'Suppose you're wanting a taxi.'

Valerie's chin dipped and she stepped backwards. 'Never mind.'

'No, wait. Wait.' Max pressed her fist up against the glass. 'I'm sorry, don't go.'

'You need to stop trying to scare me off,' Valerie warned.

'I'm not.'

'Hmm, we'll see. Anyway, I was nowhere near the area so I thought I'd pop in and see how you're doing. Both of you.'

Max frowned, not sure what she meant. Then she realised the mumbling in the corner had stopped. Drew was watching them with glazed eyes and a slack mouth.

'Who's this? She's well fit.'

'Ignore him,' Max muttered. 'He's an idiot.'

'Don't be a bitch all your life.' He rocked the chair back on its casters till it tipped and he grabbed for the desk to stay upright. 'Okay, I'll let you have that one.'

Max's cheeks burned. She gestured to the street and manoeuvred her way through the dividing door and narrow space without touching Valerie once. She could see her smirk from the corner of her eye, but she couldn't bring herself to face her, not even when they were in the yard with an eight-foot brick wall between them and anyone else.

'You can look at me, you know,' Valerie said finally.

She swallowed and shifted herself around. With the height difference, it was guaranteed she'd end up tasting that perfume she remembered from the nature reserve car park. It forced her away another foot and Valerie chuckled.

'You don't plan on making this easy, do you?' she asked.

'Sorry, I'm not – I don't reckon –'

'Okay, this may go a little faster if I talk and you just stand still for me. These heels aren't built for chasing you around the town centre.'

Max shuffled her feet, but said nothing. She was trying to keep her attention away from the blonde hair fluttering in the breeze, looking instead at a patch of weeds taking over the bottom gate.

'You see, at first I was hurt about what happened at the hospital. I mean, there was a moment, wasn't there? A few of them, actually. I'm not exactly used to people who are attracted to me holding back like that.'

'I bet you're not,' Max murmured.

'So, I was bemused, offended even. I put you out of my mind. Or, that is, I tried to. The fact that I couldn't was proof enough that I should come down here and talk to you but . . . Well, you'd turned me down and, I have to say, I didn't like it.'

Max's eyes had drifted to her face, despite herself. Nearly everything about Valerie this minute was precise. She could be on a podium, swishing her arms around and getting votes for it. Except there was something else. A bead of sweat below her hairline, a flick of her tongue every few seconds. Max knew she was nakedly staring now.

'I started thinking about it,' Valerie continued, meeting her gaze, 'and I realised something. You rejected my invitation for the same reason you were delaying going to the hospital that night. Ironically enough, you rejected me because of the same reluctance that brought us together in the first place. Am I wrong?'

'I don't know,' she admitted.

'Well, will you take my word for it? Listen, the why doesn't matter. I've learned that it's the destination that matters, not how you get there. So, let's try this. Hi, Max, I'm Valerie. I'd love to cook dinner for you at some point soon. What do you say?'

Max opened her mouth then pressed her lips together.

'I want your first answer,' Valerie said.

She squeezed her eyes shut, but it didn't take away the glossy mental image that'd imprinted itself on her brain.

She opened her eyes to face the real thing, managing a smile.

'Sure,' she said. 'Why not?'

Max didn't go straight back to the office after she'd exchanged numbers with Valerie. She took a detour to the café a few doors down and got Drew a triple shot Americano and a vanilla latte for herself.

The phone was blaring when she elbowed her way back into the office. Drew was slumped over the desk, drool slithering along his jaw. Nudging him with her shoe didn't work, so she booted his shin and waited for the groan.

'What did you do that for. Oh . . .'

He reached for the headset, but she snatched it away. 'No, leave it alone.'

'But –'

'Drink this.' She dumped the coffee into his hands. 'We need to bloody well talk.'

'You're not my sodding missus,' he snapped.

'No, I could call her though. Let her know you've turned up and you're pissed out of your skull, screwing up the business as well as your relationship. Is that what you want?'

All his stroppiness suddenly melted away and every muscle in him drooped. He looked like he had done that night, drained of everything that made him her bloody annoying business partner. She couldn't yell at him again, but she did stretch across him and mute the switchboard, giving him no room to hide behind another call.

'So, who was the woman?' he asked eventually.

Max rolled her eyes. 'Sod that. You need to stop doing this, mate. I'm not covering for you anymore.'

'Don't be a bitch. Like you've never been worse for wear.'

'Bit more than that. You've been worse for wear for two months now.'

'What's it to you?'

'Apart from you messing around with my livelihood . . . Elena doesn't deserve what you're doing to her.'

He kicked his heel back into the chair. 'You think I don't know that? But . . . Max, she wants to try again.'

'Drew . . .' Max hesitated then tried to smile. 'She wants kids, she always has.'

'We had a kid!'

'What, and you reckon she's forgotten about him? You're being an arse.'

'Oi, just because you bought me a coffee, doesn't mean you can treat me like shit. Look, I can't – I can't go near her, not like that.'

Max snorted. 'You're being selfish.'

'Give it a rest. I mean it.'

'Well, do you love her or are you just an arse?'

He crossed his arms. 'Seriously, leave it alone.'

'No, come on. Do you love her?'

'Yes! Course I do.'

'Then why are you hurting her?'

All his rage drained away again. He shrivelled into the chair and took the odd swig of his coffee while the switchboard lights flashed like a carnival. Max just let him stew, parking up on the sofa and warming her hands through on her latte. He scraped his shoes together then looked up.

'I'm all she's got. You know what her parents are like. They're right – I'm not good enough for her. She shouldn't have picked me over them.'

'She wanted you.'

'It was the baby she wanted. Now there isn't one so what's she still doing with me?'

'Mate, I don't know what she was doing with you in the first place. But it only works if you're on the same page.'

He scuffed his hand over his nose. 'What do you know about it?'

'You don't have to have jumped out of a plane to know what it looks like from the outside. Simple question – yes or no.'

'Go on,' he muttered.

'Do you still want kids? Sometime in the future,' she added when he began to answer. 'I'm not talking now. But do you want them?'

His chin quivered. 'Yes.'

'Then you have to get past this. I know you're scared, I get it. I saw how much it hurt you –'

'It's not about me – it's what it did to her! I'm scared, yeah. I'm bloody petrified. But it's of watching her go through that again, not me. I couldn't look after her, there was nothing I could do or say that'd make it better for her. I didn't know how to help – I still don't.'

Tears bubbled in his eyes. Max groped for the box of tissues lodged on the windowsill and tossed them onto his knee. He blew his nose twice before looking at her again with his cheeks inflated like a puffer fish.

'Drew, I'm not a bloody therapist,' Max said after a minute of him staring at her. 'But you said the grief counsellor –'

'She was a right cow.'

'Yeah, maybe, but she said things are different for everyone, that grief doesn't work the way you think it should. I agree with that, I reckon. Don't you think Elena's thought about what might happen if you try again? She's just as scared. Only she's having to hold it together in front of you or you'll be all over it. You've gotta start talking to her, properly talking. Tell her what you've told me and then listen to her for God's sake.'

He yanked another fistful of tissues from the box and wiped his eyes. His attention drifted back to his coffee, then he cocked his head to the side.

'So, who was the woman?'

'Just a rep.' Max gestured to the switchboard. 'Get some calls answered now you've sobered up a bit.'

# Chapter 4

'Amy, may I have a minute?'

Dennis Cowper's voice echoed across the cafeteria. She dropped her pen as he approached then twisted her face into a smile as he sat down opposite her.

'Of course,' she replied.

'Is that my suggested reading you're working on?' he asked.

'Economics. Paula Harborough gets very excited when you actually get it done.'

'It's a teacher thing, I'm afraid.' He nestled his fingers together and peered over his beige glasses. 'I'm glad I've finally caught you. I've been trying for some time, but you've thwarted most of my attempts and I didn't feel it right to draw attention to the situation by requesting you stay after class. I'm concerned about you.'

'I don't understand. My marks are coming back okay, aren't they?'

'That as may be, but I see you struggling, Amy. I've spoken to a few of your old GCSE teachers and –'

'Excuse me?'

Dennis scratched his ear. 'I assure you, this is nothing untoward. It's standard procedure when we believe a student isn't coping very well. Throughout your time at the school, you've always been a model pupil. That's why your behaviour –'

'My behaviour?'

'Please, there's no need to be defensive. There's no shame in admitting you're struggling with your workload or that there's something else in your life troubling you. We're all human.'

'There isn't anything,' she insisted.

'Amy . . .' Dennis paused and ran his eyes over the textbooks scattered across the table. 'My understanding is that you're a bright girl. Your grades in all subjects, both at GCSE and AS Level confirm that.'

She pressed her knees together. 'Then I really don't see the problem.'

'You're not happy,' he said.

'My dad died less than a year ago and you expect me to be happy? Quite frankly, Mr Cowper, I don't care what you think about my state of mind or whatever else it is you're talking about. My mood's nothing to do with you, my grades are. And, actually, I'm offended that you think you can speak to me like this when there's nothing wrong.'

His congenial smile flickered and faded. She began to apologise, but he held up his hand.

'Yes, you could be a lawyer. You've got the capacity to do most things you set your mind to, I'd imagine. Law isn't an easy field, not in the long run. It's not something you should go into if you're not passionate about it. My feeling is that you're passionate about what it represents to you, not the profession itself. Now, so far, you've been able to put that aside, but you have exams to get through, this year and next. Many pupils have lined up internships for the summer. With your background –'

'Okay,' she interrupted. She gazed into the grains of the table and swallowed. 'I'll think about it, Mr Cowper, but, please, leave me alone.'

He eased out of the chair. 'I do understand how hard this is, however unlikely you believe that to be. Theoretically, I have no reason to call home. Don't give me one.'

'You're late, dear.'

'Sorry, Biddy.' Amy pressed a kiss to her cheek. 'What are you doing out here?'

'Enjoying the sun. I hope that's allowed.'

'I just worry, that's all.'

'Enough to let me know when you're too busy studying to come home?' Biddy tilted her hat further to the left. 'It works both ways.'

Amy shrugged and settled on the blanket spread across the lawn. Biddy had taken her sandals off, so she felt no compunction in slipping her flats off and kicking her legs out. The sun that had blighted her walk tickled her legs now she was back until the knot in the pit of her stomach gradually unwound. It only left behind one kink.

'Biddy, do you think it's too late to ask Flyman and Twine for an internship this summer? It's only just been suggested that we should try for something and I wondered if it's too late.'

'That school's slipping,' Biddy answered.

'I don't think it's their fault –'

'They have responsibilities. Anyway, I thought of it myself weeks ago and I mentioned it to your mother. I should have a word with the firm.'

Amy's fingers caught in a stray blade of grass trembling beside the blanket. 'No, Biddy, don't do that. It's an oversight, that's all. It's not the end of the world.'

'Your father always said that students should know what they're walking into, dear.'

'I know that, but I'm not just anyone. I know what his job was like and I'm ready for it.'

'You're a credit to him,' Biddy murmured. 'A real credit.'

Amy shivered as her voice cracked. She inclined her chin a touch, just to see if she was struggling to draw breath, but her cheeks were flushed and her eyes sparkling.

'Don't think I can't see you watching me,' said Biddy as she adjusted her hat again. 'There's no need to fuss.'

'I wouldn't dare, Biddy. I'm not brave enough for that.'

Valerie's presence diluted the warmth of the sunset.

The dinner table conversation followed the usual pattern of Biddy's week, local news, and updates from Valerie including the odd political anecdote. One prospective constituent had been too tactile with her during a meeting, which she'd taken in her stride at the time. Amy watched Biddy over the rim of her glass, seeing her frown sprout up as the tale wound to its conclusion. Valerie only noticed the expression when she'd regaled them with the punchline.

'You look very serious, Clarice. It's just a hazard of the job, and it very rarely turns into anything more inflammatory than that. Most people are harmless.'

Biddy brushed crumbs into her napkin and bundled it up. 'I wonder what Timothy would make of the whole idea. You're encountering all sorts of people, undesirables from all kinds of backgrounds. It can't be healthy.'

'Undesirables?' Valerie's tone was indecipherable. 'What do you mean?'

'Oh, you know. All those special cases – the ethnics and the gays.'

Amy grimaced, lowering her eyes into her soda water. She wasn't expecting the huff from across the table that made her glance to Valerie.

'Really, Clarice, I would've hoped you'd put those attitudes behind you by now. If you said things like that to the wrong person, you could cause serious offence.'

Biddy shook her head. 'They're always quick to take offence. Now, I know you have a public persona to maintain, so I'll leave it at that, but I'll not be lectured to in my own home.'

'Of course not. I didn't mean to lecture. I'm in debate mode, I suppose,' Valerie added with a deferential smile. 'Each side of the argument deserves an airing.'

Amy narrowed her eyes, but said nothing. She was focused on the way Valerie clutched at her wine glass until it seemed to absorb the tension in her hand. Then she was back to normal, sipping her Chardonnay and complimenting the moussaka. Biddy accepted the praise before putting her fork down.

'Did you ever speak to Graham Wilson about the internship I suggested?'

'Hmm?' Valerie took another sip of wine. 'Oh, they were looking more for a dogsbody than an intern and I couldn't allow Amy to work in Tim's office under such circumstances. It would hardly be appropriate.'

'That's disappointing. I should speak with him, or perhaps Murray Cox. I play bridge with his sister-in-law. I could –'

'Actually. Clarice, I'd prefer if you didn't. I'm afraid I became rather emotional with him. It was to do with Tim's loyalty to the firm and how they've altered things in his absence. I'm not sure Amy working there now would be pleasant for anyone, even if they were to agree.'

Biddy jangled her fingers together. 'A placement is vital. I won't have Amy walking into her career without a placement first.'

'I'll ask around,' Valerie promised. 'We'll do our best for her. I meant to ask, Clarice, did you see that piece in the paper about St. Michael's?'

The conversation shifted to Biddy's church and Amy's attention drifted, along with her appetite. She managed the mechanics of clearing and serving dessert, but she was grateful when Biddy excused herself from coffee and she could finally look at Valerie again.

'You never spoke to Graham, did you?'

Valerie brushed her hands together. 'Why would you assume that?'

'Probably because I know what you're like. And I know Graham wouldn't be like that.'

'You don't understand people half as well as you'd like to think. You're still a teenager, remember that.'

Amy snorted and crossed her arms. 'Come on, what did you think? That if I don't have an internship then I might just abandon the whole idea of becoming a lawyer? You're the one who doesn't know a thing about me if you thought I'd give in at that.'

'Really?' Valerie took a long sip of coffee before reaching for a chocolate mint. 'I'd say I know more than you'd like to admit. Why has it taken you until this late in the day to wonder about an internship? Did you wonder at all or is the idea fixed in Clarice's mind –'

'I was the one who brought it up,' she interrupted.

'Then I ask again – why now?'

'I've only just thought of it, that's why.'

'The school hasn't, though. It was prominently discussed in the newsletter two months ago, along with a note saying all students had been informed on several occasions. Now, either you haven't been attending college or . . .'

Valerie popped another chocolate mint into her mouth then stood. She went through the ritual of smoothing down her clothes before walking straight out of the room without a backwards glance. Amy caught up with her as she was collecting her coat from the hooks beside the door and grabbed her arm.

'You're not going to stop me doing what I want to do,' she warned.

'Then we'll both be happy in the end, won't we?' Valerie shook her off and opened the door. 'You know as well as I do that being a lawyer isn't what you want, not in your heart. You'd better open your eyes sooner rather than later. There is such a thing as going too far to fail. Believe me, Amy, I know that cliff edge well. Goodnight, sweetheart.'

# Chapter 5

Max's skin prickled as she pulled up outside 5 Geith Place.

She let the engine idle and craned her neck to clock the height of the trees lining the cul-de-sac. The sun skimming across the bonnet caught her in the eye before she could follow the trunk all the way up. She rubbed away the sunspots with one hand and tapped the steering wheel with the other.

Bouncing light off towards the house dragged her attention to the frosted glass door. Valerie was stood on the top step, motioning her into the driveway. Max hesitated for a moment then reversed in beside the BMW. She'd barely applied the handbrake when her door was plucked open and a finger trailed along her bare arm.

'Come in,' Valerie said.

The finger was gone, replaced by a breeze as Valerie swept away into the house. Max locked the car up and glanced around the sheltered garden before she followed her inside, halting when spices tickled her nostrils. She was trying to separate them out in her mind when Valerie stretched past her to nudge the door shut and their bodies pressed together.

'Am I going to have to coax you every inch of the way?' Valerie asked.

Max inhaled, tasting wine in the air. She tried to step away, but there was no moving forward or back. Her only choice was to raise her eyes and meet Valerie's. The flash of satisfaction she caught there would've put her off with anyone else, but it set her hands moving into blonde hair that slithered between her fingers now. Valerie leaned back into the touch and smirked.

'I have to say, it's reassuring to find that this isn't one-sided. I thought I may have coerced you into dinner, twisted your arm.'

'You did,' Max murmured.

'I'm used to getting what I want, that's all. I knew the moment you broke that damn tyre that this was something I needed to pursue, come what may. Now, that might make me selfish, but if you feel the same . . .'

The words dangled in the air, inviting Max one way or the other. She let her hands fall loose to test how it felt. One flicker of Valerie's eyelids and her arms wound around her neck instead, drawing her closer for a kiss that shuddered down Max's legs. A groan gurgled up, meeting the moan that passed from Valerie's mouth into her own. Fingers tightened on her belt, so suddenly that she had to pull away and search Valerie's face.

'Are you all right? Is this all right?'

Valerie ran a trembling thumb over her own lips then moved across to Max's. 'Perfectly. Believe me, you've got no reason to worry. I wouldn't have invited you into my home if I didn't want you to do just that.'

'Just that?' Max echoed. She twitched her tongue over the tip of Valerie' thumb and felt the shiver ripple through her body. 'What about more?'

'You're suddenly sure of yourself. What happened to the woman who wouldn't get out of the car two minutes ago?'

Max shrugged and bumped her towards the staircase. She landed on the third step, chest heaving and legs askew. The aroma working its way into the air was enough to set Max in motion again. She yanked apart the cream blouse, hearing the buttons rattle against the banister, then unzipped the black trousers to probe her way inside while planting her knees in between Valerie's. She caught her lips with her teeth before moving down to the hollow of her neck and teasing with her tongue. Valerie rocked against the stairs then stiffened. It didn't clock straight away that she'd stopped responding altogether but, the second it did, Max fell backwards and landed with her head on the doormat.

She jumped up, though her eyes ran with colour and her skull was throbbing. Her hand went to her pocket for her keys, but they weren't there. Valerie had them twisted around her fingers as she sat up with her lips swollen and her makeup smudged.

'Don't you dare,' she said.

'You're not into this. I'm sorry, I shouldn't have –'

'Honestly? Max – look at me. Do I look disinterested to you?'

'No,' she admitted.

Valerie rose from the stairs, more elegantly than she had a right to, and dropped the keys on the nearby cabinet. 'You can go or you can sit with me and talk for five minutes. It's your choice.'

Now that her senses weren't overloaded, Max could look around properly for the first time. The whole place glittered white and chrome, from the elaborate mirror decorated with oblong patterns down to the three-tier shoe rack underneath the side window. Off to the left there was a long room lit by sunlight that stretched further than she could fathom, while the door a length ahead of her went through to the kitchen, judging by the smell of chicken coming from that way.

'Max?' Valerie prompted.

She shook her head. 'I don't belong here.'

'The house? You mean the house?' Valerie stepped closer. 'Is that what this is about?'

'We're different, that's all.'

'That can be a good thing, believe me.'

'Yeah, but . . . We don't know the same lives.'

'I haven't always had money, Max. Besides, you came here knowing where I lived, you know more about me than I know about you. I'm not accustomed to comparing bank statements before I have someone over for dinner, but if that's what you –'

Max dug her hands into her pockets. 'I knew where you lived, but you never said what you wanted. I assumed that it was just working out an itch, something you had to do.'

37

'Oh.' Valerie pushed her hair behind her ear with one hand and pulled her blouse closed with the other. 'Is that what this is to you then – just an itch you need to scratch? Because there are better ways to do it, especially for me. I'm risking public humiliation here.'

'So, you're scared of me selling the story to the papers or something?' Max questioned.

'No, I'm not. You didn't stop in the middle of the night and push me away to sell me out now. But, the point is, you could've done and I placed myself in this situation anyway. I trust you too much to think you could do that to me – do you see?'

'Not really,' she muttered.

'Don't pretend you're stupid,' Valerie replied. She allowed her blouse to flutter open again, showing her nipples bristling through her bra. 'You can get sex in seedy bars or online with no strings. Yet you're here – because you want to be. There's no other way around it.'

Max swallowed as the heat between her thighs increased. 'Okay.'

'Okay?' Valerie repeated. 'Is that acknowledgement or capitulation? Let's be clear here.'

'I want you,' said Max after a brief struggle. 'You're gorgeous, every bit of you. All I've wanted from the minute I saw you is to feel you come around my fingers and my tongue . . . That's what I want. That's why I'm here.'

Valerie licked her lips. 'Good. Now we're getting somewhere.'

Neither of them made a move. Noises began to filter into Max's brain – the hum of music somewhere in the house and the gurgle of boiling water. It brought a smile to her face, one that made Valerie tilt her head to the side.

'What?' she asked.

'Just wondered if what we're eating involves a pan boiling over.'

'Oh, damn . . .'

She ran off into the kitchen, clutching her blouse to her chest. Max kicked her shoes off next to the shoe rack then followed her in. Valerie was over at the far side, beyond the breakfast bar, twiddling with the biggest cooker Max had ever seen. It took up a good portion of the left-hand wall, not that there was space lacking in here. So much stuff was glinting on the worktops under the down lights that she couldn't catalogue it all, never mind figure out what that third thing that looked like a blender might be. She gave up and focused on Valerie mumbling to herself across the room.

'Everything all right?' she called.

Valerie held up a finger and sprinkled something into the pan of bubbling water. She then poured in a bowl of rice and stirred it with an oversized wooden spoon. Only once she'd shuffled everything around a few times did she put the spoon down and turn around. Her cheeks were still flushed and her bra exposed. She managed to find two buttons intact on her blouse and fastened them, though the tanned skin caught the light every time she drew in a breath.

'There's some white wine cooling,' she said. 'I hope that's okay.'

'I don't really drink while I'm driving.'

'Well, it goes very well with the dish. It'd be a positive waste of a meal otherwise. So, what do you say?'

Max dug her heels into the floor until they tingled. 'Okay.'

She watched as Valerie turned to a cupboard, catching the smile on her lips even from the awkward angle. It was gone when she brought the glasses and the wine over to the breakfast bar, motioning for them to sit down. The stool was deceptively comfy, curving around her spine and putting them on a level.

'May I ask your opinion?' Valerie questioned.

'What – mine?'

'Unless I'm missing a third occupant of the kitchen.'

Max sipped her wine, feeling it tickle the back of her throat. 'Go on.'

'I'm currently in a debate of sorts with someone. She's doing something I really don't believe is right for her, aiming for a career I think she'll struggle in. I've tried explaining why I feel that way, but she's disinterested and combative. I've been given the chance to stand in her way somewhat and, at first, I wanted to. Now I'm not so sure.'

'Why did you want to?' Max asked.

'Because I know I'm right.' Valerie tapped her glass and chuckled. 'Believe me, I know how that sounds. But I do know her very well, better than she knows herself.'

Max hesitated, but Valerie flexed her palm across the table.

'No, go on. I don't expect you to censor yourself, I need an honest answer.'

'I just don't get why you think you've got the right to judge. Who is it? Someone you work with or a relative or something?'

'In a manner of speaking.'

'Well, are you close?'

'Not really,' Valerie replied. 'We haven't been for some years.'

'Then it's nothing to do with you, is it? Standing in someone's way when they really want something's not on. It's selfish, the way I see it. Like Elena and her parents.'

Valerie frowned. 'You mentioned that at the hospital. You said the relationship was bad.'

'She lost her job and moved back in with them,' Max explained, gripping the stem of her glass. 'This was just after she met Drew and they didn't like him, reckoned he was a freeloader trying to nick their money. They made her choose when they found out she was pregnant – him and the baby or them.'

'It was brave of her to make the jump,' murmured Valerie.

'That's what it takes sometimes. You know, they lost her and if – Andrew had – if he'd . . . They would've lost a grandchild as well. I mean, they did, but they don't seem too bothered by it. They still haven't got in touch and Elena went through hell after the stillbirth. She's barely back on her feet now, and Drew's still not right. What I'm saying is that imposing what you reckon's right on someone only works harder to push them away.'

The room was quiet for a minute, with Valerie chewing on her lip and the only sounds coming from the rice rattling against the inside of the pan. Max shifted on her stool and tried not to gulp the wine down. She jumped when Valerie pushed her own stool back and slipped onto the tiles. She braced herself as Valerie swept towards her then her breath hitched when a smooth hand rested on her cheek.

'Thank you,' Valerie said.

Max cleared her throat. 'What for?'

'Oh, I don't know.' She paused and stretched a finger the length of her ear lobe. 'Drinking more than one glass of my wine tonight? It seems a shame to waste it.'

'A shame,' Max echoed. 'Yeah.'

Another smile twitched over Valerie's lips and Max couldn't help herself. She leaned in to kiss her, growling when a knee pressed between her legs. Once she'd pushed herself from the stool, she reversed their positions and was only dimly aware of the wine glasses crashing to the floor as she hoisted Valerie onto the breakfast bar.

# Chapter 6

The lawns in front of the college were deserted.

Amy dodged through the collared doves making a meal of a sandwich someone had crunched into the gravel and trudged towards the main road. Every limb felt heavy, just keeping her chin up was sapping her energy. She was so focused on reaching the gate that she didn't spot Valerie until she stepped out in front of her.

'What are you doing here?' she asked.

'Charming.' Valerie gestured over her shoulder. 'Get in the car.'

'You're not kidnapping me, are you? Only I've got library books in my bag and I don't want to get fined while I'm stuck in a dark room somewhere.'

Valerie rolled her eyes and took her by the elbow. 'Honestly, how you can claim we're nothing alike is beyond me sometimes, sweetheart. Just get in.'

'Look, you'll be over tomorrow for dinner, can't it –'

'I'm afraid not. Get in.'

With two swift motions, she'd steamrollered her around the car and into the passenger seat. Amy narrowly escaped losing a fingernail as the door slammed, although she cracked her head on the rear-view mirror when she tried to dislodge her rucksack. She just managed to wedge it between her feet when Valerie slotted into the driver's seat.

'Mum, what's going on?'

Valerie fiddled with the radio until something exuberant blasted out from Classic FM then lowered all four windows down as she reversed. The assault on her senses forced Amy to lean back against the leather and let the wind whip through the car to tangle with the violins for the fifteen-minute drive to Biddy's. She sat up straight when they zoomed past the end of the track and headed for the dual carriageway.

'You are. You're kidnapping me.'

'Now, don't be so dramatic. Could you get my sunglasses out of the glove compartment? It's getting a little bright. Oh, and there's an ice box behind your seat if you want some water.'

'An ice box?' She twisted to check. 'Seriously, Mum, what's going on?'

'We're going on a picnic.'

Amy gaped at her. 'Excuse me? Have you actually lost your marbles?'

'I need those sunglasses, darling,' Valerie said, flicking down her visor.

'Stuff the sunglasses. Turn around – take me home.'

Brakes squealed as Valerie spun them onto the nearest verge. The car rocked against the bank and Amy grabbed at the dashboard to steady herself. Her heart was hammering in time to the music then, when Valerie jabbed that into silence, all she could hear was the drumming in her ears. She pressed her knees together and swallowed the lump that had risen in her throat.

'You're parked illegally,' she murmured.

'Listen to me – you may be living at Clarice's, but that is not your home. Are we clear? Do you understand me?'

Amy tilted her body away, her hand still trembling out of sight. 'It's the closest I've got. Anyway, kidnapping me probably won't help. Not unless you're looking to play the deranged mother card, but that might not play well at the polls. You never know what the public's going to go for, do you?'

'I haven't got the stomach for this, Amy. Not today.'

'Then tell me what's going on.'

'If I do, will you come quietly? I need you to be a credit to your father this afternoon, I really do.'

'When am I not?' she demanded.

Valerie held up a hand. 'That's a valid point, I apologise. It's just that we're going to the Yorkshire Sculpture Park for a picnic with Graham Wilson and his young children. He wants to talk to you about an internship through July

43

and August, only working a few days a week at the Leeds branch.'

'W-what?'

'Well, it's what you wanted isn't it, sweetheart?' said Valerie with a soft smile. 'Now, may I please have my sunglasses? All I can see at the moment at sunspots.'

Amy wordlessly retrieved them and watched Valerie as she manoeuvred the car back onto the road. It hit the tarmac with a thud then they were gliding along with the breeze rushing through the open windows. Valerie turned the radio back on and, by the time they reached the dual carriageway, she was almost conducting with her left hand. All Amy could do was fumble in the back for a bottle of icy water to make sure she wasn't suffering from dehydration and the associated hallucinations.

'The pair of you look exhausted.'

Amy levelled a finger at Valerie. 'She pushed me down a hill.'

'You fell,' Valerie retorted, yanking them both down onto the sofa. 'Honestly, Clarice, those tennis lessons went to waste. She can't balance to save her life.'

'Hey, I get that from you,' Amy shot back.

'I'll have you know I could walk a tightrope if I wanted to. Although perhaps not in these shoes.'

Biddy chuckled and started to rise. 'I'll put the kettle on.'

'Stay where you are, I'll do it,' said Amy. 'Do you want coffee, Mum?'

'That'd be brilliant, darling, thank you.'

She didn't hurry making the drinks. Companionable chatter echoed through the house as Valerie and Biddy exchanged news and anecdotes. Amy listened to the hum while preparing the coffee and digging out the strawberry creams. It was only when she noticed that she'd placed four cups on the tray instead of three that she realised where her mind had taken her. She could suddenly picture Tim sat in the corner waiting for her to deliver the biscuits, yawning behind his hand when he thought the others weren't paying attention. That had been one of their secrets, just like the Saturday morning trips for cake and the late-night renditions of Louis Armstrong on the antique record player in the study.

The tray wobbled when she picked it up, though she steadied it as she carried it into the conservatory. Her back seemed to straighten of its own accord, so much so that neither Valerie nor Biddy glanced her way. She passed out their cups and sat beside Biddy.

'What are we talking about?' she questioned.

Biddy reached for a strawberry cream. 'Thank you, dear. I was asking about John Foster, that's all.'

'Clarice . . .' Valerie murmured.

'Who's John Foster?' Amy asked, looking between them. Valerie lowered her gaze so she switched her attention. 'Biddy? Who's John Foster?'

'Haven't you heard of him? He's Shadow Environment Minister, he's got a very good reputation. From what I hear, he's making quite a name for himself, and your mother's spending a lot of time with him.'

Valerie coughed. 'Behave, Clarice. There's nothing going on, John and I are just friends.'

'That's a shame. Timothy would want you to find happiness, you know. He told me as much. I know it's hard, but you shouldn't feel . . .'

Her voice faded and Amy gently removed the cup from her quivering hands. She knotted their fingers together and squeezed until Biddy's eyes lifted to meet hers. The deep hazel was another flash of Tim in the room.

'I'm being an old fool,' Biddy muttered.

'No,' said Valerie, 'far from it. Listen, Clarice, Tim told me the same thing a hundred times and it still doesn't feel right. I'm trying to respect his wishes, but, believe me, John is not someone I'm leaning on for emotional support. I've got you two for that, haven't I?'

45

That provoked a watery smile from Biddy, although Amy's incredulity snagged in her throat. The recollection of a stranger parading around in one of Tim's dressing gowns was replaying on a loop in her head. She finally had to drop her hands between her knees to keep them from shaking.

Biddy's mood had flattened and so had the atmosphere. The moment her cup was empty, Valerie made an excuse about an early start and scurried towards the door. Amy took off after her, grabbing her arm in the hallway.

'It was nothing to do with making amends, was it?'

Valerie's face was blank. 'What wasn't?'

'The internship. You were just trying to keep me occupied so I don't ask about who you're sleeping with this week.'

'Is that how little you think of me?' Valerie queried.

'You never do anything unless there's a reason for it, something in it for you.'

'Can't you give me credit for caring? I made a mistake about the internship and I fixed it. There's nothing conspiratorial about wanting you to be happy. You're my daughter.'

Amy snorted and shook her head. 'No, there's something different. About you, about the way you're being. In the car, you were . . .'

'I was what, hmm?' asked Valerie when she trailed off. 'Some sort of ogre in heels? Really, Amy, tell me. I'm fascinated.'

'Happy,' she mumbled after a few seconds. 'You were happy.'

Tears suddenly stung her eyelids. She twisted away from Valerie, blinking at the light drizzling along the ceiling as the chandelier bobbed back and forth. Another memory washed over her; a chandelier jangling followed by Biddy's sobs, Tim's soft voice, and Valerie's silence. The other two had been crying, but not her.

46

'Sweetheart, we all deserve to be happy,' Valerie said finally. 'Clarice, me, you . . . What good are we doing your father by denying ourselves the privilege of living our lives? He couldn't so we have to –'

'Don't do that,' she warned.

'It's true, though.'

Amy brushed away the tears spilling along her cheeks. 'You're a hypocrite and you're a liar. Two things he always hated. By rights, he should've hated you. I don't understand why he didn't.'

The words lingered in the air like dust. She listened, waiting for Valerie's broadside, but the dust filtered away and left the air thick with something else. The door opened and a draught of warm air tinkled through the chandelier.

'I know you don't understand,' answered Valerie. 'But he would've wanted you to.'

# Chapter 7

'It's a woman, yeah?'

Max flinched and smashed her hand on the underside of the switchboard. They'd been so quiet this afternoon that she'd almost forgotten Drew was slumped on the sofa like a beached whale, sucking lollipops and scratching his feet. Now she looked over and caught his smirk.

'What is?' she questioned.

'You're mooning. Have been for the last three weeks by my reckoning.'

She turned the corner of her book down. 'Can't you go back to being a miserable prat?'

'Yeah, could do. Only wouldn't make a difference to you mooning. Or brooding, is it? Not the same thing, right?'

'Armchair shrink, are you? Give it a rest and I'll make you another brew.'

The cup was sticky when he handed it over, coated in a layer of damp sugar. She rinsed it off while the kettle bottle then passed him a stack of ginger nuts to go with his tea. He held the lolly between his teeth and stuffed a biscuit in alongside it, chomping on them both.

'Mooning's when they haven't called you back,' he announced once he'd swallowed everything and licked the lolly stick clean. 'Brooding – that's what you do when you're not calling them back. Come on, Max. How long have I known you?' •

'Too long,' she muttered.

He saluted her with the stick then began picking his teeth with it. 'You do neither, that's all I'm saying. You've always been happy as is.'

'Have another bloody ginger nut and chuck that thing in the bin.'

'Just call her for God's sake.'

She scrubbed her forehead. 'If I chucked a biscuit outside, would you go fetch it?'

'Catty,' he said with a grin. 'Seriously, call her. Saves me fielding her calls on switch when I'm trying to cut my toenails.'

Max's hand slipped and tea sloshed over her jeans. She winced as the burning spread down her thighs, hunting around the kitchen counters for a tea towel that wasn't encrusted with lumps of coffee. She settled on the least worst and set to work on the soggy patches above her knees. Drew just watched, demolishing the last of the biscuits then scrabbling for another lolly.

'She didn't leave her name, but I'm not an idiot.'

'Debatable,' Max snapped.

'Oh, come on, what are you doing shooting the messenger? Look, she wanted to know if you were working this aft. No bullshit about wanting a cab or anything, straight to the bullseye. I told her you were on switch till later tonight and she hung up on me. So, who is she? I'd call it a one-night stand job, but not with the way you've been looking lately. You've been pining for her.'

'I've not been pining,' she answered.

Drew snickered. 'Easier to just tell me.'

'All right, all right . . .' She took a gulp from what was left in her mug then dumped it on the side. 'That night – when you lost Andrew – I turned up looking like I'd been dragged through a hedge backwards. You probably didn't notice.'

'I didn't,' he admitted with a pained smile. 'My head was all over the place.'

'Yeah, well, I'd stopped to help a woman with a flat tyre out by the nature reserve. She came with me to the hospital, was really good about it all. When she asked me out, I said no. End of, that's what I thought. Then she turns up here a month ago. You won't remember that either. You were off your face.'

'Try me. What does she look like?'

'Blonde hair, sapphire eyes, smaller than me.' Max paused and cleared her throat. 'Looks like she's stepped out of a business magazine or something. I told you she was a rep.'

His face lit up. 'Bloody hell, she was gorgeous. You lucky cow.'

'I'll tell Elena you said that.'

'So, what's wrong? She's fit, you're needing some company –'

'I'm not, though.'

'Pull the other one. You've got it bad and she's chasing after you. Sounds spot on to me. What are you waiting for?'

Max shrugged, picking at the rust on the draining board with her thumbnail. 'Better to leave it as a one-off.'

'Why? That only pays out if you're a martyr and you're not. You don't have to make it serious, but you can have a bit of fun before you go off her, right?'

'It's not that simple,' she said. Then she threw the pack of lollies onto his lap. 'Do me a favour and leave it, all right? It is what it is.'

The lure of kebabs with Kev finally got Drew shifted. Until she handed over the switch at seven, Max kicked her feet out on the desk and buried her mind in a battered copy of *Memoirs of a Rugby-Playing Man*. She'd turned her mobile off days ago when it wouldn't stop bleeping, but it was still in her pocket out of habit. On her way into the yard, she pulled it out then stuffed it back in again before her finger hit the power button. She was just reaching for her cab keys when something snatched at her arm and dragged her into the shadow of the high wall.

'Kiss me.'

Valerie's lips were smothering hers before she could think. Hands slipped under her shirt then twisted higher, kneading her breasts, until Max forced them away. She held Valerie's wrists aloft then shivered at her expression glimmering under the fading daylight.

'You want me to touch you,' Valerie said. 'That's why you're hiding from me.'

Max let her wrists drop, tucking her arms behind her back instead. 'I'm not.'

'Then what would you call ignoring my voicemails, hmm? And not responding to my numerous text messages?'

'Proper etiquette after a one-night stand,' Max replied.

Valerie shook her head. 'No, no, you're not hiding behind that. I don't know much about you, but I'm sure of one thing. You're the kind of woman who makes things clear. Sure, you walk away, but both sides are happy with that. I'm not happy.'

'What are you after — a refund?'

'A little honesty, that's all.'

The light around her eyes had dimmed. They were just these specks of sapphire pinning Max against the wall, centring all her senses on that point between her legs that had been throbbing for over a month. She knocked her fist rhythmically back against the brick, feeling the prickle along her knuckles. She didn't expect Valerie to grab the arm and pull it clear of the wall.

'Honesty, Max,' she said, massaging the red spots on her knuckles. 'Let's go somewhere and talk. Then, if you really want me to, I'll leave you alone. Please.'

She sucked in her breath and nodded to the car. 'I'll drive.'

All the way to the nature reserve, Valerie had been the model passenger. She'd sat with her hands clasped in her lap staring out of the side window and saying nothing. Max had been able to kid herself it was a normal fare until they parked alongside the empty cars and her stomach knotted up. She tugged the key from the ignition, waiting for Valerie to leave the cab first. That gave her a moment to squeeze her eyes shut and let the green surroundings bleed into black.

'I've done some walking around here recently,' said Valerie as Max fell into step beside her. 'There's a quiet path away from the lake, we'll go up there.'

Max just followed her, first across the pebbles and then over the dirt track that stretched into the woods. Her attention was fixed on the grey kitten heels that weren't made for hiking, even though Valerie sprang over criss-crossing tree roots as if she was wearing proper boots. The feet suddenly stopped moving and Max barrelled into a suit that was brimming with sweat. Valerie grasped her waist, holding her steady somehow, then smiled.

'You're clumsy, you know. Those wine glasses were a nightmare to clean up.'

'Thought that was both of us,' she murmured.

Valerie's hand slipped inside her belt. 'Oh, you do remember. Here was me thinking I'd imagined the best sex of my life. Thank goodness it wasn't all a dream.'

'I'm sorry,' Max said.

'Don't apologise. Just explain.'

She grimaced and scuffed her hand through her hair. 'Sorry.'

'You're doing it again. Come on, Max. Why did you ignore me for three weeks? When you left, I said I'd see you soon and I meant it. Am I to assume you didn't?'

Max was struggling to breathe between the heady smell of lavender and Valerie's trademark perfume. The hand tucked into her belt moved, pressing denim into her thighs. She began to arch against it then let out a growl and stepped away.

'I'm not doing this,' she said.

'Well, at least you're talking to me now,' Valerie replied, crossing her arms. 'Keep going – what is it you're not going to do? Fuck me senseless, hmm? You've done that already. Make me ache to touch you to the point where I'm wandering around meetings with community leaders imagining my fingers inside you? Tell me it was a one-night stand for you. Tell me that was your plan.'

'I didn't have a plan,' she muttered.

'So, how can it be that difficult to adapt? Is it me? I mean, did I misinterpret what happened? If I'm coming off as a bunny boiler, Max, I'd really like to know.'

Her hands were darting around all over the place. The midges spiralling through the trees were dodging out of her way, but Max couldn't shift her eyes from the fingers running circles in the air. She took a step forward then fell back, kicking her heel through fallen leaves. They crinkled and sputtered up brittle dust that hung around their feet before crumbling back to the ground.

'Max?' Valerie prompted in a low voice.

'You're not a bunny boiler,' she answered. She finally raised her eyes and attempted to stretch her lips into a smile. 'You're gorgeous, you're – you're everything someone on your wavelength would be lucky to have. But that's not me. I'm not into politics, I'm not a poster girl. You don't want the likes of me splashed all over the tabloids as your new – new friend.'

Valerie tucked her hair behind her ear. 'It would have to be private – private, not secret – for now. It'd be inappropriate given the circumstances if we were plastered all over the front pages.'

'Inappropriate . . . Yeah, that's what I meant.'

'I don't think you understand –'

Max snorted. 'Course not. I'm thick.'

'Like hell you are,' Valerie replied. 'I mean Tim, that's all.'

'Who's Tim?' she asked then she looked down at her shoes coated in browning grass. 'Oh, I get it. You're married.'

'It's not –'

'Course you're married. What else would it be other than a straight woman looking for a bit of fun? It's been staring me right –'

'Let me finish, Max,' Valerie interrupted, snapping a twig with her heel. 'I'm not married, I'm a widow. Tim died of

53

cancer a year ago, not long at all in the grand scheme of things. He left me that wonderful house, a heap of money, and a gaping hole in my life that I decided to fill with politics.'

Max just stared at her. 'You're too young to be a widow.'

'Well, there were quite a few years between us. It didn't matter and I loved him, but I wasn't expecting to lose him so quickly. Mid-thirties and I suddenly have this label, I'm a widow and that's it. I couldn't do it. I couldn't forever be known as Tim Smythe's widow, living on the money he'd left in his bank accounts and doing nothing all day.'

She tangled her hands together as she finished and glanced around the woodland. Max's eyes were still fixed on her, drinking in every ripple along her shirt and the way her teeth nipped their way along her lower lip. It ignited a fuse in Max's body that she could feel buzzing in all directions. She took a step forward then halted.

Valerie looked back, her eyes glistening. 'Max?'

'I don't do relationships,' she warned.

'Then I'm not asking for one. I'll take whatever's on offer, as long as you stop running away from it. I can't concentrate because I'm thinking about your head between my legs every five minutes, and I need to concentrate.'

'Yeah, I get that.'

'So, we have a deal?' Valerie asked.

Max reached out and slipped a hand inside her trousers, feeling the material strain around her fingers. She wrapped her free arm around Valerie's slender shoulders and let her lips do the answering back.

# Chapter 8

'How many times have I walked in here to see you like that?'

Amy's eyes snapped open. Her spine ached pressed against Tim's desk and her head was throbbing. The last she'd been aware of, the sun was beaming into the study, but now the room was bathed in an orange glow and Valerie was leaning against the door jamb. Amy struggled to her feet, using the desk as a crutch.

'I didn't hear you come home,' she said.

'You were asleep, sweetheart. In fact, you look exhausted.'

Amy blinked to clear her vision. 'I'm fine.'

'You're not. Listen, I know you're not happy about being here for weekends, but Clarice was quite –'

'So you've said. I'm going to find something to eat.'

'No need,' Valerie said, spinning on her heel. 'I picked up a pie. I'll go and put the oven on. You can stay in here if you'd like.'

'I don't need your permission.'

The creaks on the stairs uncoiled the knot in her stomach. She closed the door and settled back against Tim's desk, though the dream she'd been enjoying before the interruption was gone. The wood was rigid now, too stiff for comfort. She tolerated it until Valerie called her down for dinner then found her shoulders easing as she flicked the light off and slipped out of the door.

Dinner was improved by the CD player humming Chet Baker in the corner, making conversation unnecessary. Amy stood to move her place and Valerie cleared her throat.

'How about a coffee, hmm?'

Amy stifled her sigh and shrugged. While the coffee brewed, she loaded the dishwasher, the few bits and pieces they'd used dwarfed by the scale of it. Then she stood in the middle of the kitchen with her toes curled into her slippers waiting for Valerie to turn around.

'Let's take these through to the living room,' she said when she did. 'I need to talk to you about a few things.'

Amy trailed after her, watching the ritual of closing blinds, lighting candles, and lowering lamps from the threshold. The room glimmered like a catalogue advert, although Valerie's motions were constrained. Her thumb strayed too close to a flame on the mantelpiece, but she didn't let out a murmur. She tucked the hand underneath a cushion as they sat down on opposite sofas with their coffee cups and Amy's eyes narrowed.

'You're not pregnant, are you?' she questioned.

Valerie chuckled. 'No, I'm not. I'm sorry about bringing Rob back that time. I embarrassed you.'

'I wasn't embarrassed, I was angry.'

'Okay, okay, I know that. I do. And I understood it in the end. I know how it looks to you and what goes through your mind, but you're wrong. I was establishing barriers, I suppose. Those one-night stands were part and parcel of that. Maybe it's because bringing someone else into this situation feels incredibly awkward. How do I explain about us, hmm?'

'Well, you could try the truth. Then again, that's never been your strong point, has it?'

'Amy –'

'Is this going somewhere? Only I've got a book to read.'

'Surely you could read it down here like you used to do, instead of hiding away upstairs.'

Amy shook her head. 'You don't get it, do you? This isn't my home. This isn't where I grew up. It's . . . something else, something you've made. It's not mine, it's not Dad's. I'm actually amazed you left my room and the study alone when you went crazy.'

'I nearly didn't.' Valerie tapped her cup then took a long sip. 'Darling, I know you think I set out to erase him from history, but that wasn't the case. Sometimes, it's easier to move on than to dwell on the past, that's all. Now, I'm not blaming you, but if you'd stayed perhaps I wouldn't have gone as far as I did. I wanted to make it new, make the memories go away. Of him – and us.'

The words stretched into the silence and Amy focused on the flickering candle to avoid eye contact. Her stomach was quivering at the images this conversation was unearthing in mind – Tim in his armchair, Tim carving the turkey, Tim falling against the window ledge. It all blended together until the flame blurred in front of her.

'I've been thinking about what you said,' continued Valerie finally. 'About giving away his clothes – do you remember that? When Rob was here.'

'Why do you keep talking about him? Are you seeing him again?'

'No, of course I'm not. It's just that was when you said it, remember? You know, those clothes were something I couldn't part with, not immediately. I think it was for your sake more than mine. I hated having them in the house sometimes, but I tried to consider your feelings, the way I did with the study. I didn't want to take everything away, I wanted you to have something to come back to. They're still in the wardrobe, sweetheart. They still smell of him.'

Tears prickled at Amy's eyelids. 'Right.'

'I think – I think the time's come, don't you? So, what I wanted to ask was whether we could do it together. He'd have liked that.'

The words hung over the room. Amy had to mentally heave herself away from the memory of leather and sandalwood whirling around her brain before she understood what Valerie had said. Then her whole body began trembling.

'You want to get rid of his clothes? What about his books?'

Valerie winced. 'The books are yours, sweetheart, of course they are. I just meant that –'

'Do you want to move someone in? Is this about that John Foster again?'

'It's not about John.'

'So, what? You just want the extra space in the wardrobe, is that it?'

The flame on the mantelpiece flickered against the marble as her voice bounced off the white walls. Amy squinted at the candle then flinched as Valerie jumped up to blow it out.

'This was a mistake. We're obviously not ready for this. I want you home, I don't want to push you further away.'

Amy rolled her eyes. 'I don't think that's possible, do you?'

'You're never going to forgive me, are you? No matter what I do, you find it cathartic to hate me. I mean, I understand – I hate my mother, remember? She was never there for me, she abandoned me when I needed her more than anything, but I didn't do that to you. You forget everything I've ever done, how much I love you. It had nothing to do with you, nothing at all. It was between me and your father, and we dealt with it.'

'Nothing to . . . God, Mum, are you serious? Look, you know what? I don't care anymore. You go and move your fancy man in. It'll give me another reason to stay away.'

Valerie shook her head. 'That's not the way I want to do this. If – and this is a big if, sweetheart – something developed to that stage, I'd want us to be a family, the three of us.'

'We're not a family,' Amy snapped. 'You don't treat family like you treated him.'

Colour flooded into Valerie's face and her eyes narrowed. Amy squared her shoulders, ready to flare back, but Valerie drooped and twisted out of the room like a wounded animal. The front door slammed and silence ruptured the house as Amy wondered where Valerie's flight instinct had materialised from. It wasn't like her at all.

Any residual anger drained away during Saturday, leaving the air stagnant.

Amy decamped to the library during the day and returned to find Valerie monopolising the kitchen table with piles of documents. They scraped through dinner with the driest conversation about road maintenance then Amy retreated to her room and wondered how she could escape from the house on Sunday.

She settled on slipping away into town while Valerie was in the shower, calling for a taxi from a leaflet she found on the hall table. Nostalgia took her towards a cosy café she'd visited with Tim for their Saturday morning cake trips. It was empty when she walked in, not even a waiter in sight. The door thudded behind her and she hesitated in the doorway until the allure of a wooden chair facing into the precinct won her over. She sat down and gazed at the cluster of shoppers swaying across from one side of the street to the other, all talk and smiles.

'It's Amy Smythe, isn't it?' a voice asked suddenly. 'Tim's daughter?'

She jumped and looked up to find a young man towering above the table. With the mop of brown hair, thick eyebrows, and fuzzy goatee, he looked more like a scruffy mutt with piercings than a human being. She couldn't say she recognised him, although he obviously worked here from the apron hooked around his waist.

'I'm sorry about your dad,' he went on. 'I would've said that before, but you haven't been in since. I bet you don't remember me, do you?'

Amy gestured to the chair opposite. 'Ed, right?'

'You read that on my name badge,' he replied as he sat down.

'Yes, but I do remember coming in here with him, he was actually really religious about it. Every morning for a year, we'd sit over there and read.'

'Him the paper, you some thick book. He never told you why he came in, then?'

'Well, I know he liked the coffee, though it did seem a bit far to come every week.'

Ed twisted a dishcloth from his belt and began twirling it around his hands. 'He bailed me out, gave me a loan to stop us going under after my dad passed away. They were old mates from school so he took a punt on me when no bank'd look twice.'

'He loaned you money? But you can't have been more than . . .'

Now she remembered him. He'd been clean-shaven a few years ago, still gangly, but a bit of a klutz. Her coffee had ended up on the floor more than once and, though she hadn't minded, he couldn't stop apologising. Tim seemed to find him endearing, and they spent ages talking over at the counter while she was reading. It was always classics she brought with her, the books Tim encouraged her to read like *A Tale of Two Cities*. She'd been halfway through that when the oncologist had dropped the final bombshell and she'd never finished it.

'I was eighteen,' Ed continued, 'and I'd never paid a bill, let alone run something like this. Your dad, he came to the funeral then came by here after. I was going through the motions – you know what it's like – but he wouldn't bugger off and leave me to it. Ended up telling him everything and he offered me a loan to tide us over the sticky patch. Me and Mum, we had the funeral to pay for and all the suppliers were kicking off. The money might not have been a lot in the grand scheme of things, but it took me a while to pay it all back. Your dad said that coming in here every weekend was protecting his investment and supporting a local . . . Hey, are you all right? I didn't mean to upset you.'

Tears were dribbling along her cheeks. 'Sorry.'

'Don't apologise, it's okay. I get it. Here, wipe your . . .'

Instead of a tissue, he pressed the dishcloth into her hands. A chuckle gurgled in her throat as she took it and dabbed at her face. It came away lathered in mascara.

'You didn't upset me,' she answered with a weak smile. 'I like hearing good things about him. You just surprised me, that's all.'

He clicked his fingers. 'I know the remedy for that. Don't move.'

She dug out her make-up bag to assess the damage as he bounded off to the counter. Sure enough, her cheeks were puckered with dollops of black and she rushed to scrub them away with cleanser. Ed returned just as she finished and deposited a plate in front of her.

'Double chocolate cheesecake with cream.'

'My favourite,' Amy murmured.

'I know. Tim suggested I put it on the menu because of that. All homemade, local ingredients and all that.'

She took the spoon he waved at her. 'Homemade by you?'

'Hey, you should try my soufflé. I'll leave you in peace, but that's on the house, yeah?'

'I can't accept that. You're trying to run a business.'

'Which I wouldn't be doing if it wasn't for your dad so humour me. Which reminds me – have a look upstairs when you're done. Something else Tim suggested.'

He left her with that cryptic comment and wandered off into the kitchen. She wolfed down the cheesecake then climbed the rickety staircase to see what all the fuss was about. Her foot caught on the top step as she looked around.

What used to be an overspill area with broken chairs stacked in the corner had been transformed into an eclectic cavern. The walls bled with film posters and faded gig notices, illuminated by multicoloured spotlights while the windows onto the street were blacked out. Mismatched armchairs and sofas were boxed around low tables laden with art materials and books of every kind split into genre.

61

In the left corner, behind the staircase, there was a hollow with drapes and bean bag chairs and a wooden sign saying, "Read Here".

A smile crept onto Amy's face. She circled the tables until she came across a spiral tower of familiar titles then she plucked out *Great Expectations* and dropped her jacket across a chair. The bean bag gobbled her up as she flicked open the cover and settled down to read.

It was about twenty minutes later when Ed appeared with a large cup in one hand. He managed to bend without spilling the coffee and pushed it into hands.

'Skinny latte,' he said.

She let the book rest on her lap. 'You've got a really good memory.'

'Until it comes to the accounts,' he replied. '*Great Expectations* – nice choice.'

'You're a Dickens' fan?'

'I've read a couple, I'm up for the classics. Most of the books up here are mine or my dad's, not that I've read them all. Picked them up and put them away for when I had a chance. Not much time for reading these days. Anyway, I'll see you in a bit.'

Her eyes lingered as he returned to the staircase then she glanced down into the coffee. There was a leaf embossed into the froth that she was reluctant to destroy. She reached for her phone to take a picture of the cup before she finally relented and took a sip. The coffee was almost as gorgeous as the leaf.

A text from Valerie disturbed her reading an hour later. She'd latched herself onto a political event in Leeds so, in her words, it was safe to go back to the house. That only reminded Amy that she had the Sunday trains to contend with to get home to Biddy's so she put *Great Expectations* back onto its table then gathered up her belongings and headed downstairs with her cup.

Ed was mopping the floor. He gestured for her to stop then motioned for her to jump over the damp section by the staircase. Instead of landing gracefully, she overshot and skidded into his arms.

'Sorry, sorry,' she said as she sprang away. 'I didn't –'

'I nearly kill you, I catch you. Company policy.'

She grimaced as he took the cup from her hand. 'I'm such an idiot.'

'You're not,' Ed assured her.

'How much is the bill?' she questioned.

'Amy, no. That was on the house, I told you.'

'But –'

'Just come back,' he interrupted. 'I could do with the customers.'

Her shoulders relaxed and she finally looked at him again. There was so much of the spindly teenager left that she could see him as Tim must've seen him – anxious and eager. No wonder he'd liked him.

'I'll be back,' she promised. 'Thanks, Ed.'

## Chapter 9

'Pick up from the precinct, next to the Pink Lady. Heading to Geith Place.'

Max scrambled for the radio. 'I'll take that.'

A garbled reply came over from Pauline, but she wasn't listening. She was already easing the cab off the kerb and scuffing her fingers through her hair to persuade it to lie flat. Once she was blared at from behind, she gave it up and focused on weaving through the erratic Sunday traffic until the fountain came into view.

She craned her neck as she pulled up then cracked her head on the side window when the rear door opened. A young woman, blonde hair flung around her shoulders, was slotting into the back.

'Sorry,' Max muttered, settling down into her seat. 'Taxi to Geith Place, was it?'

'Yes, that's right.'

It only took ten minutes to get there instead of the usual twenty. The passenger was fair enough – no trouble, not eager to chat, pretty much an ideal pick-up in the normal way of things. They were just drawing into the cul-de-sac when the woman cleared her throat.

'Is there any chance you could wait? I just need to pick up a bag then I'm going straight to the train station.'

'Sure, no worries. What number is it?'

'The one on the left here with all the trees.'

Max's foot skidded off the clutch. 'This one?'

'That's right. Thanks a lot, I'll only be a minute.'

The car lurched to a halt and Max twisted around. 'I had a drop-off here a while back. Your aunt or something?'

'I wish. No, that's my mum, I found your number on the fridge.' She slipped out of the car. 'I'll be as quick as I can, I really don't want to keep you.'

A mumble came out of Max's mouth that didn't make sense to her, let alone anyone else. Her eyes followed the woman up the canopied drive and she watched her fumble with her keys, swinging her head back in a familiar way. Looking at her like this, there was no doubt they were mother and daughter. Before Max could clear the fog that caused in her brain, the daughter was back.

'Thanks for that, I really appreciate it.'

Max blinked and started the engine. 'Local or central station?'

'Local's fine, thank you.'

Ten minutes on the road this time was more like a marathon. Max kept shooting glances into the rear-view mirror, trying to get a read on everything from how old this girl was to whether she was anything like her mother. Even when she bumped the car up onto the kerb outside the station, her mind was still finding fresh questions. She couldn't help but turn around.

'Your mum's somebody, isn't she?' she asked.

The girl rustled in her bag. 'Likes to think she is. Sorry, that was uncalled for. How much do I owe you?'

'Erm, call it a straight fiver.'

'Really? Here, keep the change and thanks for waiting.'

Max pushed the £10 note back into her hands. 'Don't be daft.'

'Please keep it. You've been fantastic.'

She had no choice but to take it, smiling as the girl jumped out of the cab. Only when her blonde hair had bobbed through the snicket into the station proper did Max exhale and crumple the banknote into her fist.

The rest of her shift blurred into a mush of faces and street names. She clocked off when she couldn't see straight, stopping off at the shop for a pizza and a pack of beer. It was knocking on for 9pm when she turned onto her road.

A BMW was parked up on the verge leading to her flat. Until the door opened and Valerie stepped out, red coat flashing under the streetlights, Max hadn't decided to stop. She was forced to slam on the brakes and pull in behind the BMW, but she didn't unbuckle her seatbelt. Valerie strode over and dropped into the passenger seat with a thud.

'I've left you five messages. I was worried about you.'

Max shifted away. 'No need.'

'It doesn't seem that way to me.' Valerie stretched a hand to her thigh. 'What's wrong?'

She shook her head.

'Max?' Valerie pressed.

'Let's not do this,' she replied.

'Do what? I don't understand. What's happened?'

'I just think –'

'You're going cold on me again. Why?'

She brushed Valerie's hand away. 'It's run its course, that's all. You go back to your politics, I'll go back to my life. We've had a good run, but we said it wasn't going anywhere.'

'I don't accept that. You can't tell me you haven't been enjoying this. Look at me.'

'Let's just –'

'If you're breaking up with me, you can damn well look at me. Now.'

Max crunched her thighs together. The last of the sunlight was draining from the cab, creeping over the dashboard then the bonnet. She followed it out until fingers circled her wrist.

'Talk to me,' Valerie insisted.

'I'm not getting dragged into it,' she answered, yanking her arm free. 'All the politics. I told you – it goes straight over my head. Best to let it fizzle out now.'

'And what happens if I don't want that, hmm?'

All Max could do was shrug.

'I see. You've taken the decision of my hands. Unilaterally, you've decided that –'

'You'd better go,' Max cut in. 'Best you're not seen with me, not now.'

Valerie stared at her then finally let out a snort and forced the door open. Her coat skimmed the paintwork as she turned around to lean back into the cab, her eyes narrowed.

'Yes, you're right. I certainly wouldn't want it known that I'd wasted my time on someone who obviously doesn't give a damn.'

## Chapter 10

The house was still when Amy let herself in on Friday night. No lights were lit, although the door had only been on the latch. She pushed it closed behind her, but she didn't reach for the light switch. The idea that Valerie was occupied with another toy boy prickled at the back of her mind.

'Mum?' she called.

Nothing. She swallowed then stepped towards the kitchen, leaving her bag at the bottom of the stairs. Part of her expected to find clothes strewn over the floor or incriminating wine glasses in the sink, but, instead, Valerie was sat at the table in front of her laptop. Its screen was dark and her eyes were directed into the sunset stretching across the fields.

Amy hesitated then flicked the lights on. The dazzle brought Valerie straight to her feet, lips curling into a synthetic smile.

'You're later than I expected,' she said. 'There's a pasta bake keeping warm. Why don't you take your things upstairs and I'll serve?'

She swept over to the counter and fiddled with the CD player. As the sound of Sarah Vaughan filtered through the kitchen, Amy turned and climbed the stairs to her bedroom with her bag limp against her hip. She'd dropped it onto the bed before she realised there was something out of place, even though it took her a moment to pinpoint what it was.

A ragged owl was nestled underneath her bedroom lamp, his beak resting on a mosaic jewellery box. Neither of them had been there last week. Amy hadn't seen Wilbur since Valerie's big renovation and she'd just assumed he'd found his way into the skip. He'd been a present from Tim during a visit to an owl sanctuary in North Yorkshire, while the jewellery box was something he'd given to Valerie for an anniversary one year. From what Amy remembered, Valerie had never placed it prominently in the house, not seeming to have any sentimental attachment to it even before she'd decided to rip the place apart.

'Amy? Are you ready?'

She shook herself and returned to the kitchen, surprised to find bowls of pasta and side salad on the table.

'We're not eating in the dining room?' she asked.

Valerie settled into her chair with a glass of red. 'You invariably complain about that. I thought this would be easier, quite frankly.'

The smell of tomato and chilli curbed Amy's mistrust to the point that she devoured the meal with the accompaniment of jazz and nothing from Valerie. Once she'd set her cutlery straight, though, the sight of Valerie picking at her lettuce piqued her interest.

'Where did you find Wilbur?' she questioned.

'Hmm?' Valerie raised her chin. 'What do you mean? Who's Wilbur?'

Amy opened her mouth then stifled her response. She'd been trapped too often inside Valerie's machinations to allow herself to get caught again. So, she changed tack.

'How are things politically?'

'Fine, fine.'

'Really?'

'Yes, of course.'

'Right.' Amy paused. 'Only –'

'How were things at the office this week?' Valerie queried.

She shrugged. 'Fine.'

'I'd hoped they might be better.'

'What?' she asked, frowning.

'I know you like to think I don't pay attention, but I do. I know you've been finding it difficult there, I understand why.'

'You're not going to tell me you were trying to spare my feelings in the first place, are you?'

Valerie smiled faintly. 'I wouldn't insult your intelligence, darling. I've only been there twice since it happened, you know. Once to say thank you for the funeral flowers and then . . .'

'To talk about my internship,' she murmured. 'Thank you.'

'Well, you made it clear what you wanted.' Valerie speared a cherry tomato onto her fork. 'And what you didn't. Anyway, where did you go last week when you sneaked out of here? Please don't tell me you bought any more clothes. I'm not sure Clarice's wardrobes can cope.'

'Erm, no, I didn't.' The expectant expression on Valerie's face spurred her on. 'I wandered around, that's all. It was pretty quiet so I got a taxi and . . . Mum, are you all right?'

Valerie'd jolted against the table, rattling the frame back and forth. Nothing had tumbled then she raised a hand to her hair and it overshot, knocking over her glass of wine. The waterfall cascaded into a puddle on the floor and bubbled through the grooves until it ran out of energy. Valerie leapt across and began mopping up the mess with her napkin.

'Mum?'

'Give me a minute, I don't want it to stain.'

'Then get a proper –'

'You got a taxi, you say? To here?'

Amy stared at her. 'Why does that matter?'

'I'm interested, darling.' Valerie rested back on her heels and licked her lips. 'What company was it? Who was the driver? Did you talk?'

'What do you mean – talk? About what?'

'I don't know. Perhaps about me –'

'You're unbelievable,' Amy growled as she scraped her chair along the floor. 'Everything has to be about you, doesn't it? For the record, Mum, I don't go around gloating about being related to the great Valerie Smythe. I'm actually ashamed to be your daughter, not proud of it.'

70

'Wait a minute, Amy. I didn't –'

She snorted as she made for the stairs. 'No, you never do.'

Another Saturday hiding in the library gave way to an evening of tiptoeing around the house. Valerie didn't even insist they ate together, leaving a pan of casserole warming on the hob while she took a lengthy bath. On Sunday morning, Amy slipped out of the house again, eschewing a taxi this week in favour of walking into town. She regretted that decision when she stopped outside the café and realised her jeans were sticky against her legs. It was only Ed glancing over and spotting her that propelled her through the door.

Her entrance didn't attract the attention of the older customers huddled in the corner with empty cups. She crossed to the counter and tried to focus on the menu hooked to the wall.

'Morning,' Ed said.

She threw him a polite smile. 'Morning.'

'Do you want a skinny latte?' he asked.

'Please.' Nothing on the menu was making sense, it was all a jumble of words. 'And, erm . . .'

Ed planted both palms on the counter. 'Breakfast or snack? I can do anything. Want an omelette without the mushroom or scrambled eggs without the scrambled bit?'

The clammy sensation around her collar was intensifying. She drew in a long breath and managed to study the menu in a way that meant the letters didn't blur into gloop. Ed was watching her; she could see that from the corner of her eye, and maybe the other customers were too by now.

'I'll just have poached egg,' she said finally. 'But could I have it on a brioche bun instead of toast?'

He grinned and pressed a few buttons on the till. 'Coming up.'

Once she'd passed him a £5 note and received change, she took the stairs two at a time. It was empty up here again, with the copy of *Great Expectations* just where she'd left it. Her makeshift bookmark of a train ticket was still lodged inside and her shoulders relaxed. She took the book back to the reading nook and continued where she'd left off.

Ed arrived ten minutes later, balancing a cup in one hand and a plate in the other. He must've seen the question in her face.

'More of a challenge keeping it all steady,' he explained as he set it down on the side table between the bean bag chairs. 'My dad used to have a right go at me, said I was costing the place a fortune.'

'With respect, you were always dropping things when I was here,' Amy said.

He coughed. 'Well, I'm getting better at not doing it.'

'Why not just use a tray?' she questioned.

'Keeps things interesting. I love this place, yeah, but if I didn't have a few things to keep me on my toes, I'd go mad.'

'That's what my dad used to love about his job. Every case was different and it taught him something new, mostly about people and what they could do if pushed. It fascinated him.'

'But not you?' Ed scratched his neck and winced. 'Sorry, that's a bit –'

'Not as much,' she interrupted. 'Not yet, anyway.'

He nodded then tilted his head to the side. 'What about politics then? Does that go down in the same book?'

'You know who my mum is,' she muttered.

'Figured it was her from the name and I saw her round the precinct a few weeks ago. She's been talking to local business owners.'

'Really? Has she talked to you?'

'Now, be fair, does this place look like it'll be around by the time the election comes up?'

Amy's eyes strayed around the room and she bit her lip. 'It should be. You should be overrun with customers.'

'Well, you came back,' Ed answered with a shrug. 'That's good enough for me.'

# Chapter 11

A pair of black heels had been tossed onto the carpet.

Max halted halfway up the stairs. Her eyes raked up from the dangling ankles to the thighs pressed together on the windowsill and she swallowed hard. Her impulse to touch nearly took her over, so she knotted her hands behind her back to be on the safe side.

'What are you doing here?' she asked.

Valerie hopped down, landing on her toes. 'I thought of going to the office, but I didn't want to do this somewhere you can run from. If I called, you would've ignored me, so I took decisive action and caught the door downstairs when someone was leaving. Only it's been a long day and my feet were hurting, so I had to make myself comfortable. Oh, come on, Max. Say something.'

'You've laddered your tights.'

'That's better, that's interaction. I like it.' Valerie glanced down at her legs. 'Even if these were fresh on this morning.'

An image of her dressing suddenly lodged in Max's mind. She'd seen her rolling her tights back on, leaving her underwear nestled under the passenger seat for someone else to find. Cheeky, but Max had relished it, and had left them there most of the time. She blinked away the memory and crossed her arms.

'What do you want?'

'A glass of wine?' Valerie suggested. 'A cup of tea? Or a glass of soda water? Please, Max. Do you really want to have this conversation on a landing where all and sundry could hear?'

'Fine.' She gestured to the door. 'Two minutes.'

Walking into the flat, she couldn't help but see it through Valerie's eyes. The hallway was littered with dirty trainers and lumps of newspapers that hadn't made it as far as the bin. A spotlight had blown months ago in the kitchen, but it only pointed to the cooker so she hadn't bothered replacing it. She even had to shift a stack of rugby mags from a stool to give Valerie space to sit. Then she spun and kicked a pizza box clean across into the lounge before twisting back to put the kettle on.

'I appreciate the opportunity to talk,' Valerie said.

Max tugged two mugs from the cupboard. 'I can't see we've got anything to talk about.'

'Well, I think we have. I understand why you pushed me away again, I'll admit I deserved it. But I wouldn't forgive myself if I didn't plead for a chance to explain. At least give me that.'

'I've said all I need to. How do you take your tea?'

'A little milk, no sugar.' Valerie paused. 'Just like Amy.'

One of the teabags in Max's hand sailed to the floor. She dumped another one into the mug and focused on the gurgling of the kettle, ignoring the figure behind her.

'It's unforgivable that you found out the way you did,' Valerie went on after a few moments. 'I should've told you about her when I told you about Tim –'

'But you didn't.'

'In all honesty, I was frightened. You were already skittish about –'

'I'm not a pit pony,' Max cut in.

Valerie rubbed her forehead. 'I didn't say you were. Only you didn't want a relationship and I thought the idea of Amy might push you away completely. Besides, it isn't as simple as you might think. She doesn't – she doesn't live with me.'

The kettle clicked off and bubbled itself into silence while Max surveyed her face. All the emotion was raw, but she'd made it a rule not to be done in by people showing her what they wanted her to see. That said, she couldn't drag her gaze away from Valerie's eyes flicking around all over the place, looking everywhere except at her.

'How old is she?' Max questioned.

'Seventeen, eighteen in a few months.'

'So, why isn't she living with you?'

'After Tim died . . .' Valerie laced her fingers together on her lap, drawing flesh up around her knuckles. 'Well, she stayed for a matter of weeks before she moved in with her grandmother – Tim's mother. It's closer to her college, nearer to her friends. We have dinner once a week and I've managed to persuade her to stay weekends with me over the summer by helping her get an internship at Tim's firm. If it sounds transactional, that's because it is.'

Max frowned. 'Why?'

'Grief does funny things to people, I suppose,' she replied with a shrug. 'Look at me – I went into politics. I'm sorry, Max. I wanted to be honest about the situation, but if we were only ever going to be a temporary thing, just a bit of fun . . . I was trying to keep it all light, keep you interested. It was control in a way. I wanted to control everything, control how you were going to react, how Amy would react to it. And, you know, if I had an ounce of sense, I wouldn't be here. I would've walked away after that first time.'

'Then why didn't you?'

A shriek echoed through the kitchen when Valerie jumped off her stool. She wandered across to the lounge, looking over it like an estate agent would a demolition site, then grasped a wrinkled shirt that was slung over the sofa. It crumpled into her hands as she turned around.

'Most people I meet are . . . boring. If I'm officially there to listen to them, fine, but many of them just assume I am anyway. And, Max, they're honestly boring. Little men in their offices doing what little men in offices do. Then you've got the women – now, they won't deviate from their scripts, especially not with me around in case I take it for ammunition further down the line. I love talking to what they call "ordinary people". That's where I come from, that's what I understand. But the rest of it . . . Sometimes, it's just like dealing with a mob of suited robots. Do you know why I originally went into hospice care, hmm?'

76

Max shook her head, attention fixed on Valerie's hands kneading her shirt.

'I wanted to feel something, properly feel something. You know, I was never any good at natural responses; normal responses, Amy calls them. If there's a wrong thing to be done, I've always done it. I love her, of course I do, but I'm not what you'd call an emotive mother. My mother wasn't, I was never taught how to be. I think it's easier, actually, to open your heart to people you barely know. In the end, it all comes down to love and pain. I saw that every day at the hospice, I was privileged to be a part of it. Share in all those endings, make things slightly more bearable where I could. And then I lost Tim . . . I mean, cancer – it was the universe's idea of a sick joke. I had to detach from it – from him and Amy – just to get through. I couldn't do my job anymore. I needed something new, something that was mine and didn't remind me of him.'

The jittering that Max had taken at first to be mild shivers had turned into shaking. She stepped forward, waving to the sofa.

'Sit down or something,' she said.

Valerie crushed the shirt into her stomach. 'I don't want to sit down. Just listen to me.'

'I'm listening,' she answered and Valerie nodded a few times.

'Since Tim died, I've thrown myself into politics and one-night stands with men I knew wouldn't expect more. I enjoyed the attention, I thought I was as happy as I was going to be. Then I nearly knocked you out with that jack handle and something changed. That night, I felt it – didn't you? It was though everything slotted into place for the first time. I learned to love Tim and, trust me, he was more of a husband than I ever deserved. But with you . . . Max, you could've carried on driving that first night and I wouldn't have complained.'

Max shifted her weight. 'I don't –'

'Don't want to hear it, I know.' Valerie straightened her spine, tossing the rumpled shirt onto the floor. 'It'd be better for you if I walked away, wouldn't it? If I had any self-respect, I wouldn't do this to myself. I wouldn't be here, I wouldn't need you to touch me, but I do.'

'Valerie –'

'I love you,' she interrupted. 'I know you'd rather not believe it, but I love you.'

The words sucked the air out of her then hovered in the room like a grenade. Any movement would detonate the damn thing, so, as long as she stayed still, she'd be safe.

'Max . . .'

It was the quiver that did it. She couldn't help stepping forward and gathering Valerie up in her arms. Everything from the way she burrowed into her chest down to the pressure of their legs as they slotted together hit her all at once. It was natural to press a kiss to her hair, natural to sweep a tear away from her cheek. She almost heard the click when their eyes met.

Valerie rested their foreheads together. 'What was I meant to do, hmm?'

'What do you mean?' Max asked.

'There I was, falling for you, and you just seemed to be in it for the sex. You wouldn't even hold me for a few minutes in the backseat of my car when I was drifting off.'

Max stroked her cheek. 'I held you for twenty minutes, maybe a half hour.'

'You told me you woke me up straight away,' Valerie murmured, drawing back to look at her. 'Why did you lie?'

'Seemed easier,' she replied.

'Than what?'

'I don't know.'

Valerie gripped her wrist until the skin bunched up. 'No, you can do better than that. Talk to me, explain what's going on in that head of yours so we can fix it.'

'I don't do relationships,' she muttered.

'That's not a response, that's a manoeuvre. If you don't want a relationship then there's a reason behind it, there's some logic. Don't come out with any rubbish about you being thick either. You're not and I'm sick of the implication you are.'

Max managed to peel away, making it as far as the counter before a hand yanked her back.

'Don't run,' Valerie warned. 'It won't solve anything. You're afraid of something, just be honest with me.'

She turned, ready to argue the toss, but the determined sparkle in Valerie's eyes shut her up. Being looked at like that caught in her throat like a gulp of perfume and all her words disintegrated. Her fingers slipped into Valerie's hair and she dropped a kiss onto the tip of her nose. She felt Valerie's smile and it bled into her own.

'Why does it scare you?' asked Valerie softly.

'It doesn't,' she answered.

'Max –'

'You don't have to catch the plague to know it's a bad idea.'

Valerie growled and dragged herself away. 'That's what I am to you? The plague?'

'I didn't mean it like –'

'Oh, I'd love to know how that could've been meant in a positive way. Honestly, tell me. How is comparing me to the plague a compliment?'

'I can't get you out of my head,' she snapped.

Her voice echoed around the room, making them both jump. The flash of satisfaction that crossed Valerie's face was compounded by the way she straightened her shoulders. Max's stomach muscles contracted, but she couldn't stop the words spilling out.

'My parents – they do the normal thing pretty well. Colonel Peter Jarvis, respected staff officer and all that rubbish. Mrs Sadie Jarvis, model Army wife. Only child, Maxine Jarvis, expected to follow in her father's footsteps. Practically written for me, except I wasn't interested in getting my legs blown off. We were stationed in Cyprus, yeah, but everything was kicking off when I was growing up. The Gulf War, the IRA, the Balkans – everything. So, I'm looking at that and wondering whether I'll end up dead before I hit twenty. But my parents have got it all mapped out for me.'

Valerie's gaze was unwavering. 'Go on.'

'Enlist, do my time and work my way up. That was my dad's way of thinking. My mum threw meeting a bloody Major and getting married into the mix. Everything was building up ahead of me, and there was bugger all I could do about it. When you're in a community like that, there's pressure to believe in the ethos and everything – believe in what's going on. I couldn't. And I definitely wasn't going to be marrying any officer my mum would've had her eye on. I knew that age fourteen. None of it was ending – it wasn't ending well.'

Her burst of energy had crumbled as the memories began hitting her one by one. She grabbed onto the counter to steady herself and lowered her chin to ward off Valerie's piercing eyes. That worked until a hand wound its way around her neck, tickling her hairline.

'What happened?' Valerie questioned.

Max closed her eyes. 'I put them straight – so to speak. I didn't want to join up and I was gay so, the way things stood back then, I wasn't getting married to any officer either. Pissed off the pair of them in one swoop. We were based in Germany by then and the last thing they wanted was gossip getting around the base. So, they sent me back here.'

'What, alone?'

'To stay with my Great Aunt Bea in Harrogate, my dad's aunt. They reckoned it might sort me out, living with someone like her, but it went the other way.'

Valerie pressed a kiss to her cheek. 'Someone like her?'

'Completely wacko,' Max replied, opening her eyes and managing a smile. 'No discipline, no kowtowing to anyone else's prejudices, and do what you wanted to make yourself happy. She was seventy one when I moved in with her. Been married four times, no kids of her own.'

'They really thought that would fix you? She sounds like she lived life to the full. Wouldn't that be ideal for a teenager wanting to get away from the Army?'

Max shrugged. 'Yeah, I've thought about that. Talked about it with Bea as well. She said that my dad reckoned I'd miss the discipline and realise I didn't have any other options in life. I'd never done well academically, so if I didn't go into the Army then what was I going to do?'

'Become a cabbie,' murmured Valerie.

'Wasn't planned, but that's how it worked out. Once I'd left school, I passed my test because Bea suggested it. Then she took me on as a private chauffeur, so to speak. Driving Aunt Bea – it was like a comedy show sometimes. But I liked it, and I like being a cabbie.'

Valerie tucked a thumb underneath her chin and forced her to look up. 'I never thought you didn't. But I understand it more now. It symbolises freedom to you, doesn't it?'

'I'd never say it like that but, yeah, I suppose so.'

'And relationships . . . You perceive them as constricting, prescriptive even.'

'Maybe.' She paused and grimaced. 'All right, yeah.'

'Here's my problem, though,' said Valerie as she stroked her cheek with the back of her hand. 'In this context, you're equating me with your parents. Why not equate me with Bea, hmm? I don't understand that.'

Max felt a flush creep across her face, burning especially under Valerie's hand. She extracted herself just enough to duck her head away and clenched her jaw. Being transparent wasn't something she appreciated, but she couldn't control the way her body was giving her up any more than she could control how much she wanted Valerie near her. There was no room for compromise so she cleared her throat.

'You're more like my dad than Bea,' she admitted.

Valerie's lips parted. 'Oh.'

'I'm sorry,' Max muttered, but Valerie just shook her head.

'No, don't be. I – I get it, I think. I manipulated you into this in the first place –'

'It wasn't like that –'

'I should've heeded you when you rejected me the first time. I pushed matters and that reminds you of a situation where you had no control. I understand why you'd feel as though I was forcing you along. Not telling you about Amy was simply another nail, wasn't it?'

She pulled away completely, her hands shaking. Max watched her across the room then found herself following her. She wound up almost boxing her in, so there was nowhere to go when she turned around, and the look on her face was insecure, scared even.

'That's why you wouldn't let me touch you,' she whispered. 'You didn't trust me.'

Max stretched a hand onto her cheek. 'It wasn't you.'

'You don't trust yourself,' said Valerie slowly. 'Why not?'

'Because . . .' She swallowed down the lump in her throat and met her eye. 'Because loving you scares me. I don't know what to do with it.'

A smile slipped onto Valerie's face, opening her up so much that Max's breath caught. They moved together in sync with fluid heat sweeping through her body the moment their lips touched. It was all she could do to keep them both on their feet when Valerie's hand plunged down into her underwear. She let out a groan and tilted her head back, giving her room to pepper kisses along her throat.

'We'll work it out,' Valerie promised as her fingers curled and Max reeled against her. 'Right now, just give into it. Give in.'

# Chapter 12

September brought a return to college and no more weekends at Geith Place, at least until her birthday spa trip at the end of the month. That was Biddy's idea, and Amy just went along with it, eager to keep a lid on the questions that now sprouted up daily about college, university applications, and anything else Biddy could think of. A break, even one with Valerie, was a welcome distraction.

Her own birthday present to herself was to skip Law on the Friday afternoon. She knew that Valerie would be elsewhere so she went back to Geith Place with plans to watch a film in the living room and eat her weight in popcorn. However, she'd barely made it into her pyjamas before she heard the front door open downstairs. She hesitated on the landing as she realised Valerie was on the phone, uncertain why her stomach was suddenly tingling. Then it hit her: this wasn't the Valerie she knew. It was a voice from a memory.

In the months after the terminal diagnosis, whenever she'd thought no one else was around, Valerie had spoken to Tim like this. Her voice had been a collage of affection, vulnerability, and flirtation that struck Amy at the time like a revelation. She'd perched on the stairs, leaning her head against the banister to listen to the warmth bouncing back and forth between them until her eyes had prickled with hot tears. That Valerie had vanished before the funeral, and Amy had barely thought about her since.

The recollection gave way to ice settling in the pit of her stomach. She groped for the banister and lowered herself onto the stairs, tucking her elbows between her knees. Valerie's ritual of putting the kettle on was unwavering, whether she'd been to the shops or for a fortnight in the Maldives. All Amy had to do was sit quietly and she'd hear everything.

'She's bound to be nervous,' Valerie was saying. 'When I had my first scan, my head was all over the place, and I hadn't been through everything she has . . . Let me know how it goes. Are we still set for Wednesday? It seems an age away . . . No, no, she'll be back later, she's got Law this afternoon. I've only just walked through the door myself, I'm aching to get my shoes off so . . . It's not the weekend for it, that's all. I will tell her, I promise . . . I promise. Listen, darling, I'll call the switchboard on Wednesday when I know where I'm going to be. And Max? I love you.'

Amy flinched and knocked her head against the banister.

The thud brought footsteps from the kitchen and she immediately jumped up to make it seem like she'd been walking down the stairs. Valerie appeared in the hallway with one hand pressed to her throat then her expression softened as she spotted her.

'You scared me, sweetheart. I thought you were arriving tonight.'

'I didn't feel very well so I came home early,' she lied.

'How are you feeling now?' Valerie asked. She climbed to meet her on the stairs and pressed a hand to her forehead. 'You are a little warm.'

'I'm fine, I'm better. Just a bit . . . nauseous.'

'Well, have you been sick at all? Have you taken anything?'

'No and no.'

'I'll get you some tablets from my bathroom, I'll be right back.'

Amy turned as she passed her. 'Mum?'

'Yep?' queried Valerie, spinning back to face her.

'Thank you.'

Valerie's face split into a genuine smile. 'Of course.'

The moment she disappeared, Amy's legs began to tremble. She hauled herself up to the landing and steadied herself on the wall. Her brain was skimming through everything that had happened in the last few months, analysing everything that Valerie had said – or avoided – saying. Then it struck her.

During the summer, Valerie had been spooked by the mention of a taxi firm. It'd been one of the last candid conversations they'd had, although it'd been curtailed by Valerie knocking a glass of wine over. Amy had put her questions about the taxi driver down to narcissism at the time, but now she was wondering if there was more to it. After all, she'd told Max she'd call the switchboard – the connection was there, albeit not exactly a plausible one.

The door creaking signalled Valerie's return and Amy did her best to clear her face.

'Right,' Valerie said as she handed over two pill boxes, 'if you take two of these and one of these, you should feel better. I was thinking lamb casserole for dinner – how about it?'

Amy nodded and started towards her room. 'Thanks for the . . . Thanks.'

Even closing her bedroom door couldn't restore any equilibrium. Wilbur was still resting where Valerie had placed him months ago, his embroidered eyes weeping threads of cotton, and the yawning silence was shattered by jazz rattling through the house. Amy collapsed onto her bed then rolled over and grabbed her phone from the bedside table.

Months ago, she'd stumbled across an unofficial party forum that dealt equally in policy and personal gossip. She'd bookmarked it to keep track of the fawning, occasionally explicit, comments about Valerie, and she navigated to the gossip section now.

A search produced eleven recent entries, most of them connected with another name. That discovery didn't settle her stomach, and she stewed until dinnertime when she couldn't hold her curiosity in check any longer.

'You've been spending a lot of time with John Foster lately,' she said.

Valerie's head snapped up. 'What makes you say that?'

'Nearly every official campaigning you've done recently has been with him. It says so on the forum.'

'Oh, that thing,' answered Valerie with a chuckle. 'I only venture on there when it's absolutely necessary. Believe me, it rarely is.'

Amy squashed a carrot into her fork. 'But it says you've been out with him a lot. Are you seeing him?'

'No, sweetheart, we're just friends.'

'Are you seeing anyone?' she persisted.

'Why do you ask?' Valerie returned as she reached for her wine and took a sip. 'Honestly, after the way you've reacted in the past –'

'When you brought that idiot back, what did you expect?'

Valerie waved her glass in the air. 'Exactly.'

'Exactly?' Amy repeated. 'What do you mean? Don't you think I deserve to know?'

'It works both ways, doesn't it? While you were here over the summer, you disappeared every Sunday without any explanation. Clarice tells me you're still doing it. She thinks you're studying with friends, but I don't think that's the case. I have to guess, though, don't I? If you won't be honest with me, why would you expect me to be honest with you?'

'Are you seriously going down that route?' she demanded.

Valerie's eyes widened. 'I'm sorry, I didn't –'

'Forget it,' Amy interrupted, dumping her napkin on the table. 'I don't even care anymore.'

But the trouble was that she did.

No matter that Valerie wordlessly rearranged their appointments on Saturday so they were never in the same place for more than twenty minutes at a time. No matter that lunch was a series of one syllable responses to the waitress or that the drive home was punctuated by brittle silences when the songs finished. Amy still wanted to peel away Valerie's mask and work out why she was so desperate to hide this relationship she was apparently having.

On Monday, she made it as far as the college gates before spinning around and pushing back through the uniformed students heading for registration. She took a bus then a train into town, focused on the actions rather than the destination, until she found herself outside a shabby concrete block down a side street littered with beer cans and burger boxes.

The smell was the first thing that struck her when she walked into the office. It was like going into a fusty nostalgic sweet shop – syrupy with hints of mildew or maybe vomit. The room itself was a stumpy rectangle from what she could see, sliced through by a wall that tapered off into a desk at this end. The glass above it rattled when the door clanked shut behind her, just loudly enough to attract the attention of a scruffy man gnawing on a lollipop on the opposite side of the window. One look told Amy this wasn't the mysterious Max – Valerie's tastes weren't that exotic, even if she was having a mid-life crisis.

'Cars are all out,' he said, leaning back in his chair. 'Are you wanting to wait?'

Amy swallowed. 'Actually, I was looking f-for Max.'

'Oh, right.' He gestured to a thin door in the corner. 'She's in there, won't be a minute. You two mates or something?'

'W-what?'

'Mates,' he repeated.

She clutched at her elbows, unable to stop herself swaying back and forth. 'Y-yes. No. No.'

'Normally it's one or the other. Unless . . . God, she's not gone all cradle snatcher, has she?'

Heat flooded her cheeks as she realised exactly who Max was. She'd picked her up from town that time. Short hair, friendly enough, but distracted and enigmatic. Hadn't she undercharged her and mentioned Valerie in passing? Amy pressed her lips together until her jaw ached.

'You look like you're gonna throw up,' the man commented.

'I'm fine,' she muttered.

'Is there something that's happened? Only me and Max are joint owners so if you've got a complaint –'

'It's nothing like that.'

'You've got something on your mind,' he persisted.

Her legs stiffened as he hauled himself up like a baboon. There was the glass between them, but she still couldn't shake the impression of him bearing down on her. It wasn't anything about him exactly, more just the sensation of slipping underwater and being unable to find her feet. She took a deep breath and attempted a smile.

'I was looking for my mum, that's all. I know that she and Max have been seeing each other, so I thought . . .'

He tilted his head to the side. 'Max isn't seeing anyone, not that I know.'

Amy bit her lip. 'Oh.'

'If something's kicking off, you should tell me.'

'It isn't.'

'Well, what you doing here then?' he demanded.

The sudden tonal shift made her tremble. Life with Valerie might've involved Cold War manoeuvres sometimes, but outright expressions of anger were rare, and Amy stumbled away from the source, cracking her heel on the wall. She could feel tears brewing in her eyes as the man disappeared for a second, only to emerge from a door set into the wall.

He held up both hands. 'I'm sorry, I didn't mean to shout at you. My name's Drew, all right? I'm a bit on edge myself today, that's why I snapped. No excuse, so I'm sorry.'

'It's okay,' she murmured.

'What's your name?' he asked.

She hesitated then cleared her throat. 'Amy.'

'Great, now we're all right. I'll leave off badgering you. Just give it a minute and you can talk to Max.'

'I don't think that's a great idea,' she admitted.

'Why's that?' Drew questioned.

Now his voice had lowered, he seemed more congenial. He leaned his shoulder against the wall and waited for a response. After a few moments, he scuffed his heel against the threadbare carpet and opened his mouth. Whatever he was about to say was smothered under the rumble of a toilet flushing. The noise set Amy's feet in motion and she bolted out of the door, ignoring Drew calling after her.

Only when she dodged past a chugger in the precinct did she realise where her instincts had taken her. She slowed as she approached the café, unnerved by the number of customers on the ground floor. Maybe this was a weekday morning rush, but she couldn't see herself walking through the door and getting past all those pensioners without embarrassing herself. She was still equivocating when a hand brushed her elbow and she spun around to find Max breathless in front of her. The sight sent a wave of fury crashing through her body that she didn't completely understand.

'You followed me,' she growled.

'Amy –' Max began, but she cut her off.

'Drew said you weren't seeing anyone. Is he right?'

'Just calm –'

'Is he right or am I right?'

Max scrubbed at her forehead. 'You're right.'

The words blunted her anger and she stared at the woman who Valerie had kept from her. Maybe her unkempt hair had grown since the taxi ride, but, other than that, she looked exactly as Amy remembered. But there was a disconnect in her brain – she couldn't imagine Max even standing in the same room as Valerie, let alone anything else. It made her head whirl and she fumbled for one of the café's external chairs to stop herself from tumbling over.

'Steady on,' Max mumbled then she shifted her weight. 'So, how did you find out?'

Amy clenched her fingers around the metal backrest. 'I came home early on Friday and heard her on the phone. I thought . . . I don't know. She's been strange about taxis in the past. I guess I just put two and two together. Until I walked in there, I didn't realise . . .'

'That I'm a woman.' Max plunged her hands into her pockets. 'Not surprising.'

'With Valerie, nothing should be a surprise. You expect the unexpected! The second you think you know what she's going to do, that's when she lets rip and does something so crazy that you can't believe you were gullible enough to give her the benefit of the doubt in the first place. What lies has she told you about me?'

'Nothing but good things –'

Amy snorted. 'Oh, yeah, right. I bet she's said she's this miserable, misunderstood woman who's just trying to make a difference to the world. And I'm the horrible daughter who left her so why would you have anything to do with –'

'It's not like that,' interrupted Max. 'I swear, she's spent half her time telling me how brilliant you are, how much she loves you.'

'You're lying,' Amy muttered.

Max exhaled, glancing along the bustling precinct. Then she looked back and shook her head.

'All right . . . You're set on studying law at Durham. You got into it because of your dad, but your mum's not keen on the idea. She saw how hard he had to work and she'd rather you had something of a life. You're clever, she says. Though she reckons you don't get any of that from her and I disagree. You've got a scar on your left knee from falling off your bike when you were eight. You were off school for a couple of weeks and she took the time off work. So, you spent days watching *Sabrina the Teenage Witch* and you couldn't stop calling her "Zelda" after. Your favourite colour's red, you hate prawns, you've been eighteen for five days, and she got you an iPad for your birthday, even though you've kept saying you don't want one. I was sitting next to her when she ordered it.'

She fell silent with an anaemic smile, but Amy couldn't return it. Her fingers were still coiled around the chair until it slipped away from her and clattered to the floor. They both jumped and Amy's eyes flicked sideways towards the window. Ed had spotted the commotion and was watching, along with a gaggle of pensioners who probably had her pegged as a vandal.

A fresh wave of anger hit her as she righted the chair. She twisted back towards Max with her legs quivering.

'And what has she told you about why I don't live with her, hmm?' she demanded.

Max hesitated just long enough for the truth to shine from her face.

'That's what I thought,' Amy snapped as she pushed the café door open. 'She's playing you, Max. Don't be an idiot, don't fall for it.'

## Chapter 13

Clarke Hospice wasn't exactly the heart and soul at the best of times, all curtained windows and sombre faces. Max had done more than her fair share of runs down here in the past, covering for the lads who found it tough and Drew who had that annoying habit of opening his gob without engaging his brain. She had the nous to deal with it, letting people take their time and sit in for as long as they wanted. At the minute, she'd gladly stay in the car herself.

It took her two minutes to work her way up to going into reception. She'd been in here collecting people, but it was darker than she remembered. Even the stuffed teddies on the windowsill looked as though they'd been doused with cheap cola and left out to dry.

The receptionist glanced up from her computer, a warm look on her face. 'Hello. Are you here to visit someone?'

'I'm here to see Valerie Smythe,' Max answered.

'Oh. Of course.' Her voice hadn't altered as such, though her expression had flattened out. 'May I ask what it's regarding?'

Max licked her lips. 'I'm a taxi driver and she, er, left some money in my cab. I'd like to give it back to her in person if she's around. No offence.'

'No, no, I completely understand and I appreciate your honesty. She's with someone right now, but if you take a seat over there and help yourself to a coffee, she shouldn't be long.'

It was easier to get a drink than stand there twiddling her thumbs. She sank into the cosy cream sofa and warmed her palms around a cup of coffee. The receptionist seemed welcoming again, throwing her the odd smile while she waited. Two minutes stretched into ten and the stickiness at Max's collar intensified. Much more waiting and she could feel herself ready to bolt.

All that went out the window when Valerie stepped through the double doors with her arm wrapped around a colourless woman. Between them, they were clutching a ball of blankets that brought the scent of disinfectant into the reception. Valerie was so focused on bunching the blankets up before they fell apart that she didn't spot Max sat there. She halted and rubbed the woman's shoulder.

'Are you sure you don't want another cup of tea, hmm? You're welcome to stay for as long as you want, I'm happy to sit with you.'

The woman shook her head. 'We've taken up enough of your time. Thank you.'

Valerie just squeezed her arm and watched her through the doors. As they whirred shut, the room settled for a few seconds until the receptionist cleared her throat.

'You've got a visitor, Valerie.'

'Hmm?'

'A visitor,' the receptionist repeated, nodding to the corner where Max was sat.

Valerie twisted around and the compassion drained out of her face. She went from sympathetic to horrified without missing a beat, leaving Max to clamber up with her coffee sloshing around in time with her stomach.

'Can I help?' Valerie queried.

Max blinked then dumped her cup on the nearby table. 'I gave you a lift the other day. You left some money in the cab.'

'Right.' Nothing altered in Valerie's expression, she didn't even meet her eye. 'Thank you.'

'You don't usually get people that honest,' the receptionist chipped in.

Valerie tossed her a limp smile. 'No. You don't.'

That was her cue, Max realised, and she scrambled for her wallet. There was about £80 in there, a wad that made it look convincing at least. She held it out and waited. Valerie plucked it from her fingers like she would an unexploded bomb then flicked through it twice.

'I think it's short, actually. Was there anything else around the seat?'

Beyond her shoulder, the receptionist rolled her eyes and went back to her typing. Max didn't have a choice but to go outside with her cheeks burning. She couldn't look across at Valerie in case it caused her to trip over, especially when she started talking.

'Keep walking, don't look at me. What the hell are you doing here? You can't just show up at my place of work. It isn't professional, it isn't fair. I've told you what it's like in there for me. They think I'm a liability, they're looking for every reason to pounce –'

'I'm trying to bloody well help,' Max cut in.

'Well, you've got a funny way of showing it.'

She spun around to face her. 'Amy turned up at the cab office about a half hour ago. She'd heard you on the phone talking to me on Friday. Put two and two together, came up with five and landed first thing. Smart girl, like you said.'

Valerie's lips parted and she swallowed. 'I – I don't understand.'

'Like I said –'

'Keep looking. Look for the money.'

Max snorted, but opened the car door and kneeled on the gravel. It snagged at her jeans as she stretched forward to search between the seats. Her fingers caught on some coins, despite only having the cab valeted yesterday, and she brought them out onto the polyester. She scraped her nails against the fabric before she managed to find her voice again.

'Are you all right?' she asked.

'What did she tell you?' Valerie questioned.

'Nothing, not really. She's angry and upset, that's all. Like I said she'd be.'

That sounded more accusatory than she'd meant it to. Now the words were out, though, she couldn't squash down the injustice rising in her throat. She dragged herself up using the door then dumped herself in the driver's seat, gripping it with both hands as she continued.

'I didn't call because you don't always answer, not when it's me. Which is fine, except when something important happens.'

'Max —' Valerie began, but she wouldn't let her finish.

'Forget it. She's gone to the café in the precinct, the one between the barbers' and the bookies. She might still be there, I don't know.'

'Just wait and we can talk about this.'

She sniggered and reached for the door. 'It's not me you need to talk to.'

'Look, I'm sorry —'

'You're not,' Max interrupted, nudging her out of the way. 'That's the bloody problem.'

# Chapter 14

The lower floor was a jumble of voices when Amy stepped out of the toilets.

Given how she'd sped upstairs without a word, she expected some response. All those pensioners downstairs for their Monday tea and currant teacake deal had a nosy streak, but none of them had migrated up here to satisfy their curiosity. In fact, the group that had been sat around the table in the far corner when she'd arrived had gone. The idea that customers had left thanks to her emotional appearance brought a flush to her cheeks. It made it impossible to creep down the stairs and slip away before Ed noticed – she had to either walk down there and have a mature discussion about it or stay trapped up here.

She was trying to focus on a Kate Atkinson novel twenty minutes later when creaks alerted her to someone climbing the stairs. Any hope that it might be a regular customer were dashed as Ed rounded the corner of the reading nook with a cup in his hand.

'Hey,' he said.

'Hey,' she returned.

'I thought you might want . . .' He cleared his throat and deposited the cup on the table. 'I left it a bit in case you wanted to be alone then I figured you might need a drink so I –'

'I'm sorry if I've cost you any business.'

Ed's eyebrows knitted together. 'What? No, why would you say that?'

'There were people up here and they left because I ran up looking like –'

'They went downstairs because I asked them to,' he interjected.

She opened her mouth then closed it again. Nothing sprang to mind that wouldn't make her sound stupid, but he just smiled and perched on the edge of the nearest bean bag chair. It would've swallowed him up if he hadn't planted both feet on the carpet and rocked forward.

'Had an experience at my aunt's house once,' he explained, glancing over to her. 'There was me, a massive bean bag thing, and my cousin's puppy. It was a terrier, a right little scruffy thing. Got really excited and started scratching everything – me, the chair . . . So, all the stuffing starts coming out and then it wets itself as well. Brilliant day, that was.'

Amy couldn't help but grin. 'And you decided to put all these up here because you like reliving the drama?'

'Not so much reliving it as getting over it, not letting it beat me.'

'That sounds very noble and grown-up,' she replied.

'Shush, don't say that. I'm not planning on growing up.'

'You run your own business,' she pointed out.

He shrugged. 'My dad never grew up, not really. If you're not being true to yourself then what's the point? That's what he said. I've tried to put that into this place as much as I can. Reckon they'd have both been pleased with how it's gone, my dad and . . . Sorry, I've done it again, haven't I?'

Tears had begun streaming down her cheeks without her realising. She tried to mop them away with her arm, but they just dribbled onto her lap and pattered against the cover of *Case Histories*. Ed slipped from his chair and kneeled in front of her, extracting the book from her hands before rubbing her arm.

'I'm sorry,' she whispered.

'Shush, you're all right.'

She raised her chin, intending to argue, but his lopsided smile stopped her. The pressure of his hand against her arm suddenly squeezed like a blood pressure monitor and he stretched across her knees to kiss her. His elbow dug into her thigh and his lips were off-centre, but none of that mattered. It was perfect for being imperfect.

'If I overstepped, I'm sorry,' he said as he pulled away.

'You didn't, honestly. I enjoyed it.'

He sighed and rested back on his heels. 'I'm damned if I do and damned if I don't here so I might as well –'

'Ed –'

'Let me finish, please. I need to say this so it's right.'

He was chafing at his beard with his index finger until she grasped his hand and trapped it between hers. His fingers relaxed and he met her eye as he continued.

'You've been coming in here all summer and it's been nice. More than nice. With everyone else – especially my mum – I'm putting on a front, pretending that this place is doing all right when it's not. We're barely breaking even, and I'm letting my dad down – and yours – by not making a success of it. But that's not what I . . . Look, I've been working here pretty much nonstop for three years. I don't have days off, I can only afford to pay Davinder for lunchtimes and I'm too shattered by the time I get home to do much more than watch Netflix. I'm not kidding myself I'm a catch, especially not for someone like you.'

Amy stiffened. 'Someone like me?'

'No, I didn't mean . . . Just that you're going to uni, you'll be a hotshot lawyer like your dad and I'm –'

'Why does that matter?'

'I'm aware of the differences, that's all. Your mum's standing for election next year, mine works at Morrison's to pay the bills.'

'So, what?' Amy demanded. 'My mum's the snob, not me. And my dad wasn't.'

'I know that,' Ed answered.

'Then, what's the problem?'

He tugged his hand away and wrapped it around his neck. 'I've liked you since before, only it's not what you say to a sixteen year old, not when her dad's loaned you money either. It sounds creepy when you think about it like that.'

'It's not creepy,' she insisted.

'If I'd done anything about it then –'

'But you didn't,' Amy interrupted, resting a hand on his cheek and feeling the bristles against her palm. 'You've got nothing to feel guilty about.'

His brow softened and he exhaled against her thumb. The sensation tingled through her body as she leaned forward to kiss him again. She lost track of everything else until a familiar tang of perfume snagged at her nostrils and she lurched away. Ed's eyes widened as he caught sight of their visitor and he dragged them both to their feet.

'Mrs Smythe, it's nice to –'

'I didn't see your food hygiene rating on the door. You're supposed to display it prominently.'

'Er . . . Well, we do. It's right –'

'Obviously not or I would've been able to see it, wouldn't I? I like to know exactly what sort of establishment I've happened into. I mean, it's hardly the Ritz, but I'd appreciate knowing whether I can expect salmonella with my lunch or not.'

Amy prodded Ed out of the nook. 'Hey, can I get a tea please? Put it on my tab.'

'Sure thing,' he said, glancing between them. 'Yorkshire?'

She nodded and watched him edge past Valerie. They listened to every clump on the stairs then Amy braced herself, expecting Valerie's artic exterior to melt in favour of whatever was bubbling underneath the surface. Instead, she twirled and took a turn around the room in the way a building inspector might. She knocked her heel against the table legs to make them wobble and peered at the haphazard book organisation. Her expression froze when her eyes slipped back to the reading nook. She didn't even seem to hear Ed creep up the stairs with a tray. Amy relieved him of it, smiled, and gestured for him go back downstairs. Valerie's attention had been caught finally and she sniggered loudly.

'What?' Amy questioned.

'Oh, I'm astonished you pay, that's all. One of the key tenets of grooming is that they buy you things. You're doing this wrong.'

Amy gripped the tray until her fingers numbed. 'Well, you should know, you're the expert. How old was Dad when you dug your claws in and how old were you? Although, I bet it was something else you handed to him on a plate, not money –'

'At least I know where you've been running off to all summer. You have the audacity to criticise my choices when you're messing around with a –'

'Is that seriously where you're going with this? There's only one person who could've told you where I was, but, sure, I suppose trying to grab on to the moral high ground's your thing. Go for it.'

Valerie's mouth snapped open then, abruptly, her shoulders crumpled. She edged onto the nearest sofa, a frumpy blue heap that folded over her thighs, and a hiss escaped from her mouth. Amy hesitated before sitting beside her and depositing the tray on the table. She ignored Valerie until she'd made a cup of tea to her exacting standards then she pushed the cup into her hands.

'Drink,' she instructed.

'What?'

'Drink,' Amy repeated. She waited until Valerie had taken a sip and settled the cup between her quivering hands before asking, 'Why didn't you tell me?'

'I don't know,' Valerie murmured.

'No, come on, you know I won't buy that. I gave you the chance, I wanted you to tell me. I asked, Mum. I asked outright.'

'You asked about John Foster. Specifically, you mentioned him, no one else.'

Amy clenched her fists on her lap. 'Don't do that. Stop being a politician for five minutes. So, you're seeing a woman – and what? You were scared of telling me? You're ashamed of it?'

'I am not ashamed of how I feel about Max,' she insisted.

'Then I don't get it, Mum. Explain it to me.'

'Max is . . .' A growl erupted from Valerie's lips and she shook her head. 'Oh, you're too young for this.'

'That's you hiding again. I'm not a kid, I stopped being a kid when Dad stopped breathing in front of me. I went to his funeral and pretended everything was fine even though we were . . . Just stop using that excuse, stop treating me like a kid.'

Valerie pushed her hair from her face. 'I never wanted you to have the childhood I did. I knew too much and too little, as I learned in the end. You know, it's one thing to be treated like an adult when you're ready to have hold of the tools, but if you're not . . .'

'And you don't think I am?'

'You are,' Valerie replied after a moment. 'The way you've looked after Clarice since your father died is proof of that. Not many girls of your age would've sacrificed their social lives to look after a grieving grandparent with angina. I know it isn't the reason you left me, but it's admirable nonetheless. I'm proud of you for it.'

Amy blinked then crossed her arms over her stomach. 'So, be honest with me then.'

A war raged in Valerie's eyes until she reclined further into the baggy sofa and the folds swam around her shoulders as well with her thighs. Her startled reaction shattered the ice and she took a deep breath.

'Max is . . . incredibly normal and laid back. She and I met when the car broke down back in February – do you remember? She came to my rescue in the middle of nowhere, literally in the middle of the night. I'm not one for fate and all that rubbish, but I'm not foolish enough to ignore how I feel about her. She makes me laugh and she doesn't expect me to be perfect which, yes, I know is fortunate.'

Amy gnawed on her lip. 'So, are you –'

'More bisexual than anything, if that's the conversation you want to have. Look, it's – it's normal. Most evenings when I see her, she comes around and I cook. For point of reference, never leave her in the kitchen alone. It's a powder keg. We eat, we talk, we watch films. Any kind of film, though her favourite's horror.'

'You hate horror.'

'I know that, you know that . . . Actually, by now, she probably knows that too. A few too many incidents where I've hidden behind cushions or made an excuse to go to the kitchen.'

'You've got a whole other life and you didn't tell me,' Amy muttered.

Valerie sighed. 'I tried to. In the summer, I tried the hypothetical scenario of a relationship. Do you remember that?'

'Wait, that was about Max?'

'I'd already made a hash of it by then in some respects. You see, I didn't – Max didn't know you existed at that point, let alone the other way around.'

Amy gaped at her. 'Excuse me?'

'The first she heard of it was when you ordered that taxi and she pulled up outside the house. Not my finest hour. But not my worst either. I'm not sure if that helps. The truth of it is that she's less inclined to be rushed than me, and you know how terrible I am for that. I didn't want to tell her about you – or you about her – until I was certain of the outcome, whether it was going to be something serious and whether we could hold onto it.'

'And?' Amy questioned, knotting her hands together.

'I love her and she loves me.'

'But she doesn't know everything, does she? You haven't told her why I live with Biddy.'

'Not yet,' admitted Valerie. 'I will when it's appropriate.'

Amy tilted her head back, a flash of red from one of the spotlights blurring her vision until she lowered her gaze

102

again. 'You think you can have it all, don't you? Of course. You always do.'

Valerie rubbed her eyes and her fingers came away varnished with mascara. She stared at them for a few seconds then reached into her handbag and extracted her purple make-up pouch. A ritual of cleansing and painstaking reapplication ensued while Amy watched. Every deliberate brushstroke transformed Valerie Smythe, in love with a taxi driver, back into Valerie Smythe, prospective parliamentary candidate. As she snapped her compact shut, the only traces of their conversation were the cleansing wipes scrunched up on the tray.

'It's inconceivable to go public before the election. I'd need to tell your grandmother for a start, and that's going to open up an entire circus of worms. She's not from the generation that accepts it easily, you know that. There's so much casual homophobia there that I don't know where to start.'

'You'd be able to talk her round,' Amy answered. 'You could sell ice to Eskimos.'

'Well, thank you for the compliment, but it wouldn't work with Clarice, not about this. On the surface, we have a healthy relationship. But she didn't like me at first and she positively hated the fact that I'd ensnared Tim. We're cordial, we've established this relationship built on . . . I don't know . . . mutual love of you and your father. For me to do something as insane as fall in love with a woman like Max and contemplate moving her into Tim's house would be a red rag at the very least. Not to mention the fact that she's ill and this might –'

'You're not justifying your cowardice with her angina,' Amy warned.

'I do care about her, and I know how much you do. I have to tread carefully for everyone's sakes.'

Amy pressed her knees together. 'Why does it matter anyway? It's not as though she can take away anything you inherited from Dad.'

'Why do you always think it's about money, hmm?' Valerie queried with a sad smile. 'Amy, you live with her and you barely talk to me. When you go off to Durham or wherever, it'll be twice as bad. I'm not kidding myself that our relationship's going to be magically fixed. It's entirely feasible that, once you've gone, Clarice might be my only tangible link to you beyond Facebook.'

The truth of that statement made Amy shuffle in her seat. She avoided Valerie's eye and focused on ripping one of the cosmetic wipes into strips and flattening them out on the tray.

'Can I ask you something?' Valerie queried finally.

Amy nodded, keeping her chin low.

'I can understand why you didn't tell me about that man downstairs, but may I ask why you didn't tell your grandmother?'

'That was only our second kiss,' she muttered. 'Anyway, I don't think Biddy would appreciate Ed very much.'

Valerie stowed her cosmetics away slowly. 'I'm not sure I do, you know. He looks as though he's in his late twenties with all that facial hair.'

'He's only twenty one and he was a friend of Dad's. He helped Ed out, gave him a loan to keep this place going when he inherited it. This is where we came every Saturday morning before he got sick.'

'That changes things,' Valerie murmured as she looked around the room with fresh eyes.

'Yeah, the truth tends to do that.'

'Well, we can discuss that at a later date. I need to get going. I ran out of a shift and the hospice already think I'm a liability as it is. But, listen, let's see if we can do this properly.'

'What do you mean?'

Valerie cleared her throat and gazed at her. 'Amy, would you like to meet my girlfriend? Provided that she's still talking to me, that is. Because I've been a complete arse today and she'd be well within her rights not to.'

'Yes,' Amy answered with an involuntary chuckle. 'I'd like to meet your girlfriend.'

'Excellent, thank you.' Valerie stood and swept towards the staircase, sparing her one more glance. 'In return, I'll conveniently forget you should be in Economics right now, just to be generous. See you soon, sweetheart.'

## Chapter 15

'You gonna tell me what the hell's going on?'

Max collapsed onto the sofa and closed her eyes. 'Drew, leave it.'

'Who's this bird you've been seeing? What's the daughter got to do with it? Why didn't you tell me you were shagging someone?'

'You're a right old woman,' Max snapped.

'So, tell me and shut me up.'

She opened one eye. He was balanced on the rim of the switchboard chair, elbows planted on his knees and a greedy expression on his face. It was the spit of the bloke who'd conned her into going into business with him in the first damn place so she knew she might as well give in.

'Her name's Valerie,' she muttered, clumping her hands together. 'She's the one I told you about before, the blonde I said was a one-off.'

'Miss Hoity Toity Businesswoman?' he questioned.

'She's more of a politician, but, yeah.'

Drew raised an eyebrow. 'You've gone and hooked up with a politician?'

'When you say it like that, it sounds stupid.' Max paused then snickered. 'It is stupid. Was never working, so it's best it's done with.'

'I'm not following. Why's it done with?'

She shrugged and leaned back into the sofa. 'That was the first time I'd met the daughter. It's a long story, but it doesn't matter now. I'm best leaving them to it.'

'You don't get out of it that easy,' Drew replied, nudging the volume on the switchboard down to zero. 'Tell me what's gone on.'

He wasn't likely to let it go if she didn't, not when he was voluntarily losing them custom. So, she launched into a sanitised version of what'd happened since she met Valerie. Only when she said it all aloud did she start wondering what she'd been doing to herself. Drew's face matched how she felt when she got to the end of it. He kept quiet while he crossed to the kettle and made them both a cuppa then he dumped himself beside her on the sofa.

'She doesn't want you mucking up her job. That's the long and short. She's happy to keep you stringing along and jumping to her tune, but God forbid you do anything off your own bat like talking to her kid. Amy seemed nice enough, though. Was she all right when you caught up with her? I mean, bloody confused and all that, but I hadn't upset her, had I?'

Max shook her head. 'It wasn't you.'

'Not her fault she's got a crackpot for a mum. So, what now? You steering well away?'

The cuppa was still too hot to drink, but she took a sip anyway and scorched her tongue.

'You're not putting up with it,' he continued after a second. 'You're not that daft.'

'That's what I keep saying to Elena about you,' she shot back.

Drew rolled his eyes and kicked out his legs. 'At least Elena's not ashamed of me like Valerie is you. Wouldn't have thought you'd put up with that.'

Until Pauline came on shift at seven, Max covered the switchboard and blundered through the accounts. Drew had buggered off to Elena's scan then sent her a text with a grainy ultrasound picture on it that somehow managed to bring a smile and tears at the same time. Everything the first time around with Andrew had been rushed, but it was like Drew was making the most of every minute even before the baby was born. Max found herself relieved he wasn't at the office to see her emotional reaction to the blob on the ultrasound and just sent him a short text saying congratulations. Knowing him, he'd get the bigger drift.

All she wanted to do when she handed over was get home and have a few drinks. The BMW parked up across the road put paid to that. She hesitated then crossed over and rested her palm on the roof, waiting for the window to wind down. Valerie's face appeared by millimetres, pale and anxious. Max sighed and rubbed her forehead with her free hand.

'What are you doing here?' she asked.

Valerie reached out through the window to grab her arm. 'I'm sorry, Max. I truly am. I behaved abominably and I won't try and defend it. I'm sorry.'

Denial or defence she could've argued with, but not this. Max turned her hand over and let their fingers lock together while she searched Valerie's face for any discomfort. She told herself that if there was the slightest bit of public panic, that'd be it. Instead, Valerie just squeezed harder.

'Let me drive you home for a change. Stay over – you don't do that nearly enough and I love waking up next to you.'

'You never seemed to want me there,' Max replied.

'I'm scared of needing you there, that's more accurate. Please, leave the cab and come home with me. Please.'

Max drank in her jittery expression and then nodded. She cast a look over her shoulder to make sure no one was watching from the cab office before rounding the car and slipping into the passenger seat. The street was deserted bar a homeless man cocooned inside an old warehouse entrance and the drive up towards the main road passed in silence.

'I spoke to Amy,' Valerie said suddenly. 'I've calmed the waters and she wants to meet you properly. If we're still . . . Well, are we?'

'Don't know,' Max admitted.

'What can I do to persuade you?'

She snorted. 'That says it all, doesn't it?'

'What?' Valerie glanced sideways. 'What?'

'I've let you do that before. You said you'd tell Amy before it all kicked off and you didn't. It shouldn't have got to the point where she's hearing you on the phone then turning up on my doorstep. It wasn't fair on either of us.'

'No, I know that, Max. I do. But I –'

'But what?' she cut in. 'She just has to put up with it because it's part of your big plan?'

Valerie didn't answer that, choosing to focus on the road instead. They twisted through the one-way system and onto the bypass before Max was conscious they were going in the wrong direction. Once she'd clocked it, though, she knew where they were headed and sank back into her seat. It wasn't normal for her to be the passenger and, by the time they reached the nature reserve, she was itching to get back behind her own wheel.

There were a half dozen cars dotted around the nature reserve car park, all of them empty. Valerie just switched the engine off and unbuckled her belt before turning her shoulder into the leather seat.

'This isn't about us,' she said. 'At least, not wholly. It's about Amy.'

Max frowned. 'What else did you expect it to be about?'

'That's not what I mean. It isn't that she turned up at the cab office today – it's your relationship with her that's the issue.'

'I don't have one,' she pointed out.

Valerie massaged her neck and smiled. 'Exactly. It's what you said back there about me having a big plan. If you mean getting elected then, yes, of course I do. I'd be foolish not to plan accordingly for that. But you see yourself in Amy, don't you?'

'How can I do that? I barely know anything about her.'

'I've gone about this all wrong,' Valerie murmured.

Whatever she was talking about, Max couldn't grab hold of it. That left a flush on her cheeks that she couldn't get rid of sat right there so she clicked off her seatbelt and got out of the car. She crunched across to the treeline then stopped with her hands shoved into her pockets watching a blackbird prod into the earth with its beak. A dog was growling somewhere far off and there was the usual rush of traffic from the bypass. Max stiffened when Valerie appeared beside her and pulled one of her hands from a pocket.

'There I was, thinking Amy was an obstacle between us, and it was just the opposite. I still think that if I'd have mentioned her at first, you would've run a mile, but that would've been against your instincts.'

'You're not making sense,' said Max.

Valerie gripped her hand tighter. 'You want a family. The fact I was delaying telling Amy was niggling at you, and now I understand why. You're worried about her welfare as well as mine, you're ready and willing to be a part of her life, aren't you?'

'I hardly know her,' Max reminded her.

'Admit that you want to,' Valerie said.

The blackbird had hopped over the trunk of a felled tree and was now trying its luck in a different patch. Max watched until the pressure on her fingers increased to the point where she couldn't ignore it. She looked sideways into Valerie's eyes and tried to keep her voice steady.

'You can't do the family thing while you're hiding in the closet trying to win an election. Besides, I don't know what's gone on between you and Amy, but you're hardly a ready-made family. If I was looking for that, I'd look elsewhere.'

A smile tugged at Valerie's lips. 'You didn't look for this anymore than I did. It doesn't make it any less real for that. Look, it's only eight months to the election. I'm sure we can fly under the radar –'

'No,' Max interrupted.

'It wouldn't be for long –'

'I'm not shackling myself to someone who's ashamed of me. I haven't had to feel like that since I left home. And a fine example you're setting to Amy by keeping me a secret from her and everyone else. It's like Drew said –'

'Drew?' Valerie cut in. 'You've been talking to him about us?'

Max snorted and pulled her hand free. 'There you go.'

'That wasn't me being ashamed, that was –'

'Slip of the tongue?'

'I'd rather you didn't talk to Drew about this when he's got all the emotional intellect of a cockroach. I doubt he told you to jump into a family –'

'You don't know him,' Max warned.

'I know what you've told me. Anyway,' Valerie went on, groping for her hand again, 'this isn't about Drew. It's about our family. Come on, Max. You can't tell me you don't want that as much as I do. You, me, Amy – we could be good together, couldn't we?'

Somehow, the air was stifling, in spite of the breeze. Max took a step forward into the shadows and spooked the blackbird. It took off through the leaves, the worm it'd finally caught waggling in its beak. She watched it up and away then risked a glance back at Valerie. Her face was different, clouded by something like fear.

'What?' Max asked.

Valerie inhaled and managed a smile. 'I'm frightened of losing you, that's all. It's strange. I feel comfortable and alive at the same time when I'm with you. Do you know how rare that it? I've had one, never both.'

'What about Tim?' she pressed before she thought too much about it.

'Oh, I felt safe with him, yes. He was the first person I'd ever encountered who wanted to look after me and didn't want something in return. For someone as self-sufficient as I'd learned to be over the years, that took some adjusting to. He left me financially stable so I'd never need anything and yet . . . Everybody needs something, don't they?'

Max's throat was tight so she just nodded.

'I picked politics,' Valerie continued after a few seconds, 'and I believe I'm actually good at it, you know. Amy says that I am, but she means it in a derogatory way. I want to make a difference, and I think I've got a shot. This seat's a marginal for a reason. No one keeps their promises, not the council or the current MP. It's all about Westminster for him, not about anything thing going on here. I can win this.'

'I reckon you can,' Max muttered.

Valerie raised an eyebrow. 'Have you been taking an interest?'

'I've just been keeping my ears open. Some of the customers bleat on and I listen.'

'What do they say?' Valerie questioned, biting on her lip.

'That you're about, that you're paying attention. Everything you'd want them to be saying.'

Satisfaction flashed across Valerie's face. Then it was gone, replaced by that usual expression that made Max want to chuck caution to the wind and let herself get swept away. Everything that had gone on held her in check though, to the point where Valerie's chin drooped.

'I need you,' Valerie said. 'You're good for me. And – I think – you'd be good for Amy. Now, I'm willing to give that a chance if you are. Just eight months to the election, Max. We can do this. As a family.'

Max reached a thumb forward and lifted her chin up. She was searching for some hint of that shame Drew was on about, but it wasn't in Valerie's eyes – or on her lips. Once they separated, Max kept their foreheads resting together so she couldn't lose the connection.

'Well?' whispered Valerie. 'Can I tempt you into meeting my daughter and seeing what we can make of that?'

## Chapter 16

'Is it an event you're going to?'

Amy threw Biddy an indulgent look then focused on the two dresses spread on the bed. Blue stripes were more mature than red butterflies, but the butterfly dress was shorter. It was also her favourite. She put it to one side and returned the striped one to the wardrobe.

'You're being very cryptic,' Biddy persisted.

'And you're being nosy.'

'At my age, I'm allowed to be.'

'I thought you didn't agree with taking age-related liberties.'

'I'm entitled to change my mind,' she said as she loosened her collar. 'It's warm up here.'

Amy frowned and motioned her onto the bed. 'You've been off-colour all day. Are you all right?'

'It is your mother you're seeing, isn't it? You're not trying to fool me and go off with some unsuitable boy, are you?'

'Biddy –'

'I know the signs, Amy. Your father was the same before he brought your mother home. Oh, this is where we need him. I couldn't bear for you to take the wrong path –'

'I've got a feeling Mum's seeing someone,' Amy interrupted.

Biddy's eyes widened. 'Oh, is that the game? Are you going to meet him? Is it John Foster, after all?'

'No, it's not John Foster, I'm sure of that. It's just that Mum wanted to have dinner with me so maybe we'll . . . I don't know. Maybe we'll talk.'

The half-truth stung on her lips, but she ignored the gnawing in her stomach and continued packing her bag for the rest of the weekend. The jeans and pink camisole top she'd selected for her café trip tomorrow were already stowed in the bottom of her rucksack, although her make-up was still strewn all over the dressing table. She settled for bunching it all together into her case, despite knowing she'd need it to get ready for her meeting with Max.

'Well, I'm glad,' said Biddy suddenly.

Amy turned around. 'What do you mean?'

'You need to be on the ground floor with something like this. People aren't as friendly as they first appear. I'm not implying your mother's a silly schoolgirl, but she's got to keep her wits about her and you can keep her on the straight and narrow.'

'Mum knows what she's doing, I think.'

'Gold-diggers hide in plain sight. In her position, she's a prime target for that, or someone selling their story to the papers for that matter. If she was to meet a man like John Foster – now, that would be ideal. An independent income, a position of his own to maintain. That's the kind of man we want.'

'It doesn't always work like that though. What people think is unsuitable isn't always wrong.'

Biddy rolled up her sleeves. 'More often than not, it is. All I'm saying is that we should be careful for her. We both know the kind of background she comes from, it's no wonder that she struggles between right and wrong. She doesn't have it ingrained in the way you and –'

'Stop,' Amy snapped then she grimaced at the expression on Biddy's face. 'I'm sorry, I shouldn't have raised my voice. I didn't mean to – Wait there. Do not move.'

The pallor of her cheeks was enough to send Amy racing through to the main bathroom for the glyceryl trinitrate spray. She fumbled with the cap on the way back then skidded over the rug beside her bed. Biddy was leaning heavily on her arm, although her brown eyes were alert.

'Don't fuss,' she said.

Amy passed her the spray. 'I'm not. Two puffs and I'm calling Mum to cancel.'

'You are not.'

'I'm not leaving you alone. Two puffs, Biddy, come on.'

**114**

She sprayed underneath her tongue and closed her eyes, a series of deep breaths rattling her slight frame. Amy watched, ready to insist on another round, but experience told her they'd forestalled a full-blown attack. She unclenched her fist and sat down on the bed, waiting for the air to settle around them as it did every time.

'There's no need to cancel,' Biddy said eventually. 'I've invited Millicent and Roberta over for supper so I'll have company. This could be important for your mother, dear. You need to be there.'

'It's probably nothing to do with her seeing someone,' Amy lied.

Biddy tapped a hand on her arm. 'All the same, you're going.'

'Are you planning on telling me what's wrong or do I have to guess?'

The trees skidded by in a blur. It took a few seconds for Valerie's words to permeate, and even longer for Amy to drag her eyes across to the driver's seat.

'Let's just get there,' she said.

'Well, no, actually,' Valerie replied. 'It's important to me that this evening's successful. If you don't feel as though you want to meet Max right now then we can –'

'Biddy had a mild attack earlier,' Amy cut in.

Valerie eased off the accelerator. 'Is she all right?'

'She says she's fine.'

'Do you want to go back? Max won't mind if we postpone because of Clarice –'

'No, she insisted I come. I think she's finally noticed we don't spend any time together.'

The car juddered as Valerie decelerated further and looked around for somewhere to pull in. Once they were illegally parked across an access road in front of a pair of indifferent sheep, she twisted to face her.

'Sweetheart, she noticed that a long time ago.'

Amy squinted at her. 'What do you mean?'

'You give her too little credit sometimes. If I was in her position and my only grandchild wanted to spend more time with me than her own mother, I'd be flattered to say the least. I might even be smug about it.'

'You're judging her by your standards,' Amy muttered.

'Am I? I'd say I'm treating her like a living, breathing human being, something you forget to do on occasion. Anyway, the offer still stands. You don't have to meet Max tonight if you're not in the mood. I'd rather we were all at our best when it . . .'

Her voice trailed off into a limp chuckle and Amy shuffled in her seat.

'You're scared,' she said.

Valerie turned her attention to the sheep now snuffling near the bonnet. 'I'd be a fool if I wasn't, and you know how I hate fools.'

'Stop with the riddles, Mum. Just be honest with me – even if it's only for tonight. It's not like you're on the campaign trail and, anyway, I'm not going to vote for you.'

'That's a debate for another time. Yes, then, darling, if that's what you want to hear. I'm scared. I can't calculate how tonight's going to play out and I don't appreciate the uncertainty. For all I know, your big plan may be to waltz in there tonight and tell Max why – why you live with Clarice.'

Amy crossed her arms. 'Is that seriously your biggest fear? That I'll go in there and tell her the truth.'

'I can't risk that, sweetheart, not yet. I will tell her – I will. But it needs framing properly. I've already come close to losing her once this week, I can't go through that again.'

Her sincerity was unequivocal. No amount of scrutiny was unmasking a lie, and Amy had plenty of practice in that. So, she relaxed her hands onto her lap and nodded towards the sheep.

'I think if we don't get going right now, we'll have a few passengers,' she said.

Valerie's eyes flickered. 'Amy –'

'I won't tell her. It's your place to do that, not mine. And I don't want to cancel either.'

'Are you sure?'

Amy rolled her eyes and gestured to the nearest sheep. 'Okay, I'm calling that one Karl. You get to name the other one. The alternative is that you get back on the road. What are you waiting for?'

The house smelled nice – nice yet different.

Dinner was cooking, so the scent of Valerie's signature mushroom soup was drifting into the hallway, along with a main course that must've had a base in chicken. Amy hesitated in the hallway as Valerie pressed on into the kitchen, trying to identify the source of the unusual smell. Perhaps it was just the pair of scruffy grey trainers stuffed underneath the radiator or the Trespass jacket hanging beside the door.

It wasn't only the smell of the place that was different. Hairbrush pop was echoing from the kitchen instead of lethargic jazz, and the upstairs lights had been left on. The dining room was visible through the open doors at the other end of the living room with the table already set for three and a jug of water resting on the tablecloth. It was nothing revolutionary, but Amy could still feel herself quivering as she followed Valerie into the kitchen.

She caught them mid-kiss and halted by the breakfast bar.

'Sorry,' she said as they separated.

'I was just congratulating Max on not burning down the kitchen in our absence,' Valerie replied, throwing a challenging look to her left. 'It seems stirring mushroom soup is actually one of Max's skills. She didn't apply it effectively to tomato soup the other week though. I'm wondering if it's selective.'

Max snickered and crossed to the fridge. 'Your mum's had a bottle of wine cooling. Do you want a glass?'

'See how she changes the subject?' Valerie queried.

There was a lump in Amy's throat that she couldn't clear away. She attempted a smile then took the glass of wine that Max offered a minute later. It was lucky that Cyndi Lauper was warbling in the corner or the silence would've been even more awkward as the three of them just looked at each other. Valerie finally moved to stir the soup, although Max remained motionless with her hands tucked into her pockets and a flush creeping up around her ears that probably had little to do with the warmth of the kitchen.

It was seeing them together that had derailed Amy, just as she'd suspected it might. Even side by side, there was something alien about it that she couldn't connect in her mind. She was still waiting for the punchline, but that thought disintegrated when Valerie turned back from the stove and glanced at Max with more honest affection than Amy had seen from her in years. The surprise caused the wine glass to slide along her fingers and she quickly put it on the breakfast bar to prevent it crashing to the floor. She winced as both Max and Valerie pivoted towards her.

'Are you all right?' questioned Valerie.

Amy shrugged.

'Come on, you can do better than that. What's wrong?'

'This is weird,' she muttered.

Valerie's shoulders sagged. 'Oh.'

'No, I mean . . .' She trailed off then met Max's eye, anxious yet reassuring all in one. 'Most people, when their parents start dating again, this new person comes in and they have to adjust. But you're more comfortable here than I am.'

'I wouldn't go that far,' Max said.

'The house smells more like you than anything to do with me.'

'Okay, maybe, but that doesn't mean I don't tuck my elbows in when I walk into rooms.'

'That's right, you know,' Valerie chipped in. 'There was an incident with a vase.'

**118**

Amy's lips parted. 'The one on the landing? I wondered where that went. It was hideous, though, Mum.'

'That's what she said,' replied Valerie, jabbing her thumb towards Max. 'That's why I don't entirely believe it was an accident.'

'I don't buy fancy furniture for the same reason I don't buy a Merc,' Max said with a lopsided grin. 'Well, that and I don't know my arse from my elbow when it comes to it. But, honestly, that thing looked like a kid had chucked up on it.'

Valerie was unsuccessfully stifling her smile. 'That's a world-renowned artist you're criticising there.'

'You're on my side, right, Amy?'

She laughed. 'Oh, yeah. If you feel your elbows knocking near that porcelain monstrosity in the main bathroom, I'll buy you a coffee or something.'

'A coffee?' Valerie repeated. 'Is that the going rate for destroying unique pieces of my furniture these days?'

'No, you're right, that's too much,' Amy retorted.

'That's not how haggling works,' said Max, pointing a finger at Valerie. 'Didn't reckon you were teaching her to be rude.'

Valerie rolled her eyes. 'Yes, yes, that's exactly what I'm doing. I must make sure she's more polite when she goes around committing acts of vandalism and destruction.'

'Commissioning them,' Amy corrected.

'You spent far too long listening to your father's legal arguments.'

The reference to Tim landed awkwardly around them all. Amy checked first to see if Max was unsettled, but she just leaned her hip against the countertop and looked at Valerie with that same affection she'd seen operating the other way. Then she shook herself and returned her gaze to Amy.

'There are two bits of the house I haven't seen,' she said.

Amy exchanged a glance with Valerie. 'Right . . .'

119

'Your room and your dad's study,' Max explained as she straightened up. 'It didn't feel right even putting my head through the door so I said to your mum I'd wait until you wanted to show me. No pressure, I'm just saying. When I was a teenager, I would've kicked off if strangers had started going through my stuff like they had the right.'

'Thank you,' Amy said.

Max shrugged. 'So, what sort of films are you –'

'Come see the study,' she interrupted. 'How long have we got, Mum?'

'Oh, about twenty minutes if you prefer your potatoes cooked,' she replied.

'That was once,' Max returned on her way across the kitchen.

Amy smirked then motioned for Max to follow her. The smell as they passed through the hallway was more familiar now, and the lights gleaming on the landing were a welcoming sight.

'Mum's normally really pedantic about switching lights off,' she said.

'Really? She's never let on. It's not that I'm against the environment or anything like that, only . . . It's nicer, having a light on in the house to say that there's someone waiting. Then you switch it off after. My aunt was all like that, though it was probably half to do with the dodgy gin she was getting from the café down the road. Giving them signals to drop it off.'

A chuckle spluttered out of Amy's mouth. 'What, seriously?'

'Her favourite was rhubarb,' Max said.

'Rhubarb? In gin?'

'Not my thing either, but she liked it. She was one on her own, but that's why me and her got along so well. There's nothing in here I can knock over, is there?'

They'd reached the door and stopped in unison. The only alteration this room had experienced in Valerie's big renovation was the door colour – cream instead of natural wood. Beyond the threshold, everything was just as Tim had left it and Amy's stomach swirled at the prospect of showing someone else inside. It'd be like walking Max around a mausoleum dedicated to someone she couldn't compete with, and that was cruel. So, instead of opening that door, Amy backtracked several steps and nudged her own bedroom into view. She reached around the frame to turn the light on and then left Max to walk inside of her own accord.

'I don't have much stuff here anymore,' she said.

Max looked around, eyes lingering on the pink curtains and the array of ornaments on the windowsill. She made a beeline for them then faltered at the sight of something else.

'Is that Wilbur?' she asked.

'Erm . . . yeah.' Amy retrieved him and held him out. 'Be careful with his left eye. It might fall. Mum told you about my toy owl?'

Max tickled his beak. 'Is that weird?'

'I don't know,' she admitted.

'Me neither,' Max said with a wry smile. 'I've never been seeing someone's parent before. I'm not sure how this is meant to work.'

'Well, I've never had someone date my mum before. Maybe we can muddle our way through it?'

She watched as Max returned Wilbur to his station underneath the lamp, adjusting his beak to point towards the door. Then she massaged her neck with one hand while taking in the rest of the room. Amy could almost hear the barcode scanner beeping and found herself bouncing on her heels until Max turned back fully, a pensive expression playing across her face.

'I'm not out to cause problems,' she said.

'I know that,' Amy replied.

Max nodded slowly. 'And I've never done this before – not a proper relationship with a woman, never mind her kid. So, if I muck it up, can you tell me? I've watched

Drew lurch his way through it with Elena, but the day I start treating him like a role model is the day you've got free rein to stick me in a padded cell. I need help to make sure I'm doing this right and I've no one else to ask.'

'You want me to be the barometer for your relationship with my mum?' Amy questioned.

'Sounds daft when you say it like that.'

'It doesn't, honestly. I'm just not sure I'll be any good at that either.'

'So, we're even,' said Max.

'I like that,' Amy murmured. She hesitated then held out a hand. 'Deal.'

'Deal,' Max echoed.

They walked downstairs a few minutes later in silence, although they were comfortable together. Valerie had taken the opportunity to switch the music back to jazz, earning an eye roll from Max when they entered the kitchen. Amy couldn't suppress her smile, and it only grew when Valerie glanced back from the stove and caught her in the act.

'I take it everything's all right?' Valerie queried.

Amy spotted the tremor in her voice; she knew Max did too. Whatever Valerie was expecting by way of response, it wasn't Max turning and striding back out of the kitchen. Her cheeks paled as she looked to Amy for an explanation.

'Max?' Amy called.

She was back almost before she was gone, throwing them both a shrug. 'Just turning the upstairs light off since we're all here. Saving electricity and all that.'

## Chapter 17

Valerie slept like a pedigree cat and woke up like a feral one. Max loved watching her come round, even if the heels kicking back against her shins were leaving bruises. Those few seconds in the morning before Valerie woke properly left her more open than Max saw her when she was fully awake. She'd let a hand rest on her naked thigh and wait for the sapphire eyes to flutter open. The only difference this morning to the other handful of times she'd stayed over is that, this time, they weren't alone in the house. That pushed Max out of the bed before Valerie had done much more than arch back into her body. On her way out of the room, she grabbed a silk dressing gown from the door hook. She was grateful of it when she walked into the kitchen to find Amy nursing a cuppa at the table.

Max cleared her throat. 'Morning.'

'You look ridiculous,' Amy said as she caught sight of her.

'Yeah, tell me about it. Do you want another drink?'

'If you don't mind. You know, you could've worn one of my dad's old dressing gowns. It was a thing with him, he had about eight of them.'

'Wouldn't have felt right.'

'Where do you get that from?' Amy asked.

Max pulled a clean cup from the dishwasher then turned back to face her. 'What do you mean?'

'You've got this filter, what's right and what isn't. Some people, they just – they can't separate it out and they hurt everyone else. You can tell when you're on the other side of it that they're wrong, but they can't see it.'

'You talking about your mum again?'

Amy scrubbed at her forehead while a blush crept up around her throat. It didn't help that Max was staring at her, so she crossed to the patio window instead and looked out across the fields. She liked this view, all rolling hills and cows dotted about in the next field but one. The last time she'd lived with a view had been in Harrogate with Bea and she hadn't realised how much she'd missed all that openness until her first morning with Valerie.

'It was what you said about being your barometer,' Amy answered suddenly.

Max winced but didn't turn around. 'That was just me being an idiot. Forget about it.'

'You do know how much she wants to get elected, don't you?'

'Yeah, she's –'

'I mean, she really wants it. I've seen her when she's ruthless and I don't want –'

'You don't have to worry about me, you know,' Max cut in, twisting back and smiling. 'I'll be all right.'

Amy shook her head. She scraped the chrome chair along the floor until it screeched then paced beyond the breakfast bar. The whole room seemed to carry with her, so, when she spun on her heel, it rocked a bit before settling. That was the passion Valerie had in life, the same energy it looked like she'd passed down to her daughter. Whatever had been going through Amy's head was stoppered when footsteps padded down the stairs in the hallway. She'd cleared her face by the time Valerie walked in, and half of Max was wondering if she'd imagined the whole thing.

'Is everything all right?' Valerie asked as she glanced between them.

'We were just about to stick the kettle on,' said Max.

Valerie's shoulders relaxed. 'Oh, I think we can do better than that. I know a café which is apparently heavenly on a Sunday.'

'Mum . . .' Amy growled.

'What?' she questioned innocently. 'I'm just saying I know the right place, that's all.'

The first thing Ed did when they walked into the empty café was drop the teapot he was drying. It shattered behind

124

the counter and he smashed his head on the coffee machine trying to grab it.

Amy darted forward, but he waved her off.

'I'm fine, I'm fine. I just wasn't expecting – Hello, again, Mrs Smythe. The – the hygiene rating's to your left right there. Four stars –'

'Thank you, Ed,' Valerie interrupted with one of her polished smiles. 'I would offer to shake your hand. Unfortunately, you do seem to be bleeding.'

Max couldn't hold in her snort, earning a glare from Amy as Ed lifted his palm up to the light coming through the window. He tilted his head to the side then licked his lips a few times.

'Right, yeah. Sorry about that. I'm not too good with blood, as it goes.'

Valerie's laugh sputtered out from behind her hand. 'I see.'

'Why don't you two go upstairs?' Amy suggested.

'I'm a registered nurse, I could –'

'Go away, that's what you could do.'

'Spoilsport,' Valerie said, grabbing Max's hand. 'Come on, we know when we're not wanted. Just make sure he doesn't get blood in my coffee, or I'll sue.'

She clattered up the stairs and Max just stumbled after her, trying not to lose her footing. Valerie turned at the top with a fresh smirk on her face, ready to draw her in for a kiss that left them teetering against the banister.

'You're acting like you're drunk,' Max murmured as she pulled away.

Valerie chuckled and kissed her again. 'I'm just happy. This is wonderful, I haven't felt so –'

'Put each other down for five seconds and let me through,' Amy cut in.

Instead of acting embarrassed, Valerie stepped aside. It took Max's brain a few seconds to catch up then she realised that both of them were off to sit down and she was stood there like a prize plum. So, she wandered after them, making a show of looking at the gig notices scattered about when what she really wanted to do was check if the pair of them were getting along okay. All this was the opposite to what she'd expected with Amy, and it wasn't much like she was used to seeing with Valerie either.

Ed trotted up the stairs and poked his head above the banister. 'Mrs Smythe, is that offer to check my hand still up for grabs?'

'As long as you start calling me Valerie,' she replied.

'Not sure about that. Here, I've got the first aid kit and I've cleaned it out.'

'I hope you're sure about that. Come – sit.'

He nearly tripped over his feet crossing to the sofa, but that was probably down to the blood as much as anything else. Max glanced at Amy to see if she minded Valerie patching him up, but she was smiling. They both watched as Valerie unrolled the bandage and smoothly wrapped the wound up, although she did stop him from moving his hand away when she'd done.

'What are your intentions towards my daughter?' she asked.

Amy groaned. 'Don't answer that.'

'Please, do,' Valerie said.

With his free hand, Ed scratched his beard. 'Mainly to make her coffee and chocolate cake.'

'Hmm.' Valerie looked to Max. 'I think we have to sample this chocolate cake, don't we?'

'Reckon so, yeah,' she said.

Ed scrambled to his feet. 'I'm on it.'

The footsteps sounded like an avalanche, but he must've landed on his feet at the end of it because he didn't make a yelp. The three of them listened to him banging around down there for a minute then Amy turned to look at Valerie and then Max in turn.

'You're evil, the pair of you,' she said.

Valerie grinned and reclined into the cosy sofa. 'Just taking advantage of the mother-in-law card. Besides, we can't have him too comfortable, can we?'

# Chapter 18

As soon as Amy walked into her Economics class on Monday morning, she was redirected to the Law Department's office with instructions to see Dennis Cowper. Her first instinct was to lock herself in the bathroom for the rest of the day, but she settled for twenty minutes perched on the sink playing on her phone instead. By the time she knocked on the open door of the Law office, Dennis seemed surprised she was there.

'I assumed you were off sick,' he said, gesturing to the chair beside the door. 'Take a seat.'

'I'm okay, thanks. I got the message you wanted to see me.'

Dennis sighed and peeled his glasses from his face. 'I've been trying to catch a moment with you after class, although I was reticent to deliberately hold you back. I know what students can be like and the last thing I want to do is cause you more stress in or out of the classroom. There's plenty of talk about your mother in the corridor these days –'

'Is there?' Amy interjected, looping her fingers behind her back.

'You must have heard it.'

'I don't really listen.'

'Is that perhaps half the problem?' Dennis asked.

She straightened her shoulders. 'I'm afraid I don't understand.'

'Amy . . .' He glanced around and retrieved a printout, holding it up towards her. It was full of notes written in Comic Sans, his usual concession to discord that made him popular with the students. 'Your Sociology records are excellent; your Economics grades are exceptional. Paula Harborough is impressed with your grasp of the subject and with your willingness to participate. Have you thought about pursuing a career in that area?'

128

'I know what I want to do, Mr Cowper. I've told you that before.'

'Just look at this for me, Amy. I don't take pleasure in writing notes like this, not for any student, but especially not one with your intelligence and potential. You're distant in class, almost lazy even. Your written work's atrocious and, yes, before you try and argue, your grades are now slipping below what's acceptable.'

'I'll pass,' she insisted.

'And then what, hmm? Continue being bored at university? I've spoken to your personal tutor, I know your plans and intentions. If you don't rethink now, you could be in for a lengthy career you find absolutely no pleasure in. That's if you get that far which, quite frankly, I doubt. Now, if you reconsider, do something at university you enjoy –'

'With respect, that's not a plan. I won't be one of those people who jumps around from career idea to career idea without sticking to anything. I'm going to be a lawyer, that's what I'm going to do.'

Dennis rubbed his chin. 'Your tutor thinks there's difficulty at home. She's asked me to hold off calling either your mother or your grandmother and to deal with this in-house if at all possible.'

'Right,' Amy muttered.

'I have to say, we may be getting beyond that point. I understand that you feel as though you're honouring your father's memory by going into –'

'You don't understand,' she interrupted, crossing her arms. 'I want to do this.'

He stared at her for a minute then replaced his glasses on his nose. 'Then get your grades up and show some enthusiasm in my class. Otherwise, we'll need to speak again before your UCAS application.'

For the second Monday in a row, Amy found herself standing outside the office of Pinder Cabs wondering whether to go inside. The interior had been an unknown quantity last week, but now she could picture the desk and the chair, even the frayed wallpaper. Her only concern about pushing the door open this time was whether she'd come face-to-face with Drew again. Max had passed on his apologies, but Amy was still worried about encountering him after the last time. From the talk over the weekend, she knew he mattered to Max, however much their relationship was apparently built on sarcasm and rugby. Getting Drew's approval felt like a hurdle she had to jump in order to be friends with Max.

The decision was taken from her hands by the door jolting open. A woman swore at her to move then lumbered towards the taxi that had just pulled up on the kerb. Amy turned to watch then checked herself when the woman glanced over her shoulder. She was left with little choice but to launch into the office, startling Max on the switchboard.

'I thought you were her back again,' Max explained, gesturing outside. 'Right one, she is. Kicks off every time about the prices then makes out like she's been hard done by if I tell her to go elsewhere. She's after a discount, but she's not getting one. Not from me, anyway. With the way she tries it on, reckon it might get her somewhere with the lads.'

Amy let the door swing shut. 'Do you get a lot of that?'

'Comes with the territory. People try their luck, it's part of the game. Come through, I'll put the kettle on.'

The door to the other half of the office was little more than a piece of plywood that quivered in her hand. It wouldn't slot back into the frame when she tried and Max came over to force it in with her shoulder.

'Nothing round here's easy to work,' she said as she crossed to the kitchenette. 'Keep saying we'll move elsewhere, but it all costs and Drew's got enough on his plate. Anyway, he'd muck a new place up like he has this one. There's peanut shells on the sofa so watch yourself. I'll get them in a minute.'

Just as she'd managed to turn the kettle on, the switchboard phone began blaring. She hesitated, but Amy motioned for her to answer the call and, while she did, set about making the tea herself. One call bled into three and she was perched on the edge of the sofa drinking from a Batman mug before Max could finally speak.

'Cheers for this. And for the peanuts as well. Saves me a job. Elena's still got all the morning sickness going on so he's shifted his bad habits here full-time. Better here than in the cab though. What's up, anyhow? What are you doing here?'

Amy shrugged and sipped her tea. 'Today's when Biddy has her church friends over for tea. They drive me mad at the best of times, I'm really not in the mood for it today.'

'How come?'

'Had enough of idiotic people for one day.'

Max grinned. 'Know that feeling. But how did you end up here?'

'Mum's in Leeds for a meeting and Ed's baking so . . . You said pop in so I did.'

'Yeah, I meant it. Saves me from going potty answering that thing.'

'I don't know how you work with people all day,' Amy admitted. 'Even if it's just on the other end of a phone. I can't think fast enough to deal with it sometimes.'

'I wasn't too dissimilar when I was your age. Didn't mind talking, but the minute it felt like I had to . . . You get there with confidence. And by not giving a toss what people think.'

Amy tilted her head to the side. 'But they're your customers. They matter.'

'Course they do, but that's not to say they've got free rein over what goes on in my head. That woman before – Ms Bawtry – she reckons she's putting one over on us every time she has a go, every time she wangles a discount.'

Fact is, we've got a policy about who we carry and who we don't, so if we wanted to ban her, it'd happen.'

'Why haven't you?'

'Because she doesn't matter. Let her think what she likes as long as we're getting her money at the end of the day. I'll play nice with her, but she's not right. Booking in customers or talking over the phone – it's just what you do.'

'I bet I still couldn't do it,' Amy said.

Max's lips twitched. 'If I take you up on that, I can nip down the road and get us some cake. What do you reckon?'

'I – I couldn't, I'd mess it up –'

'If Drew can do it, you can,' Max cut in. Then she held up a hand and continued, 'Not that I'm forcing you into doing it, just thought you might want some lemon drizzle cake, that's all.'

That made her mouth water, though she covered by taking another sip of tea.

'How did your internship work out?' questioned Max after a moment.

'I did a lot of filing and making cups of coffee,' Amy replied.

'No answering the phone?'

She shook her head. 'They didn't quite know what to do with me. It was like they were wearing kid gloves, you know? I was there, I got the tick for my CV, but they didn't want to offend me by giving me anything to actually do. I was bored.'

'Maybe they should've got you to answer the phone. That's not boring.'

'Yeah, but it is important and I'm not . . .'

'What, good enough?' Max finished for her.

'I'll mess up,' she murmured.

Max patted the switchboard then stood up. 'Not on this thing, you won't. Come on, I'm not leaving you to it, but I'm saying I could if I wanted. All you do is speak to them naturally and put the postcode into this machine. Here, I'll show you.'

Even though her stomach was churning, she found herself leaving the Batman mug on the carpet and taking Max's place in the switchboard chair. It smelled more of sugar than the rest of the office, although the backrest was deceptively comfortable. She listened attentively to all Max's instructions then nearly panicked when the machine in front of her buzzed and flashed.

'You're fine,' Max said, rubbing her shoulder. 'Go for it.'

Amy cleared her throat then pressed the button. 'Pinder Cabs, Amy speaking.'

'Oh, hiya, love,' a raspy voice replied. 'Can I have a taxi from 8 Bawlin Lane on the Cottinghill Estate?'

'Where are you going to?'

'Cat and Bottle, down Ridgeway Lane.'

She put all that into the system and clicked. 'That'll be eight minutes. Can I take a name?'

'Doreen.' There was a pause. 'Eight minutes?'

'Sorry – is that too long?'

'No, love, I'll set me stopwatch by it, that's all.'

Her gruff laugh was cut off when the call ended. Amy covered her eyes and tried to duck out of the seat, but Max pushed her back down.

'You've still got to dispatch, don't do half a job. You're giving it to Raj from where he is so just radio it through. Or it'll be more like nine minutes, come on.'

Amy couldn't help but laugh. It took a second to recall how to use the radio then she blurted out the instructions in a rush. That left her facing another lengthy pause that brought fresh heat to her cheeks.

'Erm, who's this?' Raj asked.

Max chuckled and took over. '8 Bawlin Lane, soon as, mate.'

'That was horrible,' Amy muttered, burying her head in her hands. 'I sounded like such an idiot.'

133

'You got the call dispatched, you're fine. Doreen was only taking the mickey out of you and Raj was just checking he wasn't being had. It's normal, it's good.'

'Good?' she repeated.

'Yeah, the job got done. It's that simple sometimes. Look, you could've gone off on one like Pauline did this once with her niece's ex's mother-in-law. That lost us hundreds, but she felt better after it.'

Amy smiled. 'You're not a normal boss.'

'I wouldn't wanna be. That's how me and Drew got going with this place – our old boss was a right old arsehole so we took half his lads and started out on our own. Only took two years for him to go out of business. Should feel sorry for him, but he deserved it. Here, you've done your bit and proved you can do it. I'll take back over.'

'No, I need another chance,' she replied.

Max went over to retrieve her mug from the floor and passed it to her. 'You'll need this.'

The next hour passed in a flurry of calls and a few customers appearing in person. Amy found herself almost enjoying it, especially when a woman complimented her phone manner. Instead of hovering, Max took root on the sofa with a Stephen King novel and Amy was sure she heard snoring from behind it at one point.

Her equilibrium was shattered when the door opened and Drew walked in though. She snatched the headset from around her neck, dumping it on the chair and backing away.

'I'm sorry, I didn't –'

'Whoa, hold up, I'm not a monster,' he interrupted. 'Just an idiot when I'm not asleep, if you listen to Max. Has she got you pulling illegal shifts now then?'

'Only if we're paying her in tea,' Max said as she crossed the room. She rested a hand on Amy's shoulder and asked, 'Are you all right?'

'I'm fine,' she murmured.

Drew scratched his cheek. 'It's my fault. Look, I was well out of line last week. It's no excuse, but I had a lot on my mind and I'm a prat to boot so . . . If you're a mate of Max's, you're welcome here anytime. As long as her mates aren't ashamed of her, that's fine by me.'

'I'd never be ashamed of her,' Amy answered.

'Yeah,' he said with a smile, 'you wouldn't be here if you were.'

## Chapter 19

'Drew, I swear, I'm pregnant, not terminally ill. If you lay one finger on that potato masher, you'll be wearing the turkey instead of a paper hat.'

Max winced as Elena rounded on him with a wooden spoon then she stretched to nudge him away towards the table.

'Here, pull a cracker with me,' she suggested.

'I'm only trying to help,' he said.

'Help me with the cracker then. I want a hat.'

It took until dinner was on the table for him to settle properly, but then he managed to hoover up everything that came within a foot of his plate. That shut him up for a while, giving Elena more chance to talk than she usually had when the three of them were together.

'When's Valerie picking you up?' Elena asked when the pudding bowls were empty.

'Three, so she said.'

Drew burped. 'Expecting her to be on time?'

'She is out feeding the homeless,' Elena said. 'I'm not sure punctuality comes into it today.'

'Well, she's not doing it for the love of the homeless, is she?'

'I wouldn't know. I still haven't met her, remember?'

'You're not missing much,' he muttered.

'I doubt that's fair.' Elena glanced to Max. 'Do you think she'd come up for a drink?'

Max reached for their bowls to stack with her own. 'We've only got a few hours before she goes to Clarice's with Amy, but I don't see why not.'

'Oh, do we have to?' Drew moaned.

'I want to meet her,' insisted Elena. 'I've met Amy and she's fantastic –'

'Yeah, well, the apple bounced off the tree, fell in the canal and drifted half a mile away. They're nothing like each other. Amy's lovely, Valerie's a pain in the arse. Come on, El, it's Christmas. I'm not having her in my home.'

Elena crossed her arms over her swollen stomach. 'Do I have to play the pregnant woman card?'

He groaned, but they all knew she'd won. In her text message, Max made it clear that Elena was the one doing the asking, and Valerie confirmed within two minutes. She'd had an interest in Elena since that night at the hospital, not that Drew wanted to understand that. It'd mess with that image he had in his head of her with webbed feet and bloodshot eyes.

The minutes ticked by and Drew started shredding his paper hat to pieces. Max got herself another beer then dived into a conversation with Elena about some of the vandalism down by the park. It kept them talking till the buzzer rang then Max leapt up to answer it.

Drew sniggered. 'She really has got you trained.'

Elena threw a cushion at his head, giving Max chance to slip out into the hallway. She buzzed Valerie in, unlatched the door, then spent the time till she arrived looking at the picture of the last ultrasound Drew had framed next to the kitchen.

'I promise, they look different when they come out,' Valerie said beside her.

Max jumped as she twisted around. 'You scared me.'

'Well, you were in your own little world. Are you all right?'

'Fine,' she replied. 'Eaten too much, that's all.'

Valerie wrapped both arms round her waist and pressed a kiss to her lips. She pulled away then motioned for them to move out of the hallway. Max would've hung back a bit longer if Elena's voice hadn't echoed from the living room.

'Stop hogging her,' she called.

'Is that what you're doing?' Valerie whispered.

A shiver ran through Max's body. 'Oh, yeah.'

'Later,' said Valerie as she took a step towards the living room. 'I promise.'

Walking into Drew's line of sight was the best passion-killer Max could've come across. He was watching the doorway with a snarl on his face that barely eased when Elena glanced over at him. Anyone else might've been intimidated, but not Valerie. She just nodded in his direction then turned her full attention to Elena.

'Thank you for inviting me, it's good to finally meet you. I feel as though we've spent months missing each other. You're looking remarkably well.'

Elena patted her stomach. 'I don't feel it. But I don't care. Do you want a glass of wine?'

'I think I'd better stick to water since I'm driving,' Valerie answered.

'Always on the job, eh?' Drew muttered.

Valerie ignored him and smiled at Elena. 'You're due in early April, aren't you?'

'They've got me down for the 1st, believe it or not.'

'Well, that could be interesting. Do you know what you're having yet?'

'No, we haven't asked.'

'Any preference?'

'As long as it's healthy, I couldn't care less,' Elena said.

'I understand. I'm sure you're doing everything right, it'll be fine.'

Drew snorted as he dragged himself up from the sofa. 'You can't be sure, none of us can be. Not the doctors, no one.'

The tension in the room ramped up a notch. Max exchanged a look with Elena, getting her silent permission to end this as quickly as she could, then reached for Valerie's hand. It was yanked away before she could get hold of it as Valerie rounded on Drew.

'A platitude is better than nothing, wouldn't you say?' she questioned.

'Doesn't mean anything coming from a politician.'

'I'm not a politician by trade.'

'Yeah, then why are you acting like one?'

Valerie crossed her arms. 'I wasn't aware that I was.'

'Feeding the homeless Christmas dinner? Right photo opportunity, chance to get your face in the papers again. You're sick.'

'I see you didn't bother volunteering,' she said.

'I've got responsibilities,' Drew shot back. 'Can't go swanning off when I feel like it. That's what it's like when your family lives in the same house.'

'Oi,' Max said sharply.

'It's true,' he snapped.

Valerie let out a growl that was more usual in other circumstances. 'I'd really love to know what your problem is with me. I haven't done a thing wrong as far as I can tell. We've barely spoken a handful of times.'

'A handful,' he mimicked.

'Oh, that's it, is it? Plain old leftie jealousy.'

He reared up on his heels. 'You what?'

'There we go – that's what you think it comes down to. Class war; me against you. Because I happened to land on my feet with Tim, you think I've forgotten, don't you? People don't forget.'

'Your sort do.'

'My sort?'

'Users,' he said, squaring up to her. 'You got a good home out of Tim, now you're getting a good – secret – shag out of Max every other day. You must reckon you've got it made. Only thing is, Amy can see right through you. She's a smart kid, that one. Must get it from her dad.'

Valerie twisted back towards him, every muscle in her body throbbing. Mindful that Elena had just recoiled into the sofa, Max stepped between them and held up her hands to Drew.

'Just leave it,' she said.

He shook his head. 'She's using you. Anyone can see a mile off.'

'All right, will you shut up?' Max demanded.

**139**

The voice coming out of her mouth surprised all of them, including herself. She didn't recognise it as her own, more like Colonel Peter Jarvis on loudspeaker. She shot a look at Elena to check she was okay then stretched out a hand to Valerie.

'We're going,' she said.

Drew grimaced and slumped back towards the sofa, his cheeks burning. 'I just can see what she's doing. I'm only saying this because I care, because we're mates.'

'Then be a mate,' Max replied as she nudged Valerie through the door into the hallway. 'Stop being a prize arsehole because, otherwise, I'm done. I mean it, Drew. See you tomorrow night for the shift.'

# Chapter 20

'Can you please stop smiling?'

Valerie cast a glance sideways. 'It's appropriate to smile on Christmas Day.'

'This isn't an appropriate kind of smile. Please, tone it down, I wouldn't like to have to explain it to Biddy's church friends.'

'It's not what you think,' Valerie said.

Amy tilted back her head and rolled her eyes. 'Oh, God, now that's what I'm thinking. Thanks, Mum. Just what I needed with half of St. Michael's wandering around through there.'

Valerie chuckled then turned back to watch the guests ambling around the stifling kitchen. Beyond, in every other downstairs room, there were clumps of people that Amy barely recognised, but Biddy had enough influence to encourage them to leave their homes on Christmas Day and come to her party. She eschewed an extravagant Christmas dinner in favour of this, and every year she seemed to go further, ordering more food and stockpiling bottles of questionable wines. Only this week had Amy finally realised the amount of effort that she expended on it all, and she'd been horrified. That was why she'd found herself up to her elbows in soap suds on Christmas Eve, trying to scrub scorched pastry from the rim of a quiche tin.

'Mum, I meant to say, don't have any of the Victoria Sponge. I lost a nail and I'm not sure where.'

'I'll bear that in mind,' Valerie replied with an attempt to smother her amusement. 'I'm sad to see that Ed's flair for baking hasn't quite transferred onto you. Anyway, are you okay, sweetheart? You've been quiet since I arrived.'

'Biddy's pushing herself too hard,' she muttered.

'It's only one night. It's important to her, it always has been.'

141

Amy chewed on her lip. 'I get that, I do. But I bet she's twirling around in there with a sherry in her hand, and it's not good for her. It's like I'm the only one who cares what she might be doing to herself.'

'Well, that's not true. No one would be here tonight if they didn't care about her.'

'Then where are they the rest of the year? She gets phone calls; I know how many because I answer them. Some still write, a couple of them email. That's great because she keeps accidentally deleting them. This – tonight – it's a ritual, a chance for everyone to have a party at her expense.'

Valerie twisted to deposit her wine on the counter. 'That's the way she likes it. You father always said she was happy to live the rest of the year with just us if she could have this illusion every Christmas.'

'Did he call it an illusion, or did she?'

'I doubt he plucked it out of thin air.'

'Was it him?' Amy pressed.

'Stop it,' insisted Valerie. 'I know what you're thinking and you're wrong.'

Amy fell silent, picking a thread from her robin jumper while the carols rumbled on in the living room. The image in her mind of Biddy swaying back and forth between guests was interrupted by a face hovering around the periphery of her imagination, watching and smiling. As hard as she tried to add colour to his cheeks, the blanched complexion of his final Christmas party lingered on. The memory drizzled away when a round of applause went up from next door and Amy forced herself to turn to Valerie.

'How was Max?' she asked.

Valerie's smile was back, more intimate than before. 'Good. She survived Drew's in one piece. I even went up to meet Elena for the first time.'

'How did that go? Drew's not your biggest fan.'

'Oh, I know. That aspect of it was a complete disaster, but I realised something. I mean, I know Max loves me –

loves us. But I think I doubted how far she'd go, especially if it came down to a choice. With Drew sniping over the past few months, it's crossed my mind more than once. But it's us, Amy. We matter to her as much as we mattered to your father. I didn't think that could happen again.'

'But you're still lying,' Amy pointed out.

'We're settled,' Valerie said, reaching to retrieve her wine. 'I can't afford any drama, not with the election this close. If you start rattling the table at this point, one domino might fall. I can't risk it.'

'And after the election? Will you tell her then?'

'I'm not planning on keeping it from her indefinitely, if that's what you're asking. However, I happen to think she'll understand. We've already experienced so many little hiccups and we keep getting through them. None of us are going to jeopardise what we've got as a family. Are we?'

'No, but I don't think it's that —'

'Look at you two hiding in here,' Biddy interrupted. 'Why aren't you enjoying yourselves?'

Amy jolted, spilling orange juice onto her sleeve. She hadn't noticed Biddy wander in clutching a cocktail glass in one hand and a piece of shortbread in the other. She leaned towards the glass and sniffed.

'What's this?' she questioned.

'I haven't the foggiest. Something young Paul mixed for me. He's quite a whizz.'

'Biddy, how much have you had to drink?'

She clicked her tongue. 'Oh, it's Christmas.'

'You won't live to New Year at this rate. Please stop drinking so much. You know what the doctor said about that.'

One of the cousins — Geoff, Amy thought — materialised from a corner and tucked an arm around Biddy's waist. 'You wouldn't begrudge her a few drinks on Christmas Day. She's fine, aren't you, Aunt Clarice?'

Amy opened her mouth but was checked by an elbow into her ribs. Under the guise of sipping her wine, Valerie had successfully silenced her long enough for Geoff to steer Biddy away towards the conservatory. Amy watched them go then kicked her heel back against the cabinet.

'They wouldn't mind if she dropped dead tomorrow. I'm just the killjoy granddaughter.'

Valerie rested a hand on her shoulder. 'Steady, sweetheart. I know you care, but this isn't the way.'

'Yeah, I care – they don't. You know, they think I live here because it's closer to college; you think I live here because of you –'

'I know it's not only that,' Valerie interjected.

'I'm here because she needs me. She's lost Dad and she needs me. What's it going to be like when I go to uni? She'll be isolated, she'll have an accident or she'll have to go into a home –'

'Darling, calm down. Have another drink.'

The direction of Valerie's gaze warned her that people were staring. Usually, Amy would've assumed Valerie's concern was for herself, but not in this crowd. She lowered her chin and waited for the flush to drain from her cheeks, aware of Valerie's elbow heavy against her arm. It was working to calm her when a collective gasp from the conservatory hit her like a bolt of ice.

Both she and Valerie abandoned their glasses and jostled their way through the throng. Biddy was crumpled up against the wicker sofa, everyone gawping and no one doing anything. Geoff had rocked back on his heels, as though he could lean far enough away to make the problem vanish from his orbit.

Amy pushed past him. 'Move. Get out of the way.'

'Everyone,' Valerie called, 'I think it's best if we call it a night. It's late and you've got these children to be getting home so, if you don't mind . . .'

They shuffled around collecting their things, but Amy was too focused on scrabbling in Biddy's handbag for her travel spray to pay them much attention. She pressed the tube into Biddy's hands and allowed her to administer the first spray on her own, whilst wondering whether Valerie was sober enough to drive them to the General rather than risk a wait for an ambulance. The roar of whispers faded away and she studied the creases around Biddy's eyes.

'Another spray?' she asked.

She was grateful when Biddy acquiesced without complaint, and the knot in her stomach loosened as she saw it take effect. The touch of a hand on her shoulder made her flinch, but Valerie was gazing down at her with a compassionate smile.

'Why don't you get some water?' she suggested.

Although Amy nodded, her legs trembled when she tried to stand. Valerie hauled her up then pressed her towards the kitchen with a nudge into the small of her back. The silence of the house rang in her ears as she leaned against the worktop and closed her eyes. All she could smell were the pickled onions from the buffet table that tickled her nostrils and throat, threatening to make its way further and empty her stomach.

'Amy? She's fine, the second spray worked a treat.'

She clenched her jaw, unable to straighten her spine and turn around.

'Sweetheart, it's okay,' Valerie repeated.

Every muscle in her body seemed to sag. She used the worktop to lever herself around to face Valerie, willing the tears to stay trapped in her eyes. They didn't, but the avalanche along her cheeks prompted no movement from Valerie. Amy squinted through the blur and recognised the fear colouring her expression, even as her hands worked themselves into a frenzy.

'Mum . . .' she whispered.

Valerie swept forward and wrapped her up in her arms. 'It's okay, I've got you.'

## Chapter 21

Come February, Max was spending most nights cocooned over at Valerie's, whether that was on her own or not. Now they were on the wrong side of Christmas, the election was taking up every minute Valerie had, including stopovers in places Max wouldn't have been able to find on a map if her life depended on it. That meant they spent less time with Amy, who was round at Clarice's more since her last scare, though they still kept in touch through the week for coffees and whatnot.

The last Saturday of the month was another cold one. Max was sat in the kitchen at Geith Place warming her hands round a cup when the door went earlier than she'd expected. She looked up as Amy walked in with her rucksack weighing down her shoulders.

'Wasn't expecting you,' Max said.

Amy hovered near the door. 'I needed a break. Isn't Mum back?'

'Shouldn't be too long. You want a drink?'

'I've got work to do. I'll be back down in a while.'

Max watched her out into the hallway, noticing the way her legs didn't altogether lift from the floor until she had to start climbing the stairs. The steps thumped through the house then finished off with a door slamming shut. From the sound of it, she'd gone into the study and not her bedroom, not that Max had ever disturbed her in either.

Valerie came back in her usual whirlwind and launched into a conversation before Max had even stood up from the table.

'Sorry, I know I'm late. The train down from Newcastle was delayed at York – again. But it was a fantastic day, we definitely won a few votes. There was the old man who hadn't met a canvasser in years, let alone a candidate. I think he's friends with everyone in the damn area! I brought Chinese –'

'Amy's here,' Max interrupted and Valerie's smile widened.

'Is she? That's brilliant, there's enough to go around. You know me and Chinese. Why don't you call her down and I'll get the plates?'

Since she was halfway to the cupboard already, Max didn't have chance to argue. She only got a curt response from Amy when she tried shouting her, and they were polishing off their share of the spring rolls before she made an appearance. Valerie hadn't stopped talking about what she'd been up to till then, but she trailed off when she saw Amy's face.

'Are you all right, sweetheart?' she asked.

'Busy, that's all,' Amy muttered.

Valerie nudged the platter towards her. 'Here, we saved you some. You're allowed a night off, you know. With all the work you put in, you deserve it.'

'It's fine,' she replied as she took two pieces of prawn toast.

The way she lowered her chin warned them both that conversation was off the table. Whereas every other night, Valerie would fill any silence with talk about the election, she held off tonight. Max saw her shooting Amy looks, as if what was wrong with her could be enticed out with chicken fried rice. It didn't happen, and they were almost done before any of them spoke again.

'You know, darling,' Valerie said suddenly, 'I was talking about you today.'

Amy glanced up sharply. 'You were?'

'Well, the business meeting this morning was held at Northumbria and quite a few of the faculty attended. I told them what your plans were and how exciting it was that you were so keen to follow in your father's footsteps.'

'You didn't think it was exciting before,' Amy said.

Valerie shrugged and reached for her wine. 'We've got beyond that, haven't we? You've decided what you want to do and I've accepted it.'

147

'And now you're using it for political gain.'

'What? No, of course not. I'm saying I'm proud of –'

Amy snickered. 'Right, yeah. You're proud now, when it suits you.'

'That isn't how –'

'Forget it,' she snapped.

Without giving them another look, she grabbed her wine glass and stamped across the room. Only when she'd gone all the way upstairs and the door had slammed again did Valerie finally turn to Max, her forehead creased.

'It's been a long time since I've seen her like that,' she murmured.

'She seemed a bit off when she got in. I'm not sure it was you she was having a go at.'

'Did she say why she was here? I'm delighted to see her, obviously, but she hasn't wanted to spend a night away from Clarice since Christmas.'

Max stood and began stacking the plates together. 'Yeah, I wondered that. I reckon she needed away from her for the night. How'd they seem on Thursday?'

'The same.' Valerie paused and rested her chin in her palm. 'Clarice was perhaps more demanding, I don't know. I find it difficult to judge. I know so little about their relationship when I'm not there and Amy's still inclined to put on a mask for me, even after Christmas.'

'That was a step in the right direction though,' Max pointed out.

'I'd thought so, but apparently not.'

Valerie let out a low growl then jumped up and started collecting the plates herself. Max fell back, watching her harsh movements, until a nod told her to gather up the rest and follow her through to the kitchen. It was colder in here than it had been for a while, not that Valerie seemed to notice. Once she'd dumped her load on the counter, she spun around and paced past the breakfast bar.

'I can't have this right now,' she said.

'What do you mean?' Max asked.

'That attitude, it's dangerous.'

'She's just having an off night, that's all.'

Valerie shook her head. 'It may start out that way, but these things escalate with Amy. I can't afford any form of bad – anything that might rock the boat this close to the election. I just can't.'

'Then talk to her,' Max said.

'Oh, I can't. That'll just inflame the situation.'

'I don't get it. You've been doing so much better, the two of you. Go upstairs, just talk to her like you have been doing.'

'I can't,' Valerie repeated.

As if that was it, she walked out of the kitchen. Max assumed she was just going to the loo or something, but then the front door slammed. She stood still for a good minute with the house settling around her, not knowing what was going on. Then a flurry of steps on the stairs ended with Amy bursting into the kitchen, fists clenched at her sides. Her hands relaxed when she caught sight of her, not that Max was any less confused for that.

'What's wrong? You look like you've seen a ghost.'

Amy took a step back. 'I thought you'd gone, that's all. I heard the door.'

'Yeah, your mum went – she went for a walk. She doesn't know what's going on with you, she's worried.'

'About herself, sure.'

'That's not how it is,' Max answered.

'So, why has she gone out? Why isn't she chasing me upstairs asking me why I'm upset?'

Short of fudging it, Max didn't know what to say. She let the silence do the talking then grimaced as tears welled up in Amy's eyes. The kitchen roll was closer to her, so she pulled off three strips and passed them across. Amy muttered her thanks and dabbed at her face. It didn't seem to be doing much good from what Max could see – even if tears weren't streaming down her cheeks, they were still absorbing into the kitchen roll faster than it could take.

149

She went through three dollops of it like that, until Max cleared her throat.

'Whatever it is that's going on, you can tell me. Or your mum, if that's what you want.'

Amy sniggered through the tissue. 'Yeah, that'll work really well.'

'I know she's busy –'

'Too busy to give a damn,' Amy interrupted.

'That's not how it is.'

'So, where is she?' Amy demanded.

Max shifted her weight and looked around the kitchen. The plates needed packing into the dishwasher, which was something practical she could do. She took a step forward then faltered and glanced back to Amy.

'You came back here tonight to talk to her about something, didn't you?' she asked.

Amy just shrugged.

'Is it your gran?'

'Biddy's fine,' she muttered.

'Okay, what about Ed, then?'

From the flush that settled on Amy's cheeks, Max thought she might've struck oil, but that success was smothered under the prospect of talking to her girlfriend's daughter about her love life. Maybe Amy saw how hesitant she was. She rolled up the tissues still clenched in her hand and dumped them in the bin on her way past.

'Where are you going?' Max questioned.

Amy spun around on the threshold. 'Once she's got something in her head, that's it. Nothing else matters as long as she gets what she wants. I'm not stupid enough to get in her way. I wouldn't risk it either, if I were you.'

The dishwasher was long since finished before the front door went again.

Max was lying on the sofa swilling around the dregs of her third glass of wine when Valerie appeared in the doorway. She hadn't taken a coat out with her so there was

150

a tinge to her face, as if she'd been coated in blue rinse. Max wound her legs round onto the floor, but stayed rooted to the cushion, waiting to see whether Valerie would stay put or walk through into the kitchen.

'I needed to clear my head,' Valerie explained after a moment.

'You could've said, not just walked out.'

'Because you always behave that maturely, don't you?' Valerie retorted.

'That's not fair. I'm still here now you've come back. I could easily have gone – Amy reckoned I had. She ran down here like a bullet when she heard the door go, in case it was me leaving.'

Valerie blew into her palms. 'I take it she hasn't finished with the histrionics then.'

'She's a kid,' Max argued, standing up. 'I know she acts like she's got it all worked out, but she's eighteen, that's all. I didn't have a clue what I was doing at her age, and I wasn't looking after an old woman either. There's something going on –'

'In which case, she needs to tell me,' Valerie interrupted.

'That's what her being here tonight was all about.'

'Well, that worked, didn't it? I haven't got time to decode everything, I can't physically do it. Just for the next three months, the two of you need to be straight with me.'

Max crossed her arms. 'It's not always as neat as that.'

'For now, it has to be.'

With that, Valerie stormed off towards the kitchen. Max listened for a minute, heard the cupboard open and shut then slowly followed her through. She found her at the patio window, staring into the darkness of the back garden, a whisky glass clasped in her hand. She'd heard her come in, or maybe seen her in the window, but she didn't turn around as she carried on the conversation.

'Days like today remind me why I'm doing this. Yes, I'll concede it started as something to throw myself into, to rid myself of grief, but it's beyond that now. I had nothing to lose when I was first chosen to be the candidate, you know. That's the reason they allowed me as much rope as I had at the beginning. It looked good for the local party to select a woman, especially since they've got such a poor track record regionally. But the landscape shifted – I helped with that. Before, if I didn't win, they were just going to chalk it up to Labour safe seat syndrome. But now . . . If we don't win the seat, I'll be the one who lost it.'

Max scraped her hand through her hair. 'I get that. So does Amy.'

'Then, please, let it play out. I need to win this, Max, I really do. It feels like the only tangible thing I'll ever have accomplished if I manage it.'

'Doesn't Amy count?' Max questioned.

Valerie turned around, her forehead creased. 'Now, I didn't mean that. But Amy was good luck rather than good management. This is something I have control over, and I'm damned if I'm going to fail now because I've taken my eye off the ball. Three more months, Max. That's all. Can't we hold it together until then?'

Her fingers were trembling around the glass, Max noticed. She crossed over and took it from her hand then rested her chin against Valerie's head. It was a moment before she gave in and wrapped her arms around her waist. Then Max kissed her hair and caught her own reflection in the patio window.

'Yeah,' she murmured finally, 'course we can.'

## Chapter 22

The rain overnight had left the pavements puckered with patches of ice. For the most part, Amy dodged them as she trudged through the deserted streets, but she tested her heel on a few and felt it slip away from her. She always snatched it away right before propulsion took hold, although the instant just beforehand was tantalising. Knowing you were going to fall and it could be out of your control was one way of giving over to nature. Sometimes, human beings thought they could beat it at its own game; jump up again and carry on with the match. Then something like cancer came along and proved them wrong – the heel slipped and there was no stopping the slide or where it took you.

Dawn was muted, a few rays of sunlight cracking through the clouds long enough to splash over a few window panes and that was all. The walk into town was punctuated by the odd car trundling past her, but otherwise the streets were empty. None of the shops had opened by the time she stepped into the precinct. Shutters had been raised on the bakery and the charity shop, almost by magic since there were no other humans around. It was like being sucked into another world where she could sit under the canopy of the bargain shop opposite the café and wait for some signal that she wasn't completely alone.

'Hey, you're freezing. What are you doing here?'

She jumped, raising an arm to shield herself then finding Ed gazing down at her. No words were forming in her throat, so she just allowed him to pull her up like a ragdoll and steer her across the street to the café. It must've been tricky for him to unlock the door and disable the alarm with her weight against him, but she couldn't force herself upright. He walked her over to the nearest table and deposited her in the chair before shrugging out of his coat and wrapping it around her shoulders instead. The scent of his aftershave around the collar brought a fresh round of tears to her eyes that became even harder to contain when he kneeled in front of her and rested a hand on her cheek.

'Has someone hurt you?' he questioned.

'No,' she murmured.

'That's – that's good.' He paused and searched her face. 'So, what is it? What's going on? Have you had a row with your gran or something?'

'I stayed at Mum's last night.'

'Have you had a row with her?' he pressed.

She shook her head, but that unleashed the tears from her eyes as well. They splashed everywhere, landing on her cheeks and catching in Ed's beard, until the deluge was over. He moved long enough to get some paper towels from behind the counter then pulled a chair up beside her.

'Tell me what's wrong, Ames,' he said, rubbing circles into her wrist.

'Everything,' she whispered.

'Like what?'

'Like . . . Mum and Max.'

He frowned. 'How do you mean?'

Amy squinted at their hands and the way one of his covered almost both of hers. She could feel the slender scars along his thumb from a soufflé gone wrong, jarring against her skin then giving way to the furrows of his thumbprint. The mechanical motion soothed her until he squeezed her hand and let go.

'Give me a few minutes to get everything warmed up and I'll get you a coffee,' he said.

She clutched at his arm. 'Wait, I need to ask you something.'

'Go on then,' he replied with a lilt in his voice. 'It's all right. Whatever it is, it's all right.'

'Do you just feel sorry for me? Is that – why you – you're not –'

'Whoa, whoa, hang on, is that what you think?'

More tears congregated in her eyes and she took a swipe at them with her sleeve.

'Oh, Amy . . . Come here.'

Even though she tried to block him, he managed to tuck one arm around her neck and the other one followed. Warm against his shoulder, still in the cocoon of his coat, she gave into the shuddering and cried herself out. Only when she'd stopped sobbing did he pull away slightly and stroke her hair.

'You're an idiot,' he said.

She sniffed and reached for the stack of papers towels on the table. 'Thanks.'

'Well, we both are. I mean, I was trying not to push it, that's all.'

'You don't have to –'

'Listen for a minute,' he cut in, tilting her face towards his. 'I've got to say this otherwise I'll make a bigger idiot of myself. It's what I said right back at the start, remember? About being damned if I do and damned if I don't. All right, you're eighteen and that makes it all right legally and all that, but it's not just about ticking a box and getting it over with. You've got enough going on in your head, what with college and everything. I was trying not to lay the pressure on more. I wanted it to be right, I didn't want to scare you off.'

His eyes were bright and honest. That was what she'd liked about him from the beginning, even if she'd been aware she was never completely honest with him. The half-truths that shielded the truth from Biddy and Max had transferred onto him as a matter of course.

'My first time was a nightmare,' he continued with a wry smile. 'My dad had not long died and I was looking to be normal again. You know how it is. Last thing I wanted was to be pushing you to make the same mistake I did. I'm sorry if I went about it the wrong way, but I was trying to do the right thing. I should've asked, only I wasn't sure how that conversation would've worked. I'm not good at this.'

'You seem to be,' she murmured.

**155**

Ed leaned forward to press a kiss to her lips. 'I'm muddling through it like everyone does. I'm not making a perfect job of it by any stretch, but I do love you.'

The words seemed to stick in the air before sinking into her head. She couldn't conjure up a response that didn't sound too much like reality television so she just burrowed back into his neck instead. Then she stiffened and pulled away.

'I'm not going to Durham,' she said.

He frowned. 'You're not staying here on my account, no chance.'

'No, I can't go to Durham. You don't understand.'

'Try me,' he replied, stroking her cheek.

'You can't – you can't go to a university you haven't applied for.'

His eyebrows contracted then he urged her back into his arms. The simple act of saying nothing brought a wave of relief crashing over her and, slowly, she became aware that she was shivering, that the café was cold and her eyes were stinging.

'What was that about coffee?' she mumbled.

Ed chuckled. He drew back and kissed her forehead then stood and went about getting the machine working and the room warmed up. She watched everything he did, every practiced motion that he instigated with a gentle touch. It was only since getting to know him that she'd understood not everyone had the same attitude towards making coffee and baking cakes. Other people in the chain shops around town just punched buttons and passed over the results. Ed made it look like an artform.

By the time he brought two coffees over, she could look at him properly. Anything she'd imagined about him rejecting her the moment he found out about Durham vanished with his small grin and she tucked her hands around her cup while she worked out how to explain. It took several minutes, but he pretended to be fascinated by the sprinkles on his cappuccino. The moment she started talking, all his attention was on her.

'I don't know what I'm going to do. I kept thinking that, if I just carried on, it'd be okay, but then Mr Cowper said he couldn't endorse my application, that I'm not going to get the grades. I'll pass Law, just not with an A*. Anyway, it's almost guaranteed that I failed the LNAT, so I just didn't bother trying to apply. There would've been no point.'

'Not to be daft, but what's the LNAT?' Ed asked.

'It's the national test you do to get on a Law degree. I probably muddled through the multiple choice – I couldn't get them all wrong – but I froze during the essay. I just couldn't write it, I only got a couple of paragraphs written and then I lost it.'

Ed rubbed her shoulder. 'Why?'

'Because Dennis Cowper was right,' she answered. 'I don't like Law. I think I hate it, actually.'

Saying the words aloud set off a bomb inside her head. The roar drowned out Ed's response and it took him scooping her into his arms for the noise to fade. He dropped a few kisses on her head then waited until her trembling had subsided before speaking again.

'You wanted to do it because of your dad, didn't you?'

She nodded into his chin. 'Like you did.'

'Oh, sweetie . . . Difference is, I love this place. If I didn't, I wouldn't have sunk everything into it, I definitely wouldn't have borrowed anything off your dad to keep afloat. If I'd kept it on as a memorial, it would've gone under anyway.'

'I thought I could be a good lawyer, I thought that's what he wanted.'

Ed sighed and leaned back to look at her. 'Did he ever outright say that? Come on, he loved you and you could've been a window cleaner for all he cared, so long as you were happy.'

'Even if that were true . . . It's gone too far now, hasn't it? Biddy's set on it, I don't know how to tell her that I've messed up. She'll hate me.'

'I know I've never met her, but that's not likely. It's only a job.'

Amy snickered. 'It's more than that.'

'But it's not happening,' he said gently. 'There's no way you can carry on with the lie. It's not in your control.'

'I know, I know that.'

'So, you need a plan, that's all I'm saying. What about telling your mum and Max first?'

'I tried that last night,' she said, reaching for her coffee. 'Mum doesn't care. It's all about the election for her and I'd better not get in her way.'

'If she knew the truth –'

'Then she'll really hate me for screwing up her life again.'

'What's all this about hate?' Ed questioned.

'It's accurate,' she replied.

He caressed her cheek. 'No one could hate you, especially not your mum.'

'I'm a liar,' she said.

'You've only got caught up in it. It looks like you can't get out, but you can. Just start telling the truth and it'll right itself. And I'm not going anywhere,' he added with a smile. 'There's nothing you could tell me that'd change that.'

Amy met his gaze, knowing he meant it. But the words still stuck on her tongue and all she managed to do was kiss him again. The look on his face when they separated brought with it a fresh pang – he thought she'd told him everything.

## Chapter 23

Impending fatherhood was as good a reason as any for Drew to be out in the cab well away from Max. That left her covering switchboard most days, keeping busy with the kettle and her Stephen Kings while the weather went from sleet to sun outside. The customers who came in direct through the day were usually eager to just get home, so she avoided most conversation beyond calling that their cabs were outside. She liked the solitude; it was a welcome break from all the talk of the election she had swirling around her head whenever she was near Valerie.

Mid-morning on Monday, she was surprised to find Ed walking into the office. He didn't look like he'd come for a taxi, not with only a t-shirt on and flour sprinkled over his chin, so she let him straight into the back and gestured to the sofa.

'Want a brew?'

'Yeah, that'd be great, cheers.'

It took a couple of minutes to get done – not helped by the switchboard deciding to ring off the hook for a bit – then she transferred over to the sofa to sit next to him. Something about his body language told her this wasn't going to be a casual chat across the office.

'Have you and Amy had a row?' she asked.

'No, no, we're cool.'

'So, what's going on?'

He scratched his beard. 'I'm worried for her. I'm not trying to break her trust, but I don't know what to do for the best.'

'I know there's something not right about her at the minute.'

'It's more than just now,' he admitted.

Max watched his fidgeting then took a gulp of scorching tea. 'Have you got her into trouble?'

'What? No, of course not. We haven't – not till – I mean, no. No.'

'Thank God for that,' she muttered. 'Then what do you mean that it's not just now?'

Ed sipped his coffee slowly. 'It's her career, all this Law rubbish. It's not what she wants to be doing with herself, I don't think it's right.'

'You don't or she doesn't?' Max questioned.

From the way he dipped his chin, he didn't want to answer that, which was the answer in itself. Max scrubbed at her forehead and thought back over the past few months. Given what he'd just said, Amy's attitude was starting to make more sense. The closer she'd got to the whole Law dream kicking in, the worse she'd felt. Valerie's words about being proud the other night were meant well, but Max could see how they might've looked to Amy. She took another gulp of tea as Ed raised his eyes, wondering what to say.

'Have I done the wrong thing?' he asked.

She shook her head. 'Just not sure what to do with it, that's all. You've told me this in confidence, so I can't outright talk to her about it. Not that I'm sure I'd know how.'

'It'd be better you than Valerie. With the election and everything, she thinks she doesn't care about her.'

'No, that's rubbish,' Max said.

'I tried telling her that,' replied Ed with a weak smile. 'But maybe that's the way in, I don't know. If Valerie's okay with it, maybe she'll let it go.'

After work, Max went for a drive instead of going straight back to Geith Place.

It was funny that, however many of her shirts were hung up in the wardrobe, she never felt like she was going home. Mind you, her pokey flat wasn't much more than somewhere to get some kip either. If she stopped to think about it, the last time she'd felt like she was going home was when she lived with Bea.

Driving with the window down and the cold sweeping through the car cleared her head a bit. She did another loop around the bypass then turned in the direction of Valerie's, getting there the same time as the hailstones did. It was a surprise to find the BMW already snug in the double garage, engine cold. It wasn't like Valerie to be home much before eleven most days. Max let herself in through the utility room, only to find a beer bottle being waved in front of her.

'You're late,' Valerie said.

'You're early,' Max replied.

Valerie pressed the bottle into her hands. 'Stalemate. How about we discuss it over dinner? I found this wonderful little butcher while I was canvassing today. That's why I had to come straight back – I couldn't have the steak going off on the back seat. Supporting local businesses and getting a good meal inside both of us is a price worth paying for a few lost hours. Sit down, sit down.'

She was shunted into a chair before she could say anything then Valerie was across the kitchen pulling steaks from the fridge and humming 'Ode to Joy' out of tune. It was only when the meat was sizzling that she turned around to flash one of her bright smiles. Max tried to mirror it, but her lips wouldn't stretch.

'What's wrong?' Valerie asked.

'I need to talk to you.'

The ease drained out of her face. 'Why? What's the matter?'

'Just something . . .' Max stood and tucked her arms behind her back. 'Look, Ed came to see me about Amy earlier.'

'Amy?' Valerie repeated. 'I thought – Well, what did he say?'

'He's worried about her, like we are. From what she's said to him, it looks like she's not all that keen on being a lawyer and it's getting to her.'

Valerie exhaled and turned around to tend the steaks. 'I can't say I'm surprised. I always thought it was a reaction to Tim and Clarice rather than a genuine love of the profession. She could do it if she wanted to, of course she could, but I'd rather she did something she was passionate about.'

'Any chance you could tell her that?' Max questioned.

'It's a little late for that. She's applied, she's going to Durham or another excellent university to study Law. That's all there is to it.'

Max squinted at her back. 'Hang on, she can change her mind. It's not set in stone that's what she's doing.'

'It might as well be. She knew what she was getting into, you know. There were plenty of opportunities to turn back before we got to this stage and she kept right on. She told me she knew what she wanted then and she needs to follow through on it now.'

'That's a bit harsh for a teenager.'

Valerie twisted to face her, looking exasperated more than anything. 'You don't understand that world. Clarice has told everyone about her successful granddaughter following in her son's footsteps. Amy knows that and she won't let her down. She daren't.'

'Daren't?' Max echoed.

'Perhaps that's the wrong word. What I mean is that Amy cares too much about Clarice to risk hurting her. As heartless as it sounds, that's not a permanent problem and then she can extricate herself if she truly wishes to.'

With a shrug, Valerie's attention returned to her cooking. Max was speechless for a minute, watching her carry on as if she hadn't just basically said her daughter was stuck with her choices until Clarice died. Even while the smell of succulent beef drifted round the kitchen, Max couldn't tear her gaze away from the back of Valerie's head. It went unnoticed for so long that her disbelief worked its way up to her throat.

162

'Okay, so I don't understand that world – as you put it – but I know what it's like to be pushed into something you don't want. If I'd followed what my dad wanted, I'd have probably had a leg blown off in Iraq.'

Valerie shook her head. 'That's entirely different. You didn't take all the steps towards making his dream a reality. Amy did.'

'She's eighteen!'

'Yes, that makes her an adult,' Valerie snapped, spinning on her heel with the spatula clenched in her hand. 'That means taking responsibility, doesn't it? I had to when I was her age. So did you, come to that. If she wants advice, if she wants help, why doesn't she come direct to me, hmm? She talks to Ed, he talks to you, you talk to me. It's ridiculous.'

Max just stared at her again, but Valerie growled.

'Don't look at me like that. I told you on Saturday – we need to get through the next few months without anything going wrong. All it takes is one slip and it's done with, the whole thing's gone. They'll pick up on anything – that's what these vultures do. Only a few months more, Max. That's all.'

'Amy not going to uni isn't anything to –'

'Of course it is. I've written about her, I've spoken about her. If she doesn't go then I look like a liar, don't I? Not to mention the fact that I've raised a child who'd rather give up at the first hurdle than try and forge a life for herself. That reflects on me.'

'It's not about you,' Max pointed out.

Valerie snorted and pivoted back towards the frying pan, but her hand overshot. She staggered with her hair near to the flames that licked around the rim of the pan and Max darted forward to pull her clear. They lurched away from the cooker, falling against the worktop instead. Max's spine took the impact, although she was more focused on Valerie shaking in her arms. She wrapped her up properly, the whiff of steak more than a reminder of what could've

163

happened. Valerie finally pulled away, cheeks pinched and her lip still trembling.

'Thank you,' she murmured.

'You need to be careful,' Max said as she stroked her neck.

'I know.' Valerie hesitated and met her eye. 'I do know. I'm sorry if I sound harsh, I don't mean to. But if Amy's got a problem, she needs to come to me. I've tried putting myself in her way so many times and it doesn't work. We're the closest we've been for years, yet she still doesn't want to talk to me. I can't force her into it nor do I think I could talk her out of becoming a lawyer. She might be wobbling about it, Max, but that's the only thing she's doing. She'll follow through on the ambition because of Clarice.'

'What if she doesn't get the grades?' Max pressed. 'What if she can't go to uni?'

Valerie rested her head against her chest. 'I know my daughter. She's not in the habit of giving up.'

# Chapter 24

On March 20th, Max's birthday, Amy let herself into the house and paused in the hallway. She hadn't expected fanfare, but the complete silence unnerved her. With the election in full swing, it was a given they wouldn't be dining out, so she'd anticipated Valerie would cook as recompense. Instead, the only smell drifting through the house was the vague whiff of bleach. Amy took off into the kitchen then stopped short as she found Max sat at the table. The room was cold, but she seemed oblivious to it as she stripped the label from a beer bottle with her thumbnail while staring into space.

'Where's Mum?' Amy asked.

Max flinched, dragging her gaze up. 'Oh, hiya.'

'Where is she?'

'There's a bottle of wine in the fridge if you want a drink. Not something I've heard —'

'I don't give a damn about wine. It's your birthday — where's Mum?'

'She can't make it,' Max said after a moment. 'There's an event she's got stuck at so I'm having a few beers here then going back to mine for a curry.'

Amy frowned at her. 'What, on your own?'

'It's no big deal.'

'You're not eating alone on your birthday,' she insisted, dropping her bag on the floor. 'You want curry? We'll get curry.'

'I'm not in the mood for company,' Max muttered.

'Well, tough, because I'm not letting you spend your birthday alone.'

'It wouldn't be the first time.'

Amy dug into her pocket for her mobile. 'That's not the point. I'll call Bengal's and get our usual banquet. You can get me a glass of that wine if you want to be useful.'

Max threw her a look then just shuffled across the room and followed her instruction. By the time she'd poured the wine, the food was ordered and Amy was already pulling a lumpy package from her bag.

'This is for you,' she said as she passed it over. 'Sorry, I'm hopeless at wrapping.'

The way Max began picking apart the paper suggested she didn't unwrap presents very often. She finally worked a hand inside and teased the shirt loose, shaking it out and gaping at the array of signatures.

'Where the hell did you find this?'

Amy bit her lip. 'Do you like it? I mean, it's not a complete set of signatures, but it's close and it didn't cost thousands like the others.'

'I bet it cost enough. I can't accept it.'

'Do you like it?' Amy repeated.

Max motioned her into a clumsy hug and squeezed hard. 'Best present I've ever got, honestly. How did you know?'

'Elena said you used to go to matches with your aunt.'

'Drew must've told her. First time he's kept back something useful in his life. Thank you.'

Amy's cheeks were burning as she pulled away. 'You're welcome. Tell me more about Bea. You always drop in these little titbits and then . . . Well, usually the election gets in the way. Come on, I'd like to know more about her.'

Although Max was reticent at first, a few pointed questions set her down the right track. In the forty minutes until their food arrived, Amy had never seen her talk so much or so animatedly. It was obvious from the way she spoke that Bea had been more of a parent to her than anyone else, and a crazy one to boot. The conversation continued as they ate, trailing off naturally when Max came to the end of one story just as their plates were clear.

'And I had to bail her out,' she said. 'This sixty four year old woman with an artificial hip and all the man on the desk said to me was "try to keep her clothes on in future, ma'am".'

Amy grinned and straightened her cutlery. 'What on earth was she protesting?'

'No idea. She was big into local conservation though. I got left all these guide books to old buildings and that. I've still got them in the spare room.'

'I wouldn't mind seeing them.'

'Fancying a career in stately homes now, are you?'

'Well, everyone needs a backup plan,' she muttered.

Max shuffled her elbows onto the table. 'That's right. As long as it's not something you'd rather be doing instead.'

'I don't know anything about heritage.'

'So, not heritage, but what about something else? You're smart, you can do whatever you want. Honest to God, you can. It's not like me with no qualifications and no hope of getting any. You set your sights on something and you go and do it. No matter whether you think your gran won't like it – or your mum, come to that. Do what's right for you.'

'You don't understand,' Amy replied with a weak smile, but Max just shook her head.

'I know you don't want to be a lawyer, so get out of it while you can. Whatever anyone says about it, you've got Ed, you've got me. We can work out a way past it. It'll be okay.'

Amy snatched up her glass, more to hide behind than anything else. A minute ago, they'd been casually talking about Bea, and now the reality that she tried to avoid was crashing over her like an avalanche. The glass wobbled between her fingers then toppled to the table and shattered.

Max planted her forearm down to stem the flow of wine. It stained the fabric pink, snaking towards her elbow and through to her skin. Amy was transfixed, right until Max flinched away and she spotted a shard of glass hanging from her arm. That image brought Amy's dinner into her throat and she was fortunate to make it to the downstairs bathroom before it bubbled up further than that.

Crumpled on the floor a few minutes later, she stared through her tears at the gentle knocking on the door. There was a patch of vomit seeping into her thigh, but that was nothing compared to the acrid smell that'd spread across the tiny room. She closed her eyes and tried to conjure up the picture of Max on the other side of the door.

'Is your hand okay?' she called.

The knocking halted. 'Yeah, it was more caught in the shirt than anything else. How are you feeling? Can I get you some water or something?'

'You should go,' Amy said in a steady voice.

'I'm not leaving you chucking your guts up.'

'I want you to go.'

'Let me just get you —'

Amy cracked her fist against the floor tiles. 'You're not my mum. Just go home, okay?'

There was a long silence. Now she could really picture Max's face, flickering with hurt even as she pretended it hadn't bothered her. She wanted to take back the words, but it was easier to let them stay there stagnating. A minute later, Max muttered a goodbye then her footsteps faded away. Amy heard the door to the utility room close and the rumble of the taxi as it moved first out of the garage and then out of the drive. She strained her ears until the noise must've been only in her imagination.

'You talked to Max, didn't you?'

Ed spun around, a tea towel dangling over his arm. Even underneath the beard, she could tell his cheeks were ashen. That was his guilt proven and she couldn't breathe suddenly. She twisted away from him and rested her palms flat on the nearest empty table. The early-morning customers were probably staring at her from across the café, but she didn't care.

'Why did you do it?' she demanded.

'I was trying to help. I didn't know what to do.'

'It wasn't your place to do anything.'

'That's not fair. What was I meant to do? Sit back and watch you tearing yourself to pieces? It was coming out at some point. I just thought that Max might –'

'You shouldn't have told her anything. If you were going to screw things up, why not go to Mum?'

'Because you don't get on properly and you like Max. Out of the two, if you'd listen to either of them, I thought it'd be her.'

Amy absorbed that then swivelled back towards him with a frown. Everything about his expression was sincere. She wanted to see some mark of the betrayal in his face, but she couldn't find it, and that brought a new rush of words out before she could stop them.

'You've got no idea what you could've done. You talking to Max like that – what if she'd decided it was too much and walked away? Thanks to you, she still might. I yelled at her to go, I didn't want to talk to her.'

Ed edged forward, stretching for her arm. 'Sweetie, you're putting too much on yourself.'

'You don't understand,' she said as she took a step backwards.

'I'm trying, but you're not making sense. Max isn't going anywhere, she loves you guys.'

Amy shook her head. Another step brought her spine against the corner of the table. She leaned back into it until her ribs growled then she pivoted away towards the door.

'Wait,' Ed said, darting after her, 'where are you going? We need to talk about this.'

'Talking's what you do before you screw up someone's life.'

'No, come on. I was worried, I wanted to help. Yeah, I screwed up, but I didn't go into it intending to. You can't hide it – not forever – and I thought we could deal with it together, sort it out like a family or something. Don't go, come on. Let's talk about this. I'll shut up the café –'

'Stop it,' she snapped. 'Stop defending it.'

169

He held up his hands. 'Okay, I'm sorry. I'm sorry.'

'Fine,' she said, even as she groped for the door handle, 'but it doesn't change anything.'

## Chapter 25

Baby Wallace was overdue and a General Election had been called.

Max was out in the cab on the first Tuesday in April when her mobile bleeped with a text. Her first thought was Drew, but it turned out to be Amy asking to see her at Geith Place, so she reassigned her job and went straight there. A summons like that, especially when they'd barely talked since that mess on her birthday, wasn't something she'd ignore.

Pounding music was audible outside the house when she pulled up into the drive. It wasn't Amy's style, more like the indie rock Ed liked to listen to. Once Max opened the door, the noise smashed into her eardrums until her head rang with it. The kitchen was the source so she followed it through and managed to switch the radio off before there was any permanent damage. Liam Gallagher was still echoing in her ears when she turned back to the doorway then she stopped at the sight of the table and floor covered in papers. A round of machine gun thumps tore her eyes away from Valerie's handwriting and she took the stairs two at a time, wondering what the hell she'd find up there. Amy scrunched up against the desk with books tossed all around wasn't what she'd expected.

'Amy? What's wrong?'

There was no answer. Max clenched her jaw then nudged her way through the antique spines to kneel next to the desk. She didn't go as far as touching her shoulder, holding off in case it set something going. With the way Amy looked, she'd either crumple on contact or explode.

'I'm here like you wanted,' Max said. 'Tell me what's going on.'

It took a few seconds for her eyes to catch on Max's then she tilted her head away. At first, Max reckoned she was trying to hide her tears, but closer inspection said it

171

was more like she was well past crying. Whatever had gone on, it'd ripped something out of her and left a hole behind.

'She's screwed it up again,' Amy mumbled finally.

Max's stomach tensed. 'You mean your mum. What's happened?'

'It was right, it was perfect. Why did she have to mess it up?'

'Come on, tell me what's happened,' Max pressed, trying to keep her voice level. 'Have you two had a row? Is she – is she all right?'

Amy snickered and clambered to her feet. 'Haven't you heard? Valerie Smythe always comes up smelling of roses because she doesn't mind who she hurts on her way.'

The bitter tone of voice warded off any relief from hearing that Valerie was okay. Max followed Amy in getting up then glanced around at the mess on the floor. It was too intrusive to start tidying up, what with these being Tim's books, but it looked worse than if it'd been just a clump of her paperbacks scattered everywhere. She was shocked when Amy kicked one of them into the wall and crunched over the others to get to the doorway. Max was more cautious on her way out, tiptoeing through the spines and giving her a head start down the stairs. She'd hardly got into the kitchen when Amy pushed a piece of paper into her hands.

'Read it,' she said.

Max tried to pass it back. 'I can't.'

'Read it,' Amy repeated.

'It's private,' she replied.

Amy snorted and pushed it towards her again. 'Not if she had her way. Go on. Read it.'

Short of chucking it in her face, there wasn't much alternative. Max lowered her eyes to the paper and read the first paragraph of the email. Then she blinked and read it again. She had to do the same with the second paragraph before the rest started swimming on the page and Valerie's handwritten notes in the margin bled into the main text.

172

Max let the paper drift back onto the table. 'It's just an opinion piece or something.'

'Do not do that. I'm sick of you excusing her. Read it again! She actually calls it the 'homosexual lifestyle' – she actually uses that phrase. Who does that? Who'd do that when they're in a relationship with another woman? You've been together for a year and she still thinks it's okay to call it a lifestyle? What planet is she on?'

'I don't know,' Max admitted, her throat burning. Her attention strayed back over the scattered papers and she asked, 'Are they all like that?'

'Same vein. There's a real beauty on immigration, just banging on about integration without saying anything that's technically racist. It's dog-whistling, that's what it is.'

'But she doesn't believe that. I've heard her after she's been down the community centre, she respects people who've dragged themselves up out of nothing.'

Amy shook her head. 'Oh, that's her preaching to the crowd. She knows what she's doing when it comes to manipulation.'

'That's not what I take from it. She likes them, genuinely likes them. There's no need to put on the mask, not with me.'

'Why – because you'd forgive her whatever she did? So, she misses your birthday and that's fine because she sort of apologised. She's late for everything, she keeps cancelling on you, but that's all right because she doesn't mean to. She knows exactly what she's doing and I'm sick of covering for her, pretending she's not messing this up when she is. There's a guy, Max; another politician. Someone that she's always with, someone she's . . .'

Max swallowed as she trailed off. Something was itching at her chest, gnawing its way inside. Instead of giving in to the question, she crossed the kitchen and turned the kettle on. She flinched when Amy stomped over and jabbed it off at the plug.

'Aren't you listening?' she demanded.

'Yes,' Max muttered.

'Then ask me about him. Ask me about John Foster.'

'Amy —'

'You can't, can you? Why do you let her do this to you? If you knew everything —'

'Just calm down for a minute.'

'No, you don't get it, you don't understand w-why . . .'

More might've coming, but it smothered itself under her tears. Max stood helpless until Amy shuffled forward and then she couldn't help gathering her up like she'd done with Valerie over the last year. She cried herself out pretty quickly, though she didn't let go.

'I miss Ed,' she whispered.

Max squeezed her tight. 'You have broken up then. I did wonder.'

'We wouldn't have if it wasn't for . . . It's her, it's always her.'

There was nothing to say to that, not if she didn't want to get her going again. So, Max just rubbed her back and hoped she was helping until a bleeping from her jacket pulled them apart. She tugged out her mobile and scanned the message with fresh panic swirling around her gut.

'It's Elena,' she said to Amy. 'Something's wrong.'

## Chapter 26

All the roads to the hospital seemed to be populated by idiots who couldn't drive properly. Amy kept her hands locked together on her lap, almost soothed by the sound of Max swearing at every car getting in their way on the bypass. It distracted her from the crushing memories of driving this way with Tim for his check-ups and treatments, ready to keep him company in the waiting room for appointments. He'd never suggested she stay at home, in the same way that it hadn't seemed to occur to Max that she should leave her behind.

The car park was crowded, but they managed to wedge into a space between a transit van and a Vauxhall slanted across the lines. It took Max a few seconds to manoeuvre her way out of the driver's seat then she rushed off towards the main building, dodging puddles and lumps in the tarmac, with Amy on her heels. They made it through the clumps of visitors hovering in the atrium and into the lift, although they both swayed on the spot when it lurched into life.

Max's speed ebbed the closer they got to the entrance of the Carless Wing. As they reached the reception desk, Amy found herself ahead and it was natural for her to take the lead with the nurse gazing expectantly over her computer.

'We're here for Andrew Wallace, Elena Marshall's partner. He didn't leave details, but he asked us to come straight here.'

The nurse checked a notepad. 'I'm expecting a Max Jarvis.'

'Yes, this is Max.'

'And who are you?'

'I'm a – a friend. I was with Max when . . . Well, I'm a friend of Drew's too.'

'Unless you're a family member, I think you might be better waiting downstairs –'

'No,' Amy interrupted.

'Given that the circumstances are –'

'Do you know who Valerie Smythe is?'

A frown stretched over the receptionist's face. 'Excuse me?'

'Valerie Smythe. She's a candidate in the election next month, she's probably going to win. She's a friend of Elena's as well, and I'm her daughter. I can call her if you want – to vouch for me.'

Out of the corner of her eye, Amy saw Max's head snap sideways, but she didn't care anymore. She instead focused on the nurse, holding her gaze and hoping that she was doing a passable impression of her mother for the first time in her life.

'Do you have any ID?' the nurse queried finally.

A flash of her student card was enough to get them through the door. Amy grabbed Max's arm to hurry her along, although they both faltered at the sight of Drew drooped into a seat at the far end of a bank of chairs. Other people in the waiting room were flicking through magazines and checking their phones, but Drew was staring out of the large window towards the greyish town without blinking. Amy glanced sideways, finding Max's face frozen too. Amy just about managed to steer her in front of the chairs then she let go of her arm and kneeled on the hard floor.

'Hey, Drew,' she said softly.

He tilted his chin up. 'You came.'

'Of course we did. But, listen, you didn't . . . Well, you weren't very specific in your message. What's happened?'

'They – they've taken her for a C-section,' he said as he jammed his knuckles into his kneecaps. 'Something to do with the cord. It wasn't right so they needed to . . . There was something wrong. Something not right, they said.'

Max sat next to him with a thump. 'But they're operating, yeah? That's good, mate. That means they're getting it sorted.'

'No, it's like last time, it's like that. I should – I should've been watching. I've missed something, that's what it is. I've missed –'

'You've been watching like a hawk,' Max cut in. 'You've been driving us all potty with it. Look, have they said how long it'll be?'

He chafed at his beard, working a few hairs loose. 'Soon, it'll be soon. Unless there's . . . I said I wanted to be in there, but they said no. That's not good, is it?'

'Mate, I wouldn't let you anywhere near anything important looking like you do this minute. They probably saw your history and reckoned it'd be best to keep you out of the way. Best for Elena, yeah? So she's not worrying about you when there's more important stuff to be thinking about. Isn't that right, Amy?'

'Definitely,' she replied. 'They do these operations all the time, Drew. It'll be okay.'

His speech seemed to have dried up again. Amy shifted from her kneeling position to take the seat on the other side of Max while keeping one eye on Drew hacking away at his palms with his fingernails. She watched until he drew blood then averted her gaze to Max, receiving a feeble smile in return. However long they stayed like that, it startled them all when a nurse walked in front of them.

'Mr Wallace?'

Drew stumbled to his feet. 'Yes?'

'Mother and baby doing fine,' the nurse said without preamble. 'Your daughter's beautiful, Mr Wallace. 7lb and 3oz and a tremendous set of lungs on her. Do you want to come through?'

Both Amy and Max jumped up, grabbing his arms as he threatened to topple over.

'She's okay?' he croaked. 'They're okay?'

The nurse patted his shoulder. 'They're doing very well and Elena's asking for you. Come and see. Your friends can wait here for you.'

'Go on, you idiot,' Max said, prodding him.

**177**

Every step he took was sluggish, but he made it through the door with the help of the nurse. As it swung closed, Max crumpled back into her chair and covered her face for a second. Then she straightened up and fumbled for her phone.

'I should call your mum,' she said. 'It's only polite since we used her name to get in here.'

Amy snatched the phone away. 'Tell me you're not serious. How can you carry on as if nothing's happened?'

'What she wrote wasn't nice but –'

'Not nice? Is that it? She's a hypocrite, Max. What about all the homophobia?'

'She's not homophobic. We know that.'

'What, so that's all that matters? That lets her off the hook?'

'Amy, it's not –'

'No, no, I've had enough. You don't want to jeopardise it so you don't push, that's how she wants it. I haven't wanted to screw it up either so I kept things to myself and – No, I lie. That's what I do. Thanks to her, that's what I've had to do for years. And I didn't want to – I couldn't tell you the truth because I love having you around. I love pretending we're some sort of family. It's not even like it was with Tim because then I didn't know everything. I was a kid and it – it changes things, about how I think about everything. You don't know. It changes everything.'

Tears scorched at her eyelids and she tried to swipe them away with the back of her hand. She suddenly realised she was still clutching Max's phone and dumped it in her lap. Although Max picked it up, she stuffed it straight into her pocket and retrieved a box of tissues from a nearby table instead. They were probably causing a real scene, but Amy couldn't see beyond the creases in Max's face as she blew her nose.

'What lies?' Max questioned.

Amy crumpled the tissue into her fist. 'Can I ask you something first?'

178

'Go for it,' she said.

'I know that we – we met because you were seeing my mum and we wouldn't have talked otherwise but . . . I mean, are we only friends because you're with her?'

Max shook her head. 'We get on, don't we? I reckoned so.'

'What if you broke up?' Amy asked.

'You and me are mates, it's nothing to do with your mum. But I'll just talk to her –'

'Don't,' Amy interjected.

'I can't say nothing. She'll see the state of the house.'

Amy clamped her fingers together and forced her eyes up to Max's. Those things she wrote . . . There was one about families. Real families.'

'You mean against gays?'

'No, not directly. But s-she makes a big deal about me being born into a secure family. That's what I mean when I say she's a hypocrite, not just the homophobia. That's bad enough, but she lied, Max. She said she was married to my father when I was born.'

Max sighed. 'Is there something about the dates then? They didn't get married in time?'

'The dates,' Amy said with a snigger. 'Yeah. Problem being that the date I was conceived was about two months before Valerie Gordon ever met Tim Smythe. He wasn't my biological father.'

'But that's . . .' Max trailed off and squinted at her. 'No, that's not –'

'She was seeing this married man. That's all I know about him – that he was married. After she got pregnant, he didn't want anything to do with her and she didn't want to end up like the rest of her family, stuck in dead-end jobs and pokey flats. So, she panicked. She latched onto the first decent man she found and married him. She landed completely on her feet, as per usual.'

'How could Tim not –' Max began, but Amy cut her off. 'Of course he knew.'

**179**

'And he just went along with it?'

She nodded, managing a smile. 'It never really mattered to him, not until the end. I didn't know then . . . It was practical, that's all. He thought I had a right to know and he didn't think Mum would ever tell me, even if I needed a kidney transplant or something. He was right. She'd let me die before telling me the truth.'

'That's not true,' Max murmured.

'Isn't it?' she retorted.

'You know it's not.'

'It'd screw with the image she paints of herself as the perfect widow, wouldn't it? You don't print on leaflets that you got knocked up at seventeen and then jumped on the first man that had the misfortune to walk past. It wouldn't play well with the voters – or Biddy.'

Max's chin lifted. 'So, she doesn't know?'

'I couldn't tell her, even Dad was too scared to. That's what Mum reminded me of when she warned me to keep quiet.'

'Warned?' Max repeated. 'Did she threaten you?'

'That sounds harsh,' she conceded then she snickered and rolled her eyes. 'God, why am I defending her? She basically said I keep quiet or I'd lose Biddy and the money and – and everything Dad wanted me to have. This was before she met you, when she suddenly decided to become a politician. It's why I moved out.'

For a minute, Max turned her head away. Amy sniffed and focused on the view across the town, counting the lights that were springing from the grey skies as they faded to black. She kept losing her thread somewhere near the spire of St. Catherine's and starting over again.

'Who's John Foster?' Max asked abruptly.

Amy swallowed down the lump in her throat. 'Whenever she's at an event or meeting with someone else, it's usually him. Even on your birthday, she was with him. You don't check up on her – I do. He's always there in the background, every time she's campaigning.'

'That doesn't mean she's seeing him.' Max hesitated, rubbing her throat. 'If there was something going on, I'd know.'

'How?' Amy queried.

'Because there wouldn't be a point, that's why. Keeping me around doesn't help. It gets in her way if what you're saying's true.'

'But she loves you, Max. Really, she does. Before today – before I saw those articles – I would've said she was being honest about what was going to happen after the election. She said she'd tell you about my biological father, that she had no intention of hiding it from you forever. She said she'd be open about it, that you'd move in and we'd be a proper family. No more sneaking around and pretending we weren't. But if she'd published those articles . . . That would've been it. She couldn't go back on something like that, and I – I don't want to see you get hurt. You don't deserve to be messed around.'

Max looked away again and Amy glanced around the waiting room. Most people were lost in their own little worlds, although one middle-aged couple nearby were gawping. Even if they'd heard enough to cripple Valerie's career, Amy couldn't care less.

'I shouldn't have told you, should I?' she questioned when the silence dragged on.

'You did right,' Max replied.

'I'm sorry.'

'Hey, don't you dare,' said Max, turning back sharply. 'She's put you in this position, it's not your fault. You've done your best to hold it together and you've done a bloody good job. But you shouldn't have had to. It's done with now.'

'Done?' Amy echoed. 'Does that mean you're out finally?'

Max shifted in her seat. 'I don't know. But you can be. You don't have to put up with it. Just get to uni and away from her full stop, it wouldn't do her any good threatening you then.'

Until she said that, Amy had almost forgotten under the weight of everything else that had happened today. The truth crumbled around her shoulders and she jumped up, more to distance herself from reality than Max. She saw the flash of hurt in her face, but it was too late to explain.

'I've got to get back to Biddy's,' she said.

Max's shoulders sagged. 'Call the office. Tell them to put it on account.'

All Amy managed to do was nod before she stumbled towards the door. More people were staring now; she felt the eyes burrowing through her, but it didn't matter. The only tangible thought she could muster when she forced the door open was that she was still trapped by Valerie and her lies. There was no way out of it now she'd screwed up her career prospects.

## Chapter 27

'Amy gone?'

Max jolted out of her trance to find Drew wavering in front of her, a stupid grin splattered across his face. She didn't know how long she'd been sat there, though the whole waiting room seemed quieter now than it had before. Despite the gnawing in her chest, she had to smile along with him as he plonked himself next to her.

'She had to get back to her gran's. How they doing?'

He yanked his phone from his pocket and fiddled his way through the gallery. There were at least a dozen pictures of Elena clutching this wrinkled thing to her chest and one of Drew pressing a kiss to the baby's button nose. Max looked up and met his eye.

'She's gorgeous,' she said.

'They both are,' he answered.

'Have you got a name yet?'

His attention had caught on the screen again. 'Hannah Elizabeth.'

'And she's healthy, yeah?' Max asked.

'Oh, yeah,' he said with a chuckle. 'Ten fingers, ten toes, right set of lungs on her.'

'What about Elena?'

'Shattered, bit sore, but other than that . . .' Tears suddenly sprang into his eyes and he mopped them away with his thumb. 'It happened, Max. It's okay.'

The knot in her stomach untangled a bit. 'Told you so.'

Exhaustion took her home and she got drunk for good measure. Only when she woke up the next morning did she check her phone, finding a load of missed calls from Valerie and two voicemails she deleted without listening to. There was a message from Drew asking her to come in for lunchtime visiting, so she took off to cover the morning switchboard shift and then arranged cover for the afternoon. She was working on the basis that carrying on like nothing had happened was the right way to go, especially since she didn't know where to start approaching everything that had happened yesterday.

Drew was waiting for her by the main entrance when she got to the hospital. He looked dead on his feet, even if that goofy grin was still plastered to his face.

'Elena says to get a coffee and leave her to get some peace,' he explained.

'You're doing her head in already then.'

He wafted her towards the canteen. 'Oi, the nurses are already calling me Super Dad.'

'Probably to shut you up.'

With him, it was easier to act like nothing had gone on. They got a coffee and he spent a good twenty minutes rabbiting on about Elena and Hannah, getting too close to the mechanics of a C-section for Max's liking. She steered him back onto how gorgeous the kid was until he'd finished his Americano and, by then, she wanted to see Hannah instead of hearing about her. Drew was all for that – jumping up and knocking into an old lady stuttering across the canteen with an orange juice. Once he'd paid for another drink for her, they were set to go.

The nurse on the maternity reception seemed on edge when she buzzed them through. Max glanced over her shoulder once Drew had pushed open the door and found her picking up the phone. Another nurse was ready and waiting with the ward door open and, finally, Drew cottoned on that something wasn't right. He picked up speed, bolting into the ward, taking a left then skidding to a halt so fast that Max barrelled into him. Before she could ask what was going on, she caught sight of the scene in front of her.

A cameraman and a soundman were on one side of the bed, filming a wailing Hannah while Elena stuttered something inaudible to Valerie. She was dressed for business in a black suit and crisp blouse that Max recognised from the wardrobe, but it was the stocky man

184

next to her who was hogging the limelight. It was the politician that Amy had mentioned – John Foster. Max would bet her life on it.

'What the hell's going on?' Drew demanded.

Foster stepped forward with a wide smile. 'This must be the proud father. Let me shake your hand, sir. It's a pleasure to meet you.'

Drew snatched his arm clear and grabbed the soundman instead. While he yelped about his equipment, the cameraman sensed the gig was up and backed away sharpish. Valerie just straightened her sleeves and murmured a goodbye to Hannah. It was only when she reached the door that she acknowledged Max at all.

'Oh, I'm sorry,' she said. 'May I get past?'

Max took two steps back and her spine cracked into a trolley. Valerie didn't say a word, just breezed off out of the ward with Foster and the crew in tow.

Drew rounded on Max. 'Was this your doing?'

'Course not, I wouldn't – Elena, I didn't –'

'I know it wasn't your fault,' she cut in.

'Like hell it wasn't,' Drew spat.

Elena cleared her throat and motioned for him to take Hannah. 'Maybe you can calm her down for me.'

It was meant to work both ways and it did. He sat in the armchair rocking Hannah back and forth until her cries trailed off into coos. Out in the corridor, three nurses were gossiping without any attempt to keep it hidden and other patients were peeking out of their doors. Max tried meeting Drew's eye, but his cheeks were glowing so she looked to Elena instead.

'I don't get how she even knew you were here,' she said.

'Maybe Amy told her,' Elena suggested.

'No, they're not speaking at the minute. I'm sorry.'

Drew growled. 'Doesn't change it.'

Max rocked back on her heels, sneaking a glance at the grizzling baby in his arms. The phone pictures last night hadn't shown the way Hannah's fingers curled around the hem of her blanket or how her tiny eyelids fluttered open and shut. Now she'd settled, Max could appreciate how beautiful she was, only the screaming that had greeted them before wouldn't stop ringing in her ears.

'I'm sorry,' she muttered.

'Deal with it then,' replied Drew.

She nodded and backed out into the corridor. 'I will.'

All the patient rooms were marked with labels, but there was a visitor lounge off near the waiting room and a flash of blonde hair caught Max's attention as she walked past. Valerie was in there, framed through the porthole, Foster with her. He was pacing around, rolling his shirt sleeves down as if he'd delivered a baby not five minutes ago instead of just causing merry hell for a newborn. As Max watched, he stopped fidgeting and twisted towards Valerie. His arms slipped around her waist as he leaned in for a kiss that wasn't solicited but sure as hell wasn't rejected. It was all Max could do to keep herself upright, though her knee cracked against the door frame and the two of them sprang apart.

Foster darted forward and yanked the door open. 'Excuse me, this is private.'

Behind him, Valerie's mouth was working like a goldfish's.

'If you've got some sort of problem with our meet and greet, put it in writing,' Foster continued. 'We haven't done anything wrong, there's nothing to get worked up about.'

Max inhaled and the stench of his sweat lodged in her nostrils. She looked past him to Valerie's rigid figure, focusing on her pale eyes.

'You're right,' she said. 'We're done here.'

Valerie's jaw clenched, but she said nothing.

'Good,' Foster replied, wafting her away. 'Off you go then.'

Max didn't need telling twice. Her feet took her straight past the reception desk where the nurse buzzed her out without a word then she lurched into the same stairwell as last year. She was halfway down the stairs before an arm yanked her back up and it took prising the fingers off one-by-one to get Valerie's claws out of her.

'I'm sorry, Max. I'm so, so sorry. I didn't mean –'

'How did you know they were here?'

Valerie blinked. 'I was called this morning by the local paper, telling me that my friend, Elena, was in hospital and asking whether I'd be visiting. I was with J-John at the time and he suggested that –'

'You were with him?'

'Not that way,' Valerie insisted, shaking her head. 'Never that way. It's always been platonic with John – always. I wouldn't do that to do. Please, Max, you have to believe that. But, look, you must've used my name as currency last night or –'

'I didn't,' she interrupted. 'Amy did.'

Valerie's mouth snapped shut, just long enough for Max to realise something.

'You haven't been home since last night,' she said.

'W-what?'

'You haven't been home. You wouldn't have risked doing this if you had so that means you were with him.'

'No, Max, it was separate rooms, I promise. You can see my credit card statement if . . .' Valerie trailed off and a frown flickered over her face. 'What do you mean? Why wouldn't I have risked it if I'd been home?'

'I got a message from Amy last night,' Max explained, somehow keeping her voice level. 'She's trashed the study and left your papers – your articles – all over the kitchen floor. You'd have known if you hadn't been with him.'

Valerie's whole body quivered. She looked up and down the stairwell then inched closer.

'I wasn't going to use them,' she said.

Max sniggered.

'No, listen, I was just getting the arguments straight in my head. I would never have published them. I promise. I wouldn't –'

'What – use us? Use Amy? The one where you called this – you and me – a lifestyle, that wasn't the one she was upset about most. It was the lies about her dad that really got to her.'

Valerie reached a hand out to the banister and steadied herself. Nothing about her screamed high-flying politician now. Even the suit just looked like it was hanging off a cracked porcelain doll that had the last of its colour draining away. She clung to the banister then raised herself up.

'I can't believe she told you after all this time.'

'She was trying to do me a favour,' Max said with a grim chuckle. 'But I still wasn't sure. I didn't want to do anything daft so I was thinking about it. All that crap you spouted at the beginning – about me not running off – I'd listened. Well done, you'd got it through my thick skull.'

'Max, you're not –'

'Then you turn up with him and pull a stunt like that? No, I'm done. I'm out.'

Valerie groped for her elbow. 'You don't get to do this to me. Three weeks to the election – you can't force me to choose, not now.'

'You never would've,' Max said as she shook her off and carried on down the staircase. 'So, I'll make it easy and you can just tell yourself I walked. Problem solved.'

## Chapter 28

'Pass the salt, dear.'

'Hmm?'

'The salt,' Biddy repeated. 'Honestly, you've been miles away all evening.'

Amy roused herself long enough to pass the shaker over then she speared more asparagus onto her fork and continued with the mechanics of eating. She managed to tune out Biddy's chatter across the table, concentrating instead on the worries that had been festering all last night and through today too.

'What do you think of lavender?'

'Erm . . .' Amy looked up and shrugged. 'I don't really know.'

Biddy's brow furrowed. 'You haven't been listening to me, have you?'

'Of course I have. You were talking about the garden.'

'You would only have had to listen to one word in twenty minutes to work that out. What's wrong? Is something amiss with your revision?'

Amy straightened her cutlery. 'It's fine. Do you want ice cream?'

'I haven't finished my chicken yet.'

For the next three and a half minutes, Amy did her best to concentrate. She offered her unbiased and ignorant opinion on lavender and jasmine, plus the quality of the asparagus, and was answering a question about soil consistency when the doorbell rang. Her stomach dropped as Biddy's chin lifted.

'Are you expecting someone?' she queried.

Amy stood, nearly tripping over the chair leg. 'I think Mum said she might be passing. Just passing, not coming in. I'll go see. You stay here.'

She was gone before Biddy could object. Fear of being followed took her straight to the door, but she regretted the haste when she encountered Valerie on the doorstep. It

189

was as though she'd been stripped down and reassembled into the woman she'd been over a year ago. Her cherry blouse had three buttons open instead of one, exposing the trim of her matching bra, and she held herself differently. Even her expression was glazed.

'Let's step into the car, shall we?' she suggested. 'We don't want to impose on Clarice. I assume you've just eaten.'

Amy pulled the door to, her stomach already whirring. Each step she took towards the Mercedes idle at the end of the drive just made it worse. She already knew whose car it was, even before a stubby man in a grey suit slipped out of the driver's seat. He touched Valerie's arm and murmured that he'd give them a minute before walking to the gate without sparing Amy a glance.

'So, you've been seeing him all along, have you?' she asked.

Valerie opened the rear door. 'Get in.'

More to keep it away from Biddy than anything else, she followed the order and shuffled to the furthest tip of the seat. She watched as Valerie smoothed down her skirt and slid into the car as though photographers were lurking nearby. Then she eased the door closed and left them in semi-darkness, illuminated only by the external lights flickering through the trees.

'You didn't answer my question,' Amy said. 'Have you been sleeping with him the whole time?'

'No, I haven't.'

'Then what the hell is he doing here?'

Valerie clasped her hands together on her lap. 'We're making things a little more regular. An official relationship, I suppose you'd call it.'

'You've already got one of those or had you forgotten? She's tall, short hair, bit clumsy –'

'It's over,' Valerie interjected. 'Max finished with me this afternoon. So, there. I'm not the big bad wolf in all of this. She broke up with me.'

Amy slumped against the side door, the words still echoing around the car.

'That can't be the whole story,' she muttered.

'Yes, well . . . The whys and wherefores don't mean anything. It's done now.'

Valerie's voice was clipped, detached from any sort of reality. Amy recognised the symptoms from the year following Tim's death, from the glassy eyes right down to the robotic twitch of her fingertips against her skirt.

'She told you about the articles,' Amy said finally.

Valerie stared blankly ahead. 'That was politics.'

'Like hell it was. You were pushing your luck, weren't you? Seeing how far you could go?'

'Rather like you utilising my name to gain you access to the hospital last night, hmm? If you're seeking to apportion blame here, you might start by looking in the mirror. None of this would've happened if you hadn't encouraged Max to read those articles and if you hadn't used my name as currency last night. We wouldn't be in this situation if it wasn't for you.'

Amy gaped at her. 'Excuse me?'

'I warned you not to jeopardise it, didn't I?' Valerie snapped, twisting to face her for the first time. 'A few more weeks, that was all I needed, and yet you took the unilateral decision to light a match under the whole thing. Why did you tell her everything, hmm? Why now?'

'You're not seriously blaming me,' Amy whispered. 'You – you can't.'

Valerie held her gaze. 'Make it up to me. Stay away from her.'

'Now I know you're delusional because I'm not doing that,' she replied.

'It's impractical, Amy. Sure, you might've got attached to her, but it won't work. The relationship you have with her is based solely on mine. They can't exist separately of one another.'

'That didn't apply when you were hiding her from me.'

'Don't be facetious.'

'Oh, I'm not, believe me. Come on, Mum. Make me choose. Ask me! Go on – ask me.'

Valerie licked her lips. 'Be careful, Amy. Do you really believe Clarice would tolerate your choice of friends?'

'Do you honestly want to open that can of worms?' she shot back.

'Just be realistic for a moment. You might want to sever contact with me right this minute, but Clarice wouldn't understand that either and I won't accept it.'

Amy launched the door open and a rush of air ruffled through the car. 'Push me then, go on. You've still got three weeks to the election, remember. It might be better for your career if you just back off and leave me alone. I mean, isn't the worst thing I could do right now to leak your relationship with Max to the papers?'

'You wouldn't do that,' Valerie murmured.

Amy's legs were trembled as she slipped out of the car. 'Try me.'


'What did she do?'

Max winced as she barged into the back room. 'You want a cuppa?'

'Don't dodge it,' Amy insisted, crossing her arms. 'I've been wondering all night. I've got a right to know what's going on, but she won't tell me.'

That was the golden ticket. Max nodded then reached to switch off the volume on the switchboard as a call came in. The trilling faded into a dull burr and Max clamped her knees together, staring at the carpet.

'It must've been that nurse on reception. I mean, it's not normally a scoop, but maybe she reckoned it was. Friend of woman who's odds-on to win in the General Election and all that. Well, she must've called the local paper first thing, either that or she talked to someone who did. So, your mum hears and because she's with – with Foster, they decide to go see Elena for a bit of publicity. Me and Drew

192

walked in to find them there with a camera crew and Hannah screaming her head off.'

Amy's lips parted. 'No way.'

'Gets better,' Max muttered with a grim smile. 'I went after her to ask what the hell she was playing at and there she was kissing that . . . You were right about them. God knows how long it's been going on.'

'I didn't want to be right.' Amy dug her fingers into her eyes, trying to stop them burning. 'It was my fault, wasn't it? If I hadn't shown you those articles or – or mentioned her at the –'

'Where's this coming from? Hang on, has she said something? Is she blaming you?'

The fear that had been percolating in her stomach since last night evaporated at the fierce expression on Max's face. Amy's shoulders relaxed and she sucked in a deep breath.

'She came to see me at Biddy's last night. She was with him.'

Max snickered. 'What did she say to you?'

'That – that I'd been the one to mess it up,' she answered slowly. 'And that if I wanted to blame someone . . .'

'That's bullshit, you know it is,' Max said.

'I know, I know.' Amy paused and watched her. 'She said to stay away from you, that we can't be friends if you're not with her.'

Max kicked her heel back against the chair. 'That's for her benefit, not yours. But, you know, if you reckon it's –'

'No,' she interjected.

'I'm just saying –'

'And I'm saying no,' Amy interrupted in a voice they both recognised. 'So, let's just leave it at that, okay? I've already lost my dad. I'm not losing you as well.'

## Chapter 29

'You must have stuff round there, right?'

Max didn't have to stretch to work out what he was going on about. For someone who was meant to be off on paternity leave, Drew had spent a hell of a lot of time lounging around on the office sofa bitching about Valerie in the last week. It was open season now they'd broken up, though she could do without the constant reminders that she'd been dumped by a woman whose face was plastered over every other lamppost in town.

'Stop coughing doughnuts all over my floor,' she said as she lobbed a kitchen roll at his head. 'Go on, go home and let Hannah puke on you.'

He launched the kitchen roll onto the sofa. 'Elena wanted rid of me for an hour.'

'Then go down the pub and wet the baby's head again. You're in the way here.'

'You've got to have stuff round there, that's all I'm saying. You didn't move in, but it was as good as. What with stopovers and meals and all that. She had you on call practically.'

Max tapped on the switchboard. 'Bits and pieces. Few clothes, DVDs, spare phone charger. Nothing I can't live without.'

'Till when?'

'Till Amy's calmed down a bit,' she said with a shrug. 'Then I'll get her to stick it all in a bag for me. She's got to go back, she's got stuff round there herself.'

'Sounds like a cop-out to me. You've got a key. Go round there yourself and get it sorted. Unless you're holding off for a reason.'

'It's not like that.'

'What, then?'

'I don't fancy seeing her, that's all. With the election, she's keeping funny hours. I don't know when she'll be there and not.'

That shut him up long enough for the switchboard to ring and she grabbed at the call. By the time she'd dispatched the driver, he'd gobbled through another doughnut and was licking between his fingers one by one.

'What time do you finish?' he asked.

'Six. Look, Drew, use the sodding sink and not your tongue, all right? You're worse than Hannah.'

'Six? We'll go together then.'

She snorted. 'No way.'

'Why not? If you're worked up about seeing her, I'll be there. And if Foster's –'

'Drew, give it a rest,' she snapped.

He scowled and hauled himself off the sofa. 'Do it for me then. Elena's convinced you had nothing to do with what went on. Prove it.'


Even if Drew wasn't tagging along like some pissed colt, letting herself into Geith Place like this wouldn't have felt right. Neither Valerie's BMW or the fancy car that Foster probably drove were around the drive or in the garage, but Max's scalp still prickled as she walked over the threshold. That wasn't helped by Drew leaning forward to stroke the wallpaper.

'Bloody hell, no wonder you were hanging on. Maybe you could sue her or something.'

She closed the door. 'I'm not suing her.'

'Maybe we should, Elena and me.'

'Amy, remember,' Max reminded him. 'Don't touch anything. I'm off to get my clothes.'

All she caught as he wandered off towards the kitchen was a snicker. She took the stairs two at a time, still listening out for someone else being around, but she stopped thinking when she pushed open the bedroom door.

Nothing in here seemed different. The curtains were still open at the same angle and the white sheets were flush against the mattress. It didn't look like anything had been moved. One sniff brought Valerie's perfume back to her nostrils, but a second one brought something sour with it – something male. Max pressed her arm over her nose then started dragging her things from the wardrobe.

Clothes were spilling out of her arms by the time she got down to the kitchen. Drew was still in there, poking through the cupboard underneath the window where Valerie kept her serving dishes.

'Stop doing that,' Max warned. 'Pass me a black bag from under the sink.'

Her next stop was the living room, Drew trotting in on her heels. Straight off, he started scoffing at how it looked like a poncy art gallery, but Max tried to shut it out and knelt next to the DVD cabinet. They were all mixed up, so she had to go through them one at a time, pulling out her horrors and fantasies that Valerie had just about tolerated.

'Well, this is cosy.'

Max's chin lurched up. Valerie was blocking the doorway, arms crossed and a look on her face that would've given Medusa a run for her money. It fooled Drew as he spun around and scattered all the DVDs with his heel, but Max didn't rush. She rose slowly and stuffed her hands into her pockets.

'I'm just collecting a few things,' she said.

'I can see that.' Valerie's glare flicked to Drew as she raised an eyebrow. 'And you have to be here, do you?'

Drew's jaw tightened, not that Max could blame him. With that stunt at the hospital, she might've expected for Valerie to be a bit contrite, but that seemed to have gone out of the window. If she'd blamed Amy for all this last week, she probably wouldn't think twice about sticking a threatening behaviour charge on Drew. So, Max slid a loop from her keys then chucked the rest of the rings at him.

'Take that bag and I'll meet you outside in five minutes,' she said.

'But –'

'Go on,' she cut in.

His eyes swivelled between them then he took off towards the door. Valerie moved out of his way and watched him go. The emotionless mask stayed until the front door banged then it crumbled. Max couldn't hack seeing the pain etched on her forehead all of a sudden, so she knelt down again and stacked the DVDs straight.

'How's Amy?' Valerie questioned. 'I'm sure you've heard more from her than me.'

'That's just what you don't want, isn't it?' Max retorted then she checked herself. 'Forget it, I don't want a row.'

'No, you'll just walk away again,' said Valerie.

Max stood and glanced around. She'd need another bag.

'When you speak to Amy,' Valerie continued after a second, 'perhaps you could remind her of the guest pass I arranged for election night. All the paperwork has been directed to Clarice's, but tell her I'm expecting her at the count.'

Imagining Valerie as a blob just blocking the door was working wonders. Max walked straight past on her way to the kitchen, though she was held up when she couldn't rip the bag free from the roll and Valerie tugged it away from her.

'Why is it you can never manage these, hmm?' she asked as she pulled one loose. 'Will you remind Amy?'

Max grabbed the bag fluttering in the air. 'If she doesn't want to come, that's down to her. What did you expect to happen when you tried blaming her? She might act all grown-up, but she's still a kid.'

'Yes – mine. You may think you've got some sort of wonderful connection with her, Max, but you haven't. At the end of the day, you're nothing more than someone I happened to be sleeping with at the time.'

She swallowed, feeling the blow land in her gut. Then she got her feet moving and went back through to the living room. She'd shovelled the DVDs into the bag and was halfway to the front door when fingers clawed at her arm.

'I didn't mean that,' Valerie said.

Max shook her off. 'You don't know what you mean anymore.'

'Wait. Max – wait a minute.'

Her hand stuck on the door handle. This voice wasn't the mechanical one or the manipulative one, more like her and Amy's Valerie who couldn't stand losing at Scrabble. But Max couldn't bring herself to turn around and the silence stretched. Valerie's cough finally broke it – her politician's cough.

'The key, Max,' she said.

It was shoved in her back pocket. She tugged it out and turned it over in her palm then tossed it onto the carpet and pulled the door open. Her feet had hardly hit the bottom step before it slammed behind her.

## Chapter 30

'Amy, hey . . .'

It was the bulk of Max's body that stopped her walking along the gravel rather than hearing her voice or actually seeing her. Amy raised her eyes then clenched her fists and pushed past on her way towards the gates. Other students were milling around as usual, but she just focused on making it out onto the road.

Max jogged alongside her. 'You don't look good.'

'Go away,' Amy muttered.

'What's up? What's happened?'

She halted and twisted to face her. 'Are you serious? You said you'd call. I've been stuck with Biddy for a week thinking that you'd –'

'That I'd what?' Max cut in, grabbing her arm. 'Come on – what?'

'You weren't interested in being my friend, were you? It was all about her.'

'Course it wasn't.'

'Then where have you been?'

Max scuffed her foot through the gravel. 'At the bottom of a bottle mostly. I was trying to do you a favour and steer clear.'

'Stop thinking you know what's good for me,' Amy snapped.

'I know you've had enough of that.'

'So, why do it, hmm?' she demanded.

'Because it was protecting me as well,' Max answered with a shrug. 'I'm sorry. I'm not handling this like I should.'

Plain justification would've ignited her anger again, but that, coupled with the pained expression on Max's face, dampened it instead. Her shoulders relaxed as she looked at her properly, noticing the circles underneath her eyes and the grease at the tips of her hair. Every one of her muscles seemed as if it was being held up by sheer willpower alone.

'Okay,' Amy said.

A smile flickered over Max's face. 'Fancy a drive then?'

Now, walking to the cab, she spared a glance for the other students along the driveway. Max's appearance had garnered a few disparaging looks, not due to the fact she was a taxi driver, but because Amy was talking to her like a human being. Some of them put Biddy's church friends to shame as far as snobbery was concerned.

'I hate it here,' she said as they got into the cab.

Max started the engine. 'Not my idea of a good time. But thought you liked it.'

'I used to. When Dad was around, things were different. Now I'm just on edge all the time, feeling like I don't belong here. As if someone's going to uncover the truth and throw me out.'

The cab jolted along the driveway past a couple of curious sixth-formers Amy recognised by sight but not name. Her stomach lightened when they hit the solid tarmac of the road and began heading in the opposite direction to Biddy's. She didn't ask where they were going, just enjoyed the sensation of relinquishing control for a few minutes.

'She came to see me yesterday,' Max said suddenly. 'Your mum.'

Amy stiffened in her seat. 'Oh.'

'Wanted me to remind you of that count pass she ordered you.'

'Well, I'm not going,' she replied.

'I reckon you should think about it,' Max said.

'Why? I don't want to stand there listening to her gloat about winning. And she will win, Max. You know she will. That'll make it all worthwhile, won't it?'

'Amy –'

'No, it's not fair. Everything – this whole mess – it's her fault. I didn't ask to be born, I wasn't the one who lied to

200

Biddy in the first place. I'm just the one who has to live with it. I wasn't the one who brought you into our lives then decided I'd rather have some slimy weasel, was I?'

Max hunched further over the wheel. 'None of this is down to you. But you're right – you have to live with it. So, going to the count keeps things calm with Clarice. It makes sense. That's all I was going to say.'

'Oh,' Amy murmured.

The next right took them towards the town centre. She curled her toes into her shoes, wondering if this was accidental on Max's part, but that illusion vanished when she pulled into a short-stay space on the opposite side of the precinct. The café windows were visible in the distance as specks of glass reflecting the weak sunlight tripping across the rooftops.

'I don't want to be here,' she said.

Max didn't respond straight away. She turned off the engine and unbuckled her seatbelt, twisting to face her with a furrowed brow. Amy shifted away and crossed her arms.

'I want to leave,' she said.

'Not before you hear me out,' Max insisted in a firm voice. 'Listen, he might've done the wrong thing by coming to me, but it wasn't out of malice or anything like that. He was genuinely trying to help and he reckoned I was best placed to help him do it. Turns out he was wrong on that score since I only buggered things up more, but his heart was in the right place.'

Amy coiled her arms together. 'He still went behind my back.'

'I know –'

'Everybody lies, Max. I wanted him to be different.'

Max leaned back and tilted her chin towards the roof. 'Everybody. You mean Tim.'

'What? No. He told me the truth.'

'Like it or not, he still lied though. All that time – it has to hurt. Then he tells you the truth, just when you could really live without knowing it.'

'That's not how it was,' Amy warned.

'Isn't it?' Max retorted. 'You know as well as I do that your mum would've told you the truth if something had happened and it was necessary. You might hate her, but she loves you and she'd never put you at risk. So, that blows his reasoning out of the water, doesn't it?'

Amy shook her head and reached for her seatbelt. 'You're out of line.'

'Wait – stop. Hear me out.'

Her instinct was to tug at the door handle, but her fingers fell back when Max rested a hand on her shoulder. It wasn't rough; it would've been easier to ignore if it was. So, she had no choice but to keep still, although she refused to look over while she listened.

'I'm not saying he didn't love you or that he was trying to hurt you,' Max continued after a moment. 'Given what you've both told me about him, I reckon it was because he loves you so much that he did what he did. Better that he tells you than you finding out later when he couldn't explain what happened or why he went along with it. You can't tell me that doesn't sound like him.'

'It does,' Amy admitted.

'Anyone in your shoes would resent him a bit for telling you.'

'I – I don't –'

'Not a bit?' Max interrupted.

She wet her lips. 'Okay. Maybe.'

'Tim lied first off because he loved you and your mum. Then he told you the truth because he loved you and didn't want you thinking bad of him later. Life's more complicated than just hating people because they weren't completely honest. Ed loves you and he was trying to help. That's it.'

202

Amy absorbed that then her eyes strayed across the precinct. There were fewer people around now, and the sun had drained from the windows. She couldn't see Ed moving around inside, but knowing he was in there made her chest constrict.

'Don't take the high road for the sake of it,' Max said. 'Go after what you love.'

'Yeah, because that worked so well for Mum.'

Max snorted and rubbed her shoulder. 'She's gone after something else. You do what's right for you, otherwise you'll regret it.'

'I already do,' she muttered.

'So, fix it,' Max answered.

Amy met her gaze then fumbled for the door handle. She heard the car engine start up, but she was too busy walking straight across the uneven paving slabs to pay attention. Every step took her closer to the café until she could see Ed wiping down tables one by one. She almost faltered as she tried to work out whether he looked like he missed her, but when he glanced out of the window and saw her, her doubt disappeared. He had the door open before she reached it.

'Hey,' he murmured.

She swallowed and pushed past him into the café. It smelled of apple pie, coffee, and bleach, although even that had a sweet tang to it. The nearest table still glistened with water from his cleaning.

'Amy?' Ed asked. 'Are you okay?'

'Tim wasn't my father,' she said, focusing on the droplets wobbling on the table top. 'My mum was pregnant when they met and he raised me like his own. I only found out before he died. That's – that's why I wanted to be a lawyer so badly. I thought it'd make me more his daughter and make Biddy proud of me. But I screwed it up, didn't I? I screwed everything up.'

A hand began massaging circles into her back. 'He loved you, he was proud of you. Sweetie, anyone could see that if they spent five minutes together with you. I'm telling you, you were his daughter in the ways that matter. Is this what you've been hiding all this time?'

'I didn't know how to tell you.'

'Why? What did you think I'd say?'

She shrugged. 'If it was because of him you were —'

'I told you it wasn't.'

'Well, I didn't believe you.'

His hand stilled. The weight of it was paralysing then he moved it completely and stepped into her line of sight. She raised her chin, almost scared of meeting his eye, but his shoulders had drooped and he looked smaller than he was.

'You don't trust me,' he said with a wispy smile.

She crunched her fingers against the table. 'I want to. I'm sorry.'

'Don't be, I get it. Proved your point, didn't I?'

'No, no. You went to Max for the right reasons. I don't like that you went behind my back, but I understand why you did. They split up, you know.'

His eyebrows lifted. 'How come?'

'Make me a coffee and I'll tell you about it?' she suggested.

Although he pretended to think about the idea, she got her answer from the way his whole body seemed to lift again. He drifted his hand through her hair and leaned forward to drop a kiss onto her nose. The bristles of his beard against her lips tasted like apple pie.

With Biddy expecting her, she didn't dare stay out too late.

Ed insisted on driving her home in his decrepit Honda, promising to leave her at the end of the drive and stay out of sight. They'd talked so much that the journey was quiet, but she kept her fingers looped around his belt for the duration. It took her a few minutes to pry herself away from his warm arms then she wandered down towards the house with her hands tucked inside her pockets.

It was only when she reached the door that she realised she'd forgotten her bag. She turned around to find Ed trotting to her, but she spun back as the front door opened. Biddy was stood on the threshold, arms crossed and cardigan billowing out around her knees.

'Where have you been?' she demanded. 'Who's this – this man?'

'This is Ed, Biddy,' Amy replied.

She just pressed her lips together and Amy twisted to grab her bag from Ed's outstretched hand. A flush was creeping out from under his beard. She took the bag and tried to smile.

'Thanks. I'll see you tomorrow.'

He nodded then fled towards the car, every step clattering like a tambourine. Amy watched until Biddy coughed and she turned to face her with what she hoped was an unrepentant expression. She'd copied it from Valerie over the years.

'Who was that man?' Biddy queried.

'I told you, his name's Ed.'

'He looks like a drug addict.'

'Well, he's not,' Amy retorted.

Biddy growled through her teeth. 'I can't believe your mother allows you to consort with a man like that. Does she know?'

'It's nothing to do with her.'

'Of course it is – you're a child.'

'I'm eighteen.'

'Oh, you're a girl, you haven't begun to understand because you haven't been taught properly. I was married at nineteen and your mother . . . The least said about that, the better. Pregnant within a few weeks! You think about that, unless you want to end up marrying a man like this Ed because you weren't sensible enough to use protection.'

'Biddy, stop,' Amy warned, but she shook her head.

'That's your future – what do you think of it? Your father worked to give you a proper life and you want to

205

throw it all away because your head's been turned by an – an opportunist who sees you as a soft touch. Don't make the same mistake Timothy did, don't do to his memory what he did to your grandfather's.'

Amy's eyes widened. She might always have suspected that Biddy harboured resentment towards Valerie, but it was something else to hear it expressed so virulently on the doorstep like this. She took a step backwards as Biddy rubbed her forehead.

'I didn't mean to –'

'I'm tired,' Amy interrupted. 'May I get past and go to bed? Please.'

Biddy pulled herself aside and gestured into the house. 'You may.'

## Chapter 31

Switchboard had been quiet all morning. Max was buried in a reread of *Misery* when the door clanged. She stuck her thumb on the page to save her line then let the cover slip shut when she found Amy and Ed on the opposite side of the glass. Seeing them together brought a smile to her face, but only till she spotted the matching looks on theirs.

'What's up?' she asked.

Ed wrapped his arm around Amy's shoulders. 'We need your advice.'

Max motioned them through and turned the volume down on the switchboard. They picked their way through Drew's rubbish, perching on the edge of the sofa and exchanging a glance. Odds on, if it wasn't for the fact she'd asked him before, Max would've sworn this was the usual.

'Hit me then,' she said.

'I don't know what to do,' Amy admitted.

'Start by talking. That's why you're here, isn't it?'

Amy took a shuddering breath then raised her eyes. 'I didn't apply to Durham. My grades weren't good enough for Law and my tutor wouldn't let me apply, so I didn't. That's why – that's why Ed came to see you before. I'd just told him, but I was ashamed and I thought . . . I was trying to pretend I hadn't screwed things up for as long as possible.'

The words hung in the air, but they weren't a bolt from the blue or anything like that. It turned out that, now Max thought about it, she'd expected it. Only maybe she'd avoided it as much as Amy had, not wanting to rock the boat. With Amy blinking through tears at her, she knew she had to find something to say though.

'You've not screwed anything up,' she said. 'It'll be all right.'

'How?' Amy questioned. 'Biddy's going to hate me.'

'No, she loves you.'

'She said last night that I can't make mistakes, that I can't see someone like Ed because it's letting Dad down.'

'I gave her a lift home and we got caught,' Ed supplied.

Max scrubbed at her neck. 'It's not getting caught. The pair of you haven't done anything wrong. Look, Amy, she'll come round to all of it in time. She'll have to.'

'Not when she finds out I'm not really her granddaughter,' Amy said.

It wasn't the first time Ed had heard that titbit by the look of it, which Max was glad about. The way that ate away at Amy'd poison everything if she let it, especially her relationship with Ed. Going in honest was where Valerie always got it wrong. If Amy learned how not to do it from watching her mum then that was something at least.

Both of them were watching her, Max realised. She cleared her throat and held Amy's gaze.

'Okay, look, what's the worst that can happen? Talk it through with me, break it down.'

Amy shivered and eased away from Ed. 'I'm not going to Durham.'

'So?' Max pressed when she didn't carry on.

'I won't be a lawyer. Biddy'll hate me. If she kicks me out then I'll have to go crawling back to – to Mum. I can't do that, Max, I can't.'

'It won't come to that. There's always my spare room, that's not something to think about. What else? You won't be a lawyer so what next?'

Amy tilted her head to the ceiling. 'I'm supposed to know what I want to do and I don't. I had it all figured out and it was easy like that. I've done everything wrong, haven't I? You do the right A-Levels to get you on the right degree for your career. I planned it out and I messed it all up.'

'It's not that simple,' Max argued, motioning to Ed sat with his shoulders hunched up to his ears. 'He knows what it's like when something chucks your world up in the air. You had all these secrets going on that you had to hide, no wonder you did what was expected of you. If your dad hadn't got cancer, what would you have done for A-Levels? Would it have been Law?'

'I don't know,' she said.

'What is it you wanted to do?'

'I wanted to be like him. So, I wanted to be a lawyer.'

Max sighed and stood up. She stretched her legs across to the kitchen, filling the kettle and sticking it on to boil before she turned around. They were both still watching her from their separate cushions, looking like a pair of lost puppies.

'It doesn't follow,' she said.

Amy's forehead creased. 'What do you mean? I don't understand.'

'Wanting to be like him doesn't mean becoming a lawyer. From what I know about him, it's more like just doing something that helps other people. Like he did all that free work for charities and stuff, right? And he loaned Ed that money. That's not because he was a lawyer.'

'She's right,' Ed said.

'You've got time to figure it out,' Max continued before Amy came back with an argument. 'It's stupid, making people decide that young what they want to do. I fell into driving and I love it. You've got time and you've got options. You're bright enough to do whatever you want, whatever you're interested in. That's how you make your dad proud, I'm telling you.'

Amy wiped her eyes on her sleeve. 'But I have to tell them. I can't put it off for much longer. They'll be asking how my exams go and – and Mum! She'll probably want a photoshoot when I open my results. I have to tell them.'

'But you're not alone,' Max said.

'You're not,' Ed echoed.

Amy looked between them, maybe searching for the lie. She must've come up short because her expression hardened. It was something Max had seen with Valerie – the way she absorbed something deep inside her and

209

covered it in layers of something else. Judging from the look on Ed's face, he found it disturbing as well.

'It's best to get it done,' Max pointed out.

'Before the election?' Amy snorted. 'Yeah, right.'

'After, then,' she persisted.

'No,' Amy muttered. 'I'll do it when I'm ready.'

Max jumped as the kettle clicked off behind her then focused her attention back on Amy. 'When will that be?'

'As late in the day as possible,' she answered with a shrug. 'I'm my mother's daughter, after all, aren't I?'

## Chapter 32

'Thank you for being here.'

The gymnasium below was brimming with suited elbows colliding, occasionally on purpose. While the count staff were flicking through papers with remarkable concentration, rosettes of all different colours were glimmering under the harsh lights. Amy focused on spotting the flecks of colour to avoid looking at Valerie. That worked until she repeated her comment, coupling it with a nip to her forearm.

Amy twisted from her reach. 'I'm not here for you.'

'Oh, I know, I know. But, nevertheless, I appreciate it.'

'You didn't exactly give me a choice, calling Biddy to remind her.'

'It was a means to an end.'

'Isn't it always? Anyway, I'm not staying all night. Just long enough for them to take a few pictures, make sure Biddy knows I was here and you get your little publicity stunt too.'

Valerie tapped her fingers on the handrail. 'Sure, darling, that's fine.'

Amy shot a glance sideways under the guise of straightening her dress. This was her first direct encounter with Valerie since that night at Biddy's. Everything else she'd seen had been orchestrated for the media through interviews and statements. Then, like now, her entire attitude screamed politician-in-waiting. A second sneaky look brought an inconsistency with it, though, as Amy spotted the way her nails scraped against the threads of her jacket. It could've been nerves, but she doubted it. Nerves were something Valerie would control for the sake of the cameras; this was more primitive than that.

'Can we get a drink?' Amy asked.

Once the words permeated, Valerie acquiesced with one of her sham smiles and swished her inside the studio that was doubling as a café for the night. They settled at the most secluded table with a polystyrene cup of tea apiece, well away from the clumps of activists wearing red and yellow rosettes. They were buzzing around the television with excitement, but this little corner was thick with silence.

Valerie suddenly touched her arm. 'Amy?'

'What?'

'If this . . . I don't know. If everything goes as it looks likely to – the way I need it to – will you spend more time at home? I won't be there very much, but I'd still like to think of you there while I'm . . . You're not listening to me, are you?'

She stared into her cup. 'Don't worry, plenty of people do. And they actually voted for you.'

The hope of provoking a response faded as Valerie remained silent. Amy felt her look away again and risked another glance at her face. Her attention had wandered to the opposition activists, most of whom were glued to their phones or the television screen. They didn't give anyone beyond their cliques a second thought, but Valerie was gazing at them as if she cared what was going on in their heads. The suggestion that Valerie was playing the bigger woman here was something Amy couldn't stomach, certainly not at the moment, so she turned away.

'Amy, how is she?' Valerie asked abruptly.

Her head snapped sideways. The expression on Valerie's face had altered. It was as if the mask had cracked and emotion was seeping out through her eyes. Amy opened her mouth then closed it again, remembering the time and place. It was as likely to be a cynical ploy to work in a nice emotional mother/daughter moment for the cameras as genuine remorse.

'She's fine,' Amy answered.

'Do you . . .' Valerie wet her lips. 'Have you seen much of her?'

'Yep.'

'When – when was the last time?'

'She gave me a lift here tonight.'

Valerie brushed a crumb from the table. 'That was nice of her. Well, unless it was on the clock.'

Amy snickered.

'I'm sorry, I'm sorry,' Valerie said quickly. 'That was a bad joke.'

'Except it wasn't, was it? If this was the other way around, you probably would start charging me, wouldn't you? Or you'd refuse service, ban me from the premises – just like you tried to ban me from seeing her again.'

'That isn't fair.'

'Fair? Really, are you going down that route? You're worse than I thought.'

Valerie suppressed a sigh. 'Don't pretend you know me. You've actively tried not to, remember that.'

'So, all that time I spent with you and Max, trying to ignore everything you were saying and doing in the press and all over – that was not getting to know you, was it? I gave you the benefit of the doubt, I ignored the fact you had to be sleeping with Foster –'

'I wasn't,' Valerie hissed.

'You, me, and Max, we were a family. It wasn't even like that with Dad. So, if that wasn't being on your side, I don't know what you want from me.'

Clarity flashed across Valerie's face, but then it vanished.

'We're going over old ground,' she said. 'There's no point. Just answer my question.'

Amy squinted at her. 'What question?'

'Will you come home if I win?'

'I don't have a home.'

'You know that isn't true,' Valerie muttered.

'I might stay there more, if that's what you're asking. It's closer to Ed and Max.'

Valerie briefly squeezed her eyes closed. 'I really wish you wouldn't see her. It isn't doing anyone any good. I'm trying to help you, sweetheart. I know I hurt you, but if you'd just listen –'

'No,' she interrupted.

'Amy –'

'You don't prove something to someone by telling them. You show them. You've shown what matters to you and it's not me.'

Valerie's back straightened into her fighting stance. Then she seemed to remember where they were and raised her cup to her lips. She drained it before pushing it away and standing.

'Shall we have a wander around the count floor?' she suggested. 'I'm sure you'll enjoy it.'

'Kev didn't charge you, did he? I said to put it on account.'

Amy walked through into the back. 'You don't have to keep doing that.'

'Stick the kettle on and we're even.'

A few calls came through while she was making the tea, although Max had half an eye on the television flickering in the corner without the volume on. So far, only a handful of results had been declared and the main event was still the pundits preening themselves and crowing over exit polls. Amy passed one mug over to Max before settling on the sofa. Her wrist caught on something that looked like a lump of congealed vomit but was probably a stray ginger biscuit. She extracted it with a piece of newspaper then washed her hands and returned to her seat.

'Sorry, he's still not housetrained,' Max explained.

'I'm finding it comforting,' Amy answered.

Max tapped her thumb against her mug. 'How was she?'

'In her element. Focused.'

'Right,' Max replied.

They sat in silence for a while. Max dispatched half a dozen calls, her attention returning swiftly to the television each time. As soon as the broadcast switched to the gymnasium across town, she grabbed the remote and turned the volume up. A result was due in the next fifteen minutes and, from the downcast expression on the Labour candidate's face, it wasn't to his liking. Once the broadcast returned to the studio, Max hit the mute button again and cleared her throat.

'This is only an idea so don't feel obliged.'

'Okay,' Amy said slowly.

'Till you get your head sorted, why not work here for a bit after your exams are done with? It's some experience for your CV and Drew reckons we could do with the help. Don't worry, I didn't tell him everything, just that you might want something to do over the summer to keep yourself busy.'

Amy tilted her head to the side. 'Are you serious?'

'That depends whether you're offended or not.'

'Why would I be offended?' she asked.

'It's not exactly high-flying, is it?'

'You're mixing me up with someone else.'

'Course I'm not,' Max said, leaning back in the chair until it squeaked. 'Just doesn't have many perks, that's all. Take it from someone who spends half her life on here. You can read, that's a good one. Tea and biscuits on tap, maybe down the sides of the sofa if I don't rein Drew in. It's not a bad place to spend a bit of time and get paid for it.'

'Plus, it would really wind my mum up,' Amy pointed out.

Max shook her head. 'That's not why I'm doing it.'

'I know that, I know. But it's a brilliant side-effect.' Amy paused and let the idea swirl for a minute. 'If you're sure then, yeah, I'd love to work here. Thank you.'

'You're welcome,' Max said with the glimmer of a true smile.

Ten minutes later, the broadcast switched back to the gymnasium and Max turned the volume up again. Valerie was stood on a small stage, physically dwarfed by the other candidates but with the smugness almost radiating from her. As her name was announced with a majority of over four thousand, a grin erupted on her face that probably seemed authentic to those who only knew her politically.

To Amy, it looked as though her lips had been stretched with kitchen tongs then coated with scarlet lipstick. She shook hands with the returning officer and the other candidates before stepping forward to take the microphone.

'Now, I haven't prepared a speech or anything like that, but I obviously want to say a thank you to all the staff here for running the evening so smoothly. It's such an important job and you do it unbelievably well. Also, I must thank my agent, my family, and a few good friends who helped me to this point. They know who they are so I won't embarrass them by throwing names around. Of course, the biggest thank you must be reserved for every single member of the public who voted for me. I'll make it my mission to represent you in Westminster and repay your faith. Thank you.'

The audience began applauding and Max jabbed the television off.

'That sounded like a speech to me,' Amy said.

'Yeah,' Max mumbled.

Amy bit on her lip as she watched her quivering shoulders. 'Are you all right?'

'Doesn't matter. She got what she wanted. Sure she'll be happy with it.'

With that, she rose and took herself over to the kitchen. The kettle began boiling again and Amy's attention strayed back to the blank television screen. That woman she'd seen accepting her new role as an MP wasn't one who was capable of being happy. Amy knew that because she'd seen Valerie truly happy. That speech hadn't even been close.

## Chapter 33

The office was sticky and the best Max had was an electric fan and a cold tap for company. She'd taken to going into the bathroom once an hour and sticking her head under the faucet for a bit of relief. She was wandering back to the switchboard with beads of water dribbling into her collar when she found some welcome faces on the other side of the glass.

'Hey, what are you doing here?'

Elena nodded into the pram. 'She wanted a walk.'

'It's two miles away,' Max said as she yanked the door open and crouched down. Hannah grabbed her finger in a pudgy fist and instantly tried to stuff it in her mouth. 'Hiya, gorgeous. Hello, yeah, that's mine. You can't eat it.'

'Drew not in?' Elena asked.

Max straightened up. 'I could call him back if you –'

'God, no, we see enough of him. You know, if you could see your way to giving him jobs that mean he can't drive past the flat on his way back, we'd be grateful.'

'It's sweet,' she said, trying to smother her grin.

'Well, if it ever coincided with a nappy change, it'd be useful, but it never does.'

Max chuckled and motioned her through the door. 'Come on, I'll put the kettle on.'

'Have you seen the local today?' Elena questioned. 'It's under there. Check page four, I'll make the tea.'

There was a new column on the right-hand side, headed by a glossy photo with a fixed smile. It was the same publicity print used on lampposts and leaflets that bore no resemblance to the woman Max had shared a bed with for months. That stray thought made her toss the paper aside without reading it.

She untucked Hannah from the pram and settled down in the switchboard chair. The first call she answered got gurgles of astonishment as Hannah twitched her little head back and forth then she tried to eat the headset. As for

Elena, she made the tea then sat on the sofa and closed her eyes with a mug wedged next to her arm.

That was how Drew found them when he came in half an hour later. He scooped Hannah up and earned a squeal of either delight or irritation – Max couldn't decide which.

'This is why you weren't at home. Yes, it is. Yeah, hello, Hannah, hello.'

Max frowned at him. 'What were you doing round home? Thought I sent you to the Compton Road industrial estate.'

'Caught me,' he muttered.

'Caught you?' Elena retorted as she sat up and rescued her tea. 'We can't get away from you.'

'I'm trying to help,' he said.

'Well, help by keeping your business afloat,' she replied.

Max coughed. 'She's got a point, mate.'

'Oh, get stuffed, I'm doing my share.' He shifted Hannah into the crook of his arm. 'Besides, you're here at all hours, more than enough for the both of us. Anyone'd think you've not got a home to –'

'Drew,' Elena interrupted, 'Hannah's due a feed. There's a bottle in the bag.'

He puffed out his cheeks but got on with it. Max exhaled and shot Elena a silent thank you. She was saved doing more by the switchboard ringing then that turned into a flurry of calls and Drew was burping Hannah by the time she got a minute. She was wondering how to deflect him next when her mobile rang and saved her the trouble.

'It's Amy,' she said as she answered it. 'Hiya, how did it go?'

'Good, I think. I know I'm meant to be good at Economics but . . . I don't suppose it matters now.'

Her flat voice made Max wince, earning questioning looks from both Drew and Elena. Even Hannah seemed to notice something was up as she let out a large burp that made all of them laugh.

'What was that?' Amy asked.

218

'Burping baby,' she replied.

'Oh. Hannah's there?'

'Yeah . . . So, what are you doing now then?'

'Everyone's going to the pub then to a – a house party. Somebody's got the house to themselves, I think.'

'And you're not wanting to go?'

'I don't know them very well, they don't like me.'

'What about Ed? Or can't you go back to Clarice's?'

'He's got another private party on tonight. Biddy thinks I'm going out with Mum.'

'Was that on the table?'

'Well, it's what Biddy wanted to hear so I'm meant to be staying at Mum's. I – I thought it'd be okay at the party, but I don't want to go. And I don't want to go straight back to the house either. You know, Dad would've been waiting for me and we would've –'

'Shush, you're all right.' Max covered the phone and looked over to Elena. 'Are you two busy tonight?'

'No, we're old and boring. Why?'

'Fancy a takeaway with Amy?'

Drew shrugged. 'Brilliant, yeah. Exam went okay, did it?'

'Seems like it,' Max said as she uncovered the phone. 'Amy, how about coming round to Drew's? I'll buy in the food so the most he has to do is load the dishwasher. You can have a few drinks, get a cuddle with Hannah. I'll drive you back to your mum's afterwards.'

'Really? I don't want to –'

'Don't be daft. Just text me where you want picking up and we'll get the takeaway on the way back. And don't do anything you don't want to, all right?'

Amy muttered a goodbye then hung up. Max dumped the phone onto the switchboard and swayed from side to side in the chair.

'Been abandoned, has she?' Drew asked.

'Valerie's not in London,' she said.

'What, keeping tabs on her?'

Max fiddled with the volume control. 'I just know, that's all.'

Even with teenagers lurching around with fags in their mouths, the country pub was idyllic. Max drew the cab into a disabled bay and Amy jumped in out of nowhere, motioning for them to get going. Max indicated back onto the road and left it until they were a few miles away before pulling over into a layby.

Amy twisted her fingers together. 'Can we go?'

'In a minute. What's going on?'

'I'm fine.'

'Don't treat me like an idiot,' Max said. 'I've had enough of that.'

'Sorry,' Amy murmured, throwing her a weak smile.

'Have you spoken to your mum?'

'I – I rejected her calls.'

Max hesitated. 'I could take you there if you wanted.'

'No. I don't want to see her.'

'Fair enough, I get that. But this thing at Drew's, we don't have to do that. I could take you anywhere you want.'

'Where exactly?' Amy asked with a snicker. 'Apart from you guys and Ed, I don't have anyone else. People just know me, that's all. They don't like me, I'm just there. Even with Mum – especially with her – it's not as if she chose –'

'Hang on a second, listen to me.' Max tilted her shoulder into the seat and made sure Amy was looking at her. 'Your mum's done a lot of crappy things in her time, but she did choose you. Come on, when she found herself in that mess with your real dad, she could've got an abortion and she didn't. Yeah, she conned Tim into thinking you were his for about five minutes, but that doesn't mean she didn't want you. Far from it.'

Amy's anger had melted away into tears. She pulled out a pack of tissues and began cleaning herself up while Max turned her head towards the verge to give her some privacy, even if she couldn't stop her voice running away with her.

'Your mum chose you and so did I. What am I doing here if I didn't? I'm not here out of obligation or anything daft like that. What you said about your dad taking you to the pub and that . . . I'm honoured you called me and didn't just muck about on your own. It means something to me, okay?'

'Okay,' Amy echoed. 'Thank you.'

Max turned the key in the ignition. 'So, what do you fancy to eat?'

'Well, what do Drew and Elena like?'

'Oh, come on,' she replied. 'Drew'd eat a hamster if it sat still long enough.'

All in all, it ended up being a good one.

Drew took to shushing them every five minutes because he heard a rustle over the baby monitor and Elena pulled out a game of Yahtzee for them all to have a go at. Amy stayed tipsy, not pitching over that line between enjoying herself and burying her head in wine. Ten o'clock rolled round and, seeing Elena sway in her seat, Max suggested they call it a night.

The journey back was brighter, with Amy resting her head against the side window and tapping her fingertips together in time to Billy Joel on the radio. As they got closer to Geith Place, though, Max's stomach started to churn and her foot slipped off the clutch more than once.

'You could drop me here if you wanted,' Amy said.

Max glanced over and shook her head. 'Screw that, I'm taking you right to the door. We've not done anything wrong.'

In theory, that was all right. She had a blurry image of dropping her on the drive and going off without catching sight of Valerie. In practice, the woman herself glided down the path in her dressing gown and slippers. She must've been watching out from the upstairs window, though the creamy scent of shampoo that drifted into the cab when she yanked open the door explained that she wasn't long out of the bath.

'I've been worried,' Valerie said.

Amy slipped out of the cab. 'Well, I'm here now. Thanks, Max. Goodnight.'

'Night,' she returned.

The door was swinging shut when Valerie grabbed it with two hands. Max gestured for Amy to carry on into the house and watched her shuffle up the path, tossing anxious looks over her shoulder. It was only when the front door closed that Valerie let her iron grip on the door loosen and her head dipped into the car.

'Why?' she asked simply.

Max shrugged. 'Because she called me.'

'Well, what did you do? Where did you go?'

'To Drew's, that's all. We had a Chinese and a bottle of wine between us.'

Valerie's body sagged. 'She didn't even let me know if she was all right.'

'She's fine.' Max swallowed as the dressing gown rippled through with a breeze. 'Go on, you should get back inside.'

'Max –'

'I've gotta go,' she interrupted.

'Of course,' Valerie said. 'Thank you for keeping her safe.'

Max squeezed her eyes shut, waiting for the door to slam. 'Anytime.'

## Chapter 34

'All right, I'm here. What is it? What's the emergency?'

Valerie was hunched over the breakfast bar in her dressing gown, a recipe book open in front of her. She held up a hand while mouthing instructions to herself then she finally nodded and turned around.

'Thank you for coming,' she said.

'What is it?' Amy pressed. 'Come on, Mum, what do you want?'

'There's a dress upstairs on your bed. Get changed into that. It was the one you bought in the January sales so I'm sure it'll be fine.'

'Fine for what? You told Biddy you needed to see me urgently.'

'Well, I couldn't think of another way to get you here. We're having dinner with John this evening. He's been asking to meet you and I can't put it off any longer. So, you'll just have to grin and bear it – we both will.'

Amy frowned. 'Sorry, say that again. You've got me round here to have dinner with the man you were cheating on Max with.'

'I keep telling you, I wasn't.'

'Oh, I'll ask him that, shall I?'

Valerie spun away to wash her hands. 'He doesn't know a thing about her and I'd rather it stayed that way.'

'I bet you would. No, no chance. I'm not doing this.'

'I need your cooperation. Please, Amy, just this once.'

'Once?' she repeated, unable to repress her snort. 'No. Lie to him, you're good at that. Tell him I've got the plague or I'm looking after Biddy or something. Tell him whatever you want, except that I'm meeting him because I'm not.'

'Please, Amy, please.' Valerie clenched her jaw as she searched for a towel to dry her hands on. 'This is so important to my career, you wouldn't believe how important. Once – you meet him once, that's all.'

'Right, and what am I supposed to get out of it? I have to put up with a night watching that idiot slobber over you and I'm meant to like it because I'll get a warm fuzzy feeling of doing something for you? Don't make me laugh.'

Valerie paced across the kitchen, the towel dangling from her hand. Then she twisted around and threw it onto the breakfast bar. Amy stiffened as she watched her expression harden, unable to anticipate where the blow might land but feeling it coming.

'If we don't do this here – tonight – then I'm afraid I'll have to assent to John's other suggestion of having dinner at Clarice's. If you're telling me that's the only way this happens then I'm afraid . . .'

Amy swallowed down the bile in her throat. 'Fine. Okay.'

'And you'll be civil?' Valerie questioned.

'Sure,' Amy muttered, turning to the door. 'I've had plenty of practice being civil to people I hate.'

There was no artificial closeness on Valerie's part when she brought John through to the kitchen.

'John, this is Amy,' Valerie said.

He pulled back his shoulders and smirked. 'I was beginning to think Val was hiding you from me.'

Amy flinched at the shortened name, knowing how Valerie loathed it. John didn't notice – his attention had already drifted, first to the window and then to something on his phone. He let out a vapid chuckle as he looked at the screen then Valerie rested a hand on his shoulder and began talking about local sewage works.

A bottle of wine was cooling, Amy remembered. She retrieved the corkscrew hanging from the utensil rack and attempted to uncork the bottle without Valerie's interference, but she needn't have been so stealthy. Valerie didn't hear the pop or even notice her movements until Amy nudged a glass of wine into her hand.

'Oh,' she murmured, 'thank you, darling.'

'You're welcome,' Amy said then she forced herself to look at John. 'Are you driving?'

'I'll be getting a taxi to the station,' he replied.

'Well, we can recommend a company,' she returned.

Valerie cleared her throat and brushed John's hand with her own. 'You could always stay, you know.'

'I would if it wasn't for that meeting. Is that a Chardonnay? You might as well fill the glass properly.'

Amy followed the instruction wordlessly and poured her own glass before making a break for the living room. She paused to take a gulp in the hallway, followed in quick succession by another when she heard one of Valerie's simpering laughs. It was enough to take the edge off as she crumpled onto one of the sofas and waited for them to join her.

It didn't take long. John walked in and planted himself on the opposite sofa, not seeming to notice that Valerie put a foot of space between them when she followed suit.

He rested his arm across the cushions and zeroed in on Amy. 'So, Durham, is it?'

'That's the plan,' she muttered, even as her stomach twisted into a knot.

'Got the grades?'

'With any luck.'

'Never rely on luck. That's why people are so eager to embrace their own failures. They say it was out of their control when it wasn't.'

Valerie sat forward. 'Believe me, Amy put the effort in. I couldn't be prouder of her for it.'

The sincerity glowing on her face left a strange taste in Amy's mouth. She took another sip of wine and tried to wash it away.

'I suppose you're enjoying a break now, are you?' John queried.

'As it happens, I've got a summer job,' she answered.

'Excuse me?' Valerie said.

John's eyes narrowed as he glanced between them. 'Miscommunication?'

'Well, Mum's been in London a lot,' Amy said.

'And where is it you're working, darling?' asked Valerie.

Amy held her gaze. 'Just a cab office. On the switchboard.'

'Oh,' Valerie whispered, gripping her wine glass until her fingertips whitened.

'Sounds like charity work to me,' John commented. 'I hope they're paying you minimum wage.'

'Do you?' Amy questioned pleasantly. 'I thought I read that you wanted to scrap that.'

He coughed and turned to Valerie. 'You told me she wasn't interested in politics.'

'She isn't . . .' Valerie said. 'Not that I'm –'

'No, no, I'm not,' Amy cut in, focusing on John's glistening forehead rather than his dull eyes. 'But I thought I'd better see who my mum was spending so much time with. There wasn't much in the way of detail, though. Your official website was a little sketchy. I mean, do you have kids?'

Valerie shifted in her seat. 'Amy . . .'

'It's a valid question, Val, it's fine. Yes, I've got two boys – Joshua and Angus. They live with their mother in Aberdeen.'

'And your constituency's in Lincolnshire, isn't it?' Amy pressed.

'That's right. Say, Val, this is good wine. Is there any more?'

Somehow, the first glass had trickled down his throat while Valerie had barely taken a sip of hers. Amy raised an eyebrow as she watched her rise to get a refill then return with the bottle instead. John clicked his fingers and Valerie handed it over without comment. Then she got to work.

Everything about the next twenty minutes was calculated, right from the way she tickled her fingers along his thigh mid-sentence to the incline of her shoulders that

226

exposed her cleavage and manipulated his responses. Not only was it nauseating, it was completely unnecessary. Out of curiosity, Amy had tuned in to her maiden speech in the Commons and she'd grudgingly admit it was as eloquent as the numerous radio and television interviews she'd taken part in. It was as though she couldn't turn off the tap, Amy realised as she studied her over the rim of her glass.

The buzzing of the timer was a welcome interruption to the stale political dialogue permeating the living room. Valerie suggested they relocate to the dining room then, as an afterthought, asked Amy to help her serve. It was only when she'd slipped past the sofa under John's scrutiny that she understood why.

'Worried about leaving me alone with him?' she asked.

Valerie yanked a tray from the oven. 'Get the plates. Not the normal ones, the blue ones down there. I should've warmed them, I can't believe I didn't.'

'He's not royalty, you know.'

'He's a guest.'

Amy opened her mouth to retort then checked herself and retrieved the porcelain bluebell plates from the lower cupboard. She had barely held them out before Valerie snatched them from her hands.

'Open another bottle of wine,' she instructed.

The way they served him, he might as well have been royalty. Once they were all seated, he tucked into his dinner with revolting vigour. Amy tried to close her ears to both his gnashing and the occasional coarse comments he directed across the table. Meanwhile, Valerie was quiet – too quiet.

John tossed his napkin onto his empty plate. 'That was gorgeous, I could get used to that. Karen wasn't anything special in the kitchen, but that . . . Well done, Val.'

'Thank you,' she replied with a synthetic smile.

'The beef was lovely, Mum,' Amy added. 'The sauce had a good kick to it, you know I like that. Here, I'll give you a hand clearing up.'

227

John had closed his eyes, snorting out little puffs of air like a mangy dog curled up on a street corner. Amy almost crept past him with the serving bowls rattling in her arms. In the kitchen, she scraped the leftovers into the bin and began loading the dishwasher. She assumed Valerie was preparing dessert until she turned and found her staring into space.

'Mum?' she asked.

Valerie blinked then shook herself. 'Hmm? Listen, you've done your bit and I appreciate it. You don't have to stay for dessert, it's nothing special. Why don't you . . . call a taxi or something?'

The words wedged in the air then Amy slid the dishwasher tray back with a click. She moved to rinse her hands and reached for the towel, trying to keep her gaze from Valerie. By the time she replaced the towel on the hook, she'd expected the mask to be back on, but there were still cracks in it.

Amy cleared her throat. 'Thanks for dinner. I'll text you during the week.'

'Please do,' Valerie murmured. 'And send – send Clarice my love, will you?'

'I will,' she promised. 'Night, Mum.'


Her first instinct when Asif asked where she wanted to go was to say the cab office.

Max had her head buried in a book when she arrived, showering the pages with crumbs from a pile of custard creams on the desk beside her. She glanced up then turned down a corner.

'You look all dolled up,' she said.

Amy exhaled. 'Dinner party.'

'What, with Clarice?'

'No. Mum tricked me into a meal with him. Honestly, Max, he makes Drew look like a gentleman when he eats. It's almost like he uses up his manners with important people and then wastes the . . . Sorry, you don't want to hear this.'

Max shrugged and toyed with the edge of a custard cream. 'How does he treat her?'

'Don't,' Amy murmured.

'I'm only asking. How he treats her dictates how he treats you.'

'Yeah, but that's not why you're asking.'

'I'm not like Drew,' Max answered after a moment. 'I can't wish her pain.'

Amy rested her arms on the divide, pressing her nose against the glass. 'That's one side of it. But you don't have to wish her happiness either.'

## Chapter 35

A hot summer brought a lull in trade and Max split switchboard duties between Amy and herself. She was stuck in the office on the hottest day of the year when Drew came in late morning with a sheepish expression on his face. The last time she'd seen him with that look, he'd dropped a doughnut down the toilet and was trying to fish it out with a screwdriver.

He nudged the door shut and leaned against the wall. 'Hiya.'

'You're not on for a couple of hours,' Max said. 'Elena kick you out again?'

'No, she sent me.'

'Why? What's going on?'

'If it was down to me . . .' He trailed off and scratched his beard. 'No, actually, I would tell you. Better you hear it from us.'

Max slid the headset onto her neck. 'Hear what?'

'Take it no one's left a local today yet?'

'No, not yet. Come on, Drew, what is it?'

He tugged a crumpled newspaper out of his back pocket, drumming it against his leg for a few seconds. Then he chucked it across at her and it landed skewwhiff on the switchboard.

'I'm sorry,' he mumbled.

Every muscle in her body contracted at once. It wasn't so much the headline – 'MPs to Wed' – as much as the picture of Valerie showing off her engagement ring next to a smirking Foster. All the words swam in front of Max's eyes until she finally just screwed the whole paper up and launched it towards the bin. It caught the rim and bounced back along the carpet like a potato.

'You all right?' Drew questioned.

She pressed her knees together. 'Thanks for the heads up.'

'Does Amy know, do you reckon?'

'No, no chance. She's a good kid. She wouldn't have wanted me blindsided, she'd have told me.'

Her stomach liquified as she raised her eyes to Drew's.

'Which means she doesn't know. I've got to get to her.'

'Hang on, the paper's been out for a few hours. She probably knows by now.'

Max ripped the headset off and looked around for her keys. 'She's at her gran's. They're in a different area, they don't get the paper delivered. The first she'll know about it is when someone calls her gran. I need to get round there.'

'Go on,' Drew said, yanking the door open before she reached it. 'I'll cover the switch.'


This was the first time Max had gone all the way up to the house, though she'd been back and forth so much that she made the journey practically on autopilot. It was only when she crunched over the gravel in the driveway that her nerves caught up with her and she hesitated. The thought of Amy hearing the news from someone else spurred her on and she forced herself out of the cab.

Amy was stretched across a tartan blanket on the front lawn with her earphones in and a book under her nose. Next to her, in a chair shaded by a brolly, Clarice had her eyes shut. Max's shadow fell across Amy's book before she noticed her and tugged her earphones out.

'What's wrong?' she whispered.

Max motioned her away. 'I need a minute.'

She glanced first to Clarice to check she was still asleep then she gestured to the house. The difference to Geith Place was obvious from the second you got over the threshold, with walls and shelves littered with memories. Max followed Amy into the kitchen and took the glass of lemonade pressed into her hands. She downed it in one go and felt the tickle on her tongue.

'Have you seen the local paper today?' she asked finally.

Amy shook her head. 'Not yours, no. Wait, it's Mum's column today, isn't it?'

'Yeah, that's right.'

'What she said, Max? What has she done?'

Max scrubbed at her throat, trying to force the words up. 'The column got wiped out. I'm sorry, they got engaged.'

For a moment, Amy just seemed to waver on the spot then she crumbled. All the blood drained from her cheeks as she groped for the worktop. Max made to grab her before she fell, only Amy flinched away. It took a minute for her to recognise the response as one of Valerie's, with Amy just trying to keep a lid on everything going through her head.

'And she announced it in the paper?' Amy questioned.

Max nodded. 'Figured she hadn't told you, otherwise you'd have told me.'

'But you came here to make sure I know she's marrying the man she cheated on you with.'

'Couldn't let you walk into it blind.'

'You could've, but you wouldn't. Thank you,' Amy said.

She managed a shrug then averted her gaze while Amy put herself back together. The kitchen had all the mod cons of Geith Place, only without the chrome sparkling everywhere. Valerie went in for comfort so long as it was stylish, whereas this place had mismatched lamps on the windowsill and a National Trust tea towel flung over a chair.

'Are you okay?' Amy questioned and she tried to smile.

'It's nice here, that's all. I'd better get going before your gran wakes up.'

Amy's eyes widened. 'Oh, my God, I have to tell her, don't I? She'll be delighted. She thinks he's this high-flying minister, but he's just a drunken –'

'You don't have to tell her, it's not down to you.'

'So, what? I wait until she reads it in the paper?'

'I don't know,' Max admitted, 'but it's not your responsibility. Let your mum do what she's meant to for once. Stay out of it.'

'I was trying to before you came along,' Amy murmured.

Max grimaced, stretching out a hand then thinking better of it. 'I'm sorry.'

'I didn't mean it like that.'

'No, I know.'

Amy bit on her lip and edged forward. Max exhaled, opening her arms and squeezing hard when Amy stepped into them. She felt better for a second, as if it was what they both needed.

'Who are you?' a voice demanded suddenly.

Max spun around as Amy jolted away and wiped her eyes. Clarice was blocking the doorway more effectively than an old woman with angina should've been able to. The only sign she wasn't well came in the creases on her face, emphasised by her frown right this minute.

Clarice crossed her arms. 'I asked you a question. Who are you and what are you doing touching my granddaughter like that?'

'Biddy!' Amy said.

'No, don't try and defend yourself. If it wasn't bad enough bringing home that man with more hair than a gorilla –'

'This is Max,' she interrupted. 'One of my bosses at the taxi firm, remember?'

Even though Clarice's mouth snapped shut, the suspicion in her eyes didn't fade. It had been a while since Max had faced anything outright like this. There was the occasional loud-mouthed arse on a drunken night out, but that was just part of the job and it was mainly banter. This was visceral homophobia, the kind you grew up with and never grew out of.

'I'm sorry for intruding, Mrs Smythe,' Max said with a sidelong look at Amy.

'I assumed you were a man,' Clarice replied. 'I was never given any indication otherwise.'

'Well, I'm not keen on my full name, that's all.'

'Oh? What is it?'

She shifted her weight from her left foot to her right. 'Maxine.'

'That's a lovely name for a woman,' Clarice said.

Amy looked like she wanted a hole to swallow her up. Max knew how she felt. The silence stretched between the three of them until Amy stepped forward and cleared her throat.

'Biddy, Max reminded me I'm meant to be working this afternoon. I agreed to cover a shift.'

'I really don't see the need for this job, you know. It's not going to help you when you get to Durham, another internship would've been much more useful.'

'We've been through this,' Amy said.

'Yes, and I still don't understand. Your father would've been mortified –'

'He would've encouraged it. He always appreciated people trying to make their own way in the world and earning their own money. Anyway, it doesn't make a difference to the fact I have a shift to get to.'

Clarice turned away, brushing her fingers against the tiled wall. 'Fine.'

With that, she stalked out of the kitchen. A door slammed a few seconds later and rattled the plates in the dresser.

'You're right,' Amy said.

Max glanced over. 'Am I?'

'This is Mum's mess so let her deal with it. But I do need to get out of here before that happens, and I've just lied to Biddy that I've got to go.'

'So, where am I taking you then?' Max asked.

Amy tilted her head to the side. 'How about the pub?'

'Have you two been out boozing it up while I'm sat here working my arse off?'

Max steadied Amy through the doorway before Drew jumped up to catch her. 'Sat on your arse, more like. Besides, I'm the designated driver.'

'Getting pissed without me's not on,' he said as he clicked his fingers in front of Amy's face. 'You need coffee, yeah?'

She just blinked at him.

'Make us all one,' Max said.

Drew snorted on his way to the kettle. 'Bit of a lightweight, isn't she?'

Amy blew a raspberry at him and Max steered her over to the sofa.

'I've gotta sober you up. I can't send you back to your gran's like this, she hates me enough as it is.'

Once she was safely sat down, Amy kicked her heels together until Drew handed her a coffee and a ginger nut. She checked the biscuit for fluff before taking a bite, earning a chuckle from Drew. He settled back over on the switchboard and Max watched Amy from the other end of the sofa. It hadn't been the plan to get her drunk, but she hadn't wanted to talk about Valerie sober and then, by the time she'd had a few, she didn't want to talk about her drunk either. Max waited until the coffee had a chance to hit before she coughed.

'Ready yet?' she asked.

'I don't understand her,' Amy muttered.

'That's because you're a normal human being, not like her,' Drew replied.

'Not helpful,' Max said.

Amy hugged her mug to her chest. 'No, he's right. I think she's lost it. They've only been dating a couple of months.'

'If you believe her,' said Drew.

'Still not helpful,' Max warned him.

He shrugged. 'Just telling it like it is.'

'I don't understand her,' Amy repeated in a whisper.

Max ground her shoes into the carpet. 'Maybe she loves him.'

'No,' Amy said immediately. 'Trust me, she doesn't.'

235

'Then it's the job, isn't it?' Drew said as he wiped a ginger nut on his collar. 'Power couple and all that crap. Wait till she gets a promotion over him one day. It'll be handbags at dawn. You're well out of it, the pair of you.'

Amy sighed and took another sip of her coffee. A call came through that at least distracted Drew from chomping on his pile of biscuits for thirty seconds, but then the silence settled over the office again. It was similar to how it'd been in Clarice's kitchen, although Max didn't feel any hesitation this time about budging up and wrapping an arm around Amy's shoulder. Drew shot them a funny look, but she didn't give a toss.

'Max, what is she doing?' Amy asked.

'Whatever it is, there's nothing you can do,' she answered.

'I need to do something. She needs to know she can't do this and expect to get away with it.'

Drew coughed from across the room. 'You could spill it, couldn't you? Go to the papers, tell them your mum was practically shacked up with a woman for the best part of a year and that this traditional family crap is a load of hypocritical bollocks.'

'You've had some stupid ideas in your time, but that beats the lot,' Max said.

'What? It'd what I'd do.'

'Yeah, because that's a recommendation. If she winds —'

Amy stood up, wobbling like jelly. 'I want Dad's things. I want his pens, his cufflinks. I want everything she thinks she could get rid of and it wouldn't matter. Even if she's there — especially if she is — I want to take them. They're mine.'

'It's not the last chance you'll get,' Max said.

'You don't know that. She won't stay there, will she? Not when she can move into his mansion and have a wing to herself. It'll all go. I want to get it, I want to get it now.'

Max rubbed her neck. 'All right. Well, I'll take you.'

'No,' said Amy and Drew in unison.

'Foster might be there,' Amy added. 'It's not fair on you.'

'Yeah, I'll take her,' Drew said.

'No way,' Max replied, 'you're not getting in a scrap with her either. Raj is in the yard, he'll take you.'

Amy leaned down and hugged her. 'Thank you.'

'Call the switch when you're done and we'll get someone down,' she said as she opened the door. Once it had shut, she closed her eyes against Drew's stare. 'Don't. Just don't.'

## Chapter 36

If she did this in stages, she'd get through it.

Amy opened the door, kicked off her shoes and went straight upstairs. She veered into Tim's study and halted on the threshold, looking at the book spines glimmering under the fading sunlight. In the future she'd anticipated, all of those would've been coming with her to Durham and she would've honoured Tim every day by using them. It was only thanks to Max and Ed that she was coming around to the idea that he really wouldn't have been disappointed by her change in plans.

A door opened downstairs and spurred her over the threshold. She began emptying the desk drawers, pulling out Montblanc pens and unused moleskin notebooks. Everything in here looked the same as the day after he'd died, with the circular photo frame showing the two of them together still stuffed behind an old diary. Amy's fingertips lingered on the glass until a voice startled her.

'What do you think you're doing?'

She clenched one fist out of sight and used the other to continue rooting through the drawer. Then a hand grasped her wrist.

'I asked you a question,' Valerie said.

Amy shook her off. 'Taking what's mine. The things Dad wanted me to have before you turned into the Merry Widow.'

'You're not yourself. Wait, have you been drinking?'

'Yes, Mum, well spotted. Wow, with those powers of observation, you could work for MI5. Yes, I've been drinking. Would you like to hazard a guess at why that is?'

Valerie's lip trembled, just for a second. 'I – I couldn't think of a way to tell you without causing an argument.'

'Oh, I bet. So, instead, you chickened out, thought you'd let me read about it in the paper of all things. What kind of mother does that?'

'John wanted to –'

'I don't particularly care what John wants. Anyway, I didn't read about it in the paper. Max saw it first and rushed round to Biddy's to let me know. She thought I had the right to hear it from a human being, even if you didn't.'

Something flashed across Valerie's face then vanished before Amy could pinpoint what it was. She took a step away, running the tip of her ring finger along the mottled spines of the books until she reached the end of the row. The expression on her face when she turned back was impassive.

'That explains the voicemail I received from Clarice. She congratulated me on my engagement then suggested she was concerned about your choice of friends. I assumed she meant Ed but, no, you've been with Max and she had the temerity to get you drunk.'

Amy let out a snort. 'Don't start down that track. I mean, does that make you feel better? Standing there all high and mighty because your ex took me out for a drink. She wouldn't have had to if you'd had the guts to pick up the phone.'

'That's not the point –'

'She cares about me,' Amy interrupted. 'More than can be said for you.'

'Well, that's patently untrue.'

'Really?' she shot back, crossing her arms. 'Okay, how else would you spin it? Come on, Mum, be a politician. How would you spin it? Your phone ran out of battery and you couldn't find my number to call me from John's. Maybe you were hit over the head with a jack handle and you've got selective amnesia. That must be it – you forgot I existed. It wouldn't be the first time, would it?'

Valerie smoothed the creases from her shirt. 'Sarcasm's beneath you.'

'Who's being sarcastic? You didn't tell Max about me, remember. Because you're ashamed. You probably only told John because you didn't have a choice. Hard to play the family values card then not introduce him to me. Max is better off out of it.'

'As badly as you might wish it, she's not your mother,' Valerie snapped. 'In fact, she's nothing to you, she never was. This summer job's nothing more than a desperate attempt to keep you close and keep you away from me.'

Amy shook her head. 'If you actually believe that, you're farther gone than I thought.'

There was a moment where Valerie's eyes blazed. Then they glazed over and she walked over to the window. She straightened the curtains, trailing her hand along the fabric until a loose thread snaked around her thumb. It strained as she cracked it in two and the whole curtain billowed out with the pressure.

'What is it you want from me?' she asked, turning back. 'What is it you hoped to achieve today apart from the theft of some valuable items?'

'They're mine,' Amy said.

Valerie pressed her lips together. 'Well, that's a matter for debate. The question still stands – what do you want from me?'

'Nothing. I don't want to see you ever again.'

'Unfortunately, that's not an acceptable offer to me,' Valerie replied in the same voice Amy had heard her use on the *Daily Politics*. 'There's really no deal to be had there. You want me to agree to you taking these items and then you disappear on me completely. That's blatantly unfair, isn't it? Under those circumstances, it's really difficult for me not to share with Clarice that I have the same concerns about your choice of friends and the decisions you're making. I wonder how she'd react to that.'

Amy's jaw slackened. 'You're joking.'

'No, I'm deadly serious,' Valerie said. 'I want you back for weekends.'

'No chance.'

'Well, then, no deal.'

'You're not in Westminster now,' Amy said, trying to keep her voice steady. 'You don't get what you want by sounding nice about it.'

'It's your choice, Amy. Just think of the contrast – Max and Ed beside John. Who's Clarice going to prefer, hmm? There's really no contest. He can be very charming when he wants to be. I'm sure he could wrap Clarice around his little finger if I asked, they could become very good friends.'

Amy gripped the edge of the desk. 'Mum, don't do this.'

'Weekends over the summer,' Valerie answered with a bland smile. 'That's all I'm asking for.'

'But what do you get out of it? I'm not spending nights curled up in front of the fire while he paws at you across the room. It's not happening, not with him. We've been there and done that properly, remember.'

'You'll still be here,' Valerie said.

'And you still don't win,' Amy retorted. 'I might be here, but it's nothing more than a prison cell if you're blackmailing me into it.'

Valerie gestured around at the oak bookcases. 'This doesn't look much like a prison to me. If I'd have had this growing up –'

'What? You wouldn't have got knocked up at seventeen by a married man? I tell you something, Mum – at least I know how contraception works. It would've saved you a lot of trouble if you hadn't skipped that class, wouldn't it? Except you wouldn't have scored your meal ticket with Dad. That's the trouble with Max, isn't it? No money, no big name, nothing that can make you feel better than you are.'

She leaned back as Valerie reared up. Even at full height, she wasn't much, but the flash of fury in her eyes was intimidating. Amy's elbow cracked against the wall then, the next thing she knew, Valerie was steaming down the stairs. The house rattled as the front door slammed.

Until the noise had faded, Amy stayed perfectly still. Her elbow ached where she'd jabbed it into the wall, but her mind was fixated on the primal instinct that had triggered a reaction like that in Valerie. She'd been trying to provoke her, sure, but she'd been stubbornly stony up until that mention of Max.

Amy shook herself. It was better to take the things she'd meant to instead of trying to analyse Valerie's state of mind. So, she continued extracting Tim's personal possessions from the desk and stacked them where his computer used to sit. It ended up as a heap of pens, stress balls, and old diaries full of his precise handwriting. She couldn't resist opening one up and lifting it to her nose, tasting the aftershave on her tongue.

Time was moving on and the fear of seeing Valerie again prompted her to pick up speed. She wrenched herself away from the study and cleared the possessions she'd accumulated in her bedroom over the months of Max being part of the family. She wanted it all out of here, whatever Biddy might think about it.

It took over half an hour to pack everything into her old school rucksack and a black holdall that Valerie used for overnight trips. If she wanted to be picky, that was the only thing that could be construed as theft, but Amy was willing to risk it.

Once she was ready to go, she lingered on the upstairs landing outside the study. It was almost dark now, shadows stretching across to gobble up the bookcases. Tim used to forget to turn the light on, finally reaching for the lamp when his eyes couldn't strain through the gloom or when Amy disturbed him. She could picture him there, lifting his chin to smile and motion her inside.

The front door opened downstairs and she stiffened.

'Amy?' Valerie called.

She was about to respond when she remembered that the door had been on the latch. There was no need to alert

Valerie to her presence when she could slip away without seeing her again, at least tonight.

'Amy? Did you . . .'

Valerie's voice trailed off then ruptured into sobs. Pure, unaffected sobs.

With delicate steps, Amy crossed the landing and eased herself down until she could see through the railings of the banister. There was nothing in her line of sight, but she suddenly recalled another occasion like this, something she'd buried away. After the final diagnosis – after the doctors had admitted there was nothing else they could do – Valerie had left them both upstairs in the study to make a cup of tea. Amy had followed for some reason and heard her like this, broken and distraught. She'd never mentioned it to anyone and it'd hidden itself away underneath her anger about everything that happened next. But, now, she remembered and her chest ached.

There was no chance that Valerie knew she was still in the house and, anyway, if she'd wanted to fool her with emotion, she would've tried that earlier. Her narrative was that she'd landed her dream job, she was making a name for herself, and she was engaged to a prominent politician. It was everything she'd wanted.

Yet, here she was, weeping in her own living room. Was this what she did these days? Come home, crack open a bottle of wine, and burst into tears?

Amy rested with her forehead against the banister until the sobs began to subside. Then she realised that, should Valerie decide to clean herself up in the downstairs bathroom, she'd catch her like this. The only thing to do was slink back into the study and find a way to alert Valerie to her presence in the house.

There was a stationery caddy on the desk, empty apart from a few paperclips. It was hefty enough to cause a thud, especially when dropped from height. She also circled the desk several times before finally collecting her bags to take downstairs.

243

Valerie had reassembled herself in record time. Her cheeks were clear and she'd even managed to reapply most of her make-up too. It would've taken a telepath to recognise she'd been crying when she glanced out of the kitchen.

'Oh, I assumed you'd gone. You seemed so set on it.'

'I'm going now,' Amy replied.

'Fine,' said Valerie with a disdainful smile. 'By the way, next Friday I'm in Wolverhampton for a meeting in the afternoon. It'll be a late one so you'll have the house to yourself. We'll be back about eleven, I'd think.'

That stray comment including Foster would've ignited another burst of anger earlier, but it wouldn't even conjure itself into a spark now. All that hatred was submerged under a layer of compassion as Amy saw through Valerie's defences into the raw emotion underneath. But she couldn't let that seep into tonight, not when she needed time to think. So, she turned towards the front door and away from Valerie's placid expression.

'I've got to go,' she said.

'You'll be here Friday. Won't you?'

'Of course,' Amy answered without looking back. 'You didn't give me any choice, remember?'

'Drew's not here. Do you need him for something?'

Amy shook her head. Her attention was fixed on Hannah leaning over from Elena's shoulder, little arms chugging around in loops. She finally caught a strand of Amy's hair and stuffed it into her mouth triumphantly.

'Are you okay?' Elena questioned.

'It was you I wanted to see, not Drew,' she explained.

Elena nudged Hannah into her arms. 'Here, you take her and I'll put the kettle on.'

Cuddling Hannah was like juggling puppies. Her arms and legs, at least eight of them, were everywhere and the only way Amy found to keep her occupied was to go over to the living room window and start gibbering about the

244

colours of the cars below. By the time Elena came in with the tea, their foreheads were resting together and Hannah was gurgling her contentment. Amy relocated them both to the sofa and propped Hannah up on her knee within grasping distance of Elena's arm.

'So, what's going on?' Elena asked. 'I appreciate the company, don't get me wrong, but you look like hell.'

Amy began massaging circles into Hannah's back. 'I went to collect some things last night. Drew probably told you.'

'He mentioned it. I'm sorry about the engagement.'

'Well, that's the thing. Mum was there and we got into an argument about her letting me read it in the paper and everything. We really went at it, she was on top form. Biddy had called her already to say she disapproved of me being friends with Max and Mum turned that around on me. If I go back for weekends, she won't collude with Biddy and kick up a fuss about me being around Max.'

Elena sighed. 'I can't say I'm surprised to be honest.'

'When she's in a corner, she comes out fighting. And she can really fight, you know?'

'Mmm. I remember Christmas Day with Drew.'

'So, I wanted to hurt her,' Amy continued, focusing on the cotton of Hannah's top. 'I was actively trying to find something that would make her react and then I – I said some things about why she isn't with Max anymore and they hit home. She walked out. When she got back, she thought I'd gone and she – she broke down. I mean, really, Elena, she was distraught. She thought she was alone in the house and it's like she exploded. Everything came out.'

Elena squeezed the tips of Hannah's toes. 'Are you sure she didn't know you were there?'

'Positive. It was the way she acted when she realised I was in the house. She tried to hide it, she got herself cleaned up and everything. She was putting on an act then, not before. But I don't even think the act was for my benefit. She's miserable, Elena. I mean, I knew she wasn't happy because I've seen her happy. With Max, she was someone else. I'd never seen her like that before, not even with my dad. Then she had to go and screw it up, didn't she? I can't believe what she did to Max – and to you guys.'

'Neither could I at the time,' Elena answered slowly. 'You know, I was pretty frazzled that day at the hospital, of course I was. I'd just given birth and I looked horrific, whatever Drew said. They didn't even give me chance to brush my hair before they turned the camera on, but I'm not sure she was expecting the full works like that. She was upset. Not much, but it was noticeable if you were paying attention. He wasn't – Foster. Your mum was standing there, not saying a lot, looking pretty uneasy, and he took charge. Shoot the video, smile, have a chat. For him, it was calculated. It looked to me as though she had to force herself into it.'

Amy bit her lip. 'I've seen that a lot lately.'

'I think that she wanted to win so badly and saw that he could help her with that. The idea of her cheating on Max though . . . It still doesn't sit right with me. I saw them together on Christmas Day and it stuck with me. They were comfortable with each other. Drew couldn't see it – he never wanted to – but they were.'

'I know,' Amy muttered, 'and I'm so angry at her for being so stupid, but I . . .'

'But what?' Elena pressed.

She rested her nose against Hannah's wispy hair. 'Before – before Max – I hated her for what she'd done, the lies she'd told. I saw everything that she did as selfish. The election was pretty much an extension of that. Power-mad, narcissistic . . . I couldn't imagine why she'd be doing it if it wasn't for the ego-trip.'

'And what do you think it was now?'

'I'm not sure. She had all the money my dad left her, she didn't have to work. The diagnosis was cruel as far as her job was concerned. It would've taken a harder heart than she's got to work there after he'd died. She'd got involved in politics a few years earlier, she said it gave her something to distract her from the grief she was surrounded by every day. After Dad died and I moved to Biddy's, it's like it became an obsession. Maybe it just happened to be there and it was the perfect antidote to everything else.'

Elena nodded. 'That's an explanation. Does it make a difference if that's how it was?'

'I don't know,' Amy admitted with a weak smile. 'I saw her with Max, didn't I? That was her – the real her. I liked it at home, I liked feeling as though I was part of a family again. And all I can see in her now is how miserable she is in comparison. Believe me, I don't want to feel sorry for her. She's been completely selfish. Except, sometimes, I'm not sure it is selfishness. I think it's ambition gone wrong, something like that. And maybe fear of, I don't know, letting me in and letting Max in. That means she loses control, doesn't it? Like with Dad and the cancer and . . . I don't know what to do.'

Her last words were accompanied by tears scorching her eyelids and Elena reached across for Hannah.

'Oh, Amy . . . Here, let me take her so you can wipe your eyes.'

It was gratifying to hear the grizzling from Hannah as she was taken away. Amy watched Elena soothe her for a moment then retrieved a tissue from the coffee table. Once she'd blown her nose, she met Elena's steady gaze again.

'I never got the impression she loved me,' she said as she stretched the tissue between her fingers. 'I mean, she said she did, but you don't prove it by what you say, do you? Until Max, it was like talking to a robot. She was saying all the right things, only not in the right way because . . . Well, because she didn't know the right way. Tell me, Elena, come on. What do I do?'

Elena shifted Hannah to her shoulder again. 'You don't have to do anything. It's not your mess. They're adults, let them work it out themselves.'

'But they won't, will they? John's so self-absorbed that he wouldn't notice if Mum grew a new head unless it made it onto the front pages. And Max won't make a move – why should she after everything that's happened?'

'What about your mum?' Elena questioned.

Amy pulled the tissue until it split in pieces. 'Too proud, too ambitious. Maybe too far gone.'

'It does sound like she's realised there's a problem.'

'So, what?' Amy returned. 'There's a difference between realising it and doing something about it, isn't there?'

# Chapter 37

'Feels like I'm the Queen or something. It's my favourite meal and everything.'

Elena chuckled as she spooned more cottage pie on to the plate. 'Drew said it was and, truth be told, it's one of the only things I can make with that little madam the way she is at the moment. That's why we're living on frozen pizzas most of the time.'

'Suits me,' Drew said through a mouthful of potato.

'Yeah, it would,' Max retorted. 'Anyway, cheers, Elena. For inviting me, that is.'

'It's as much for my benefit as yours,' she replied. 'I need human interaction every now and then, and Drew doesn't count.'

The three of them fell to eating the cottage pie, though Drew somehow managed to do it while bouncing Hannah on her knee. They didn't get into anything heavy while they ate, much to Max's relief. She'd been worried about the summons over here, reckoning it might lead into a double-barrelled assault about trying to find another woman. Drew had ratchetted his nagging game up at work and she couldn't do with Elena jumping on the bandwagon.

She tagged along with Drew after dinner to bathe Hannah while Elena washed up. They settled her down then went back to the living room where another beer was waiting for the pair of them. Drew dumped himself on the sofa and began picking at his feet, only stopping when Elena chucked a cushion at his head. He grumbled about it before looking over at Max.

'You talked to Amy much lately?'

She shrugged. 'About as much as you. Why?'

'Seems off, that's all. Been snappy with the lads. They don't mind it, they're used to worse from you, but they've said it's strange. They like her.'

'Why have they been talking to you about it?' Max asked.

'They wanted to check nothing was up.'

'Yeah, why not talk to me? You're practically part-time at the minute.'

He crossed his legs. 'Well, some of them reckon that . . . I mean, they know you got her the job and she's pretty –'

'That's sick,' Max cut in. 'She's eighteen, for Christ's sake! I'm old enough to be her –'

'But you're not, are you? And, that lot, they don't know you were screwing her mum. If you showed willing about being with someone else –'

She slammed her beer down on to the table. 'Thanks for the meal, Elena. It was gorgeous.'

'Max, wait,' Elena said, but she shook her head.

'It's fine,' she answered. 'I've got an early shift, that's all. Give Hannah a kiss for me.'

Next morning, she was biting everyone's head off on switchboard. It was happening without her having any control over it, so the lads did disappearing acts when they could and the customers tended to wait outside.

It wasn't long before lunchtime when Elena arrived with Hannah. The potential for a cuddle with that little girl was the only thing that'd got Max smiling all day, so she went through and unbuckled the straps of the pram. She earned a laugh from Hannah before she even looked at Elena.

'Everything all right?' Max questioned.

'Yeah. Is Drew on a job?'

'Train station in heavy traffic,' Max said with a smirk. 'Come through, I'll put the kettle on.'

They made small talk about how well Hannah was doing until the kettle boiled then all three of them settled down on the sofa. It was enough to have the distraction so Max winced when she caught sight of the pained expression on Elena's face.

'What's up?' she asked.

Elena swept her hair behind her ears. 'I wanted to talk to you, I wanted to ask you something. I know you're not going to like it, but I think it's important.'

'If it's about that crap – sorry, rubbish – Drew was spewing last night, it's twisted –'

'I know it is,' Elena interrupted, 'I do. You're more like mother and daughter. But then that's the problem.'

'How do you mean?'

'You're still in love with Valerie,' she replied.

Max flinched and jumped up, splashing scalding tea on to her hand. She wiped it off on her trousers then rounded on Elena.

'You're out of line.'

'I understand why you think that,' Elena said.

'No, don't do that,' she snapped, provoking a wail from Hannah. 'That's what she does. Screws me around, makes me think black's white. Well, it's not. She cheated on me with that –'

'Did she?' Elena cut in.

Max opened her mouth then closed it again.

'Did she?' Elena repeated.

'No,' Max conceded. 'I don't think she did.'

'And I don't think she did either. So, sit down and talk to me.'

With Hannah crying and her brain swirling, she couldn't think of an argument. She nudged the switchboard off and sat down on the sofa again. Hannah reached for her, not relenting until she took her back onto her knee. They sat like that for a few minutes with Max knowing she couldn't break the silence. It was only a case of how long it took Elena to do it.

'Amy's falling apart,' she said eventually.

Max looked over Hannah's spurts of hair. 'I know she's got a lot going on in her head, but she's got support.'

'She's still only eighteen. Think of what she's been through in the last few years. First, she loses her dad to cancer. She falls out with her mum, moves in with her grandmother. Then you come along and you give her back this family thing that she'd been missing. I don't even think she realised how much she was missing it until then.'

'I wasn't the one who took it away again,' Max reminded her.

Elena exhaled. 'Of course you weren't. With everything that happened, no one could blame you for walking away. But you haven't, have you? You've kept Amy close –'

'She needs me,' Max interrupted.

'And you need her. She's a link to Valerie.'

'That's not why I offered her the job.'

'It didn't hurt, though, did it?' Elena questioned. 'What is it? Do you think she'll bring the two of you back together, is that it?'

Max let out a snort. 'Come on, you know what Amy's view on her is. I was hard pressed getting them talking when I was there and Valerie's blown it completely with her now. You don't let your daughter find out she's getting a stepdad from the sodding paper.'

'I think Valerie was burying her head in the sand,' Elena said.

'You hardly know her.'

Elena rubbed her cheek. 'It sounds to me like she's frightened, scared of losing control.'

'Where are you getting all this from?' Max queried.

'I've pieced it together. You get a lot of thinking done when you're rocking a baby back and forth at three o'clock in the morning. Were you her first relationship with a woman?'

Max swallowed. 'That's private.'

'Have you asked her?'

'This isn't any of your business.'

'Humour me, go on,' Elena said and she growled.

'I was the first, just not the first she's wanted. Why? What does it matter?'

Elena nodded, as if she'd finished a jigsaw puzzle. 'She fell in love with you, that's what was different about the

**252**

whole thing. Tell me, why don't you think she cheated on you?'

The image of Valerie kissing Foster flitted back into Max's head. She'd done her best to forget it over the months, but it was always there, fluttering around the edges. Instead of fighting it away, this time she let it burn through her brain.

'That kiss at the hospital,' she said finally. 'It was more like she was going along with it than anything else. But she could've gone along with more than that. How am I to know?'

'You could always ask her,' Elena suggested.

'Yeah, right.'

'Well, you'd know if she was lying,' she persisted.

Max dropped a kiss on Hannah's head. 'Doesn't matter either way, does it? She's sleeping with him now and she's lied about who she is and what she wants. I'd be a prize idiot to go chasing after that.'

'You're only a prize idiot if you let something else get in the way of how you feel,' Elena replied. 'If there's a chance, why not take it? For both yours and Amy's sakes.'

# Chapter 38

It was one thing to be prepared for John Foster arriving, but Amy hadn't anticipated the sheer level of noise he brought with him into the house. She could hear his voice ricocheting against the walls from her bedroom and she crept across to push the door closed. Her hand halted as she heard him pounding around like a baby elephant and slurring his words.

'It's namby-pamby shit. You're not telling me you agreed with any of it.'

'I see both sides,' Valerie answered in a completely sober voice.

'You barely said anything. I want to know what you think.'

'I think we voted on it, actually. You saw my vote.'

'That was you following the pack. You saw which way the wind was blowing, I know your game. Didn't I teach you it?'

'John, I listened to the debates, that's all. Now, don't you think you should lie down?'

'There's an idea . . .'

Amy cringed and made to close the door. She hesitated again when she caught Valerie's vehement reaction.

'Not while Amy's here, I told you that.'

'She's asleep! Anyway, she's a big girl. She can damn well deal with it.'

'I don't care, I said no.'

'Oh, it's an excuse. There's always a bloody excuse.'

'That's not true. Why don't you sit down and I'll make you a coffee?'

'And you'll join me.'

'Of course.'

Amy listened as he lumbered through into the living room then everything went quiet. She chewed on the inside of her cheek as she switched the light off, although she left the door ajar in case things turned nasty. What she'd do if that happened was beyond her. Foster was twice her size – and Valerie's – and sounded belligerent at best.

It was quiet downstairs for a while. Too quiet. Amy found herself perched on the edge of her bed, straining to hear any minor sound from the lower floor. It reminded her of the vigil on that long night, watching Tim's chest bubble until the air faded from his lungs. She remembered looking over at Valerie and wondering why she was the only one with dry eyes.

Everything had been silent for so long that Amy was startled when the stairs creaked. Someone was trying to be discreet, so it obviously wasn't Foster. She held her breath, expecting Valerie to go into her bedroom, but she didn't. The study door squeaked then the chair groaned as she sat down.

Amy rose and drifted along the landing as quietly as she could. She found Valerie still dressed in one of her grey suits, arms rigid and fists clenched against her temples. Her eyes were screwed shut, giving Amy a moment to watch the pain rolling across her face.

'Mum?' she murmured.

Valerie jolted as she opened her eyes. 'Oh, hello, darling. I didn't know you were still up.'

After glancing over her shoulder, Amy closed the door. She leaned back against it and crossed her arms.

'Do you remember when you told me the treatment hadn't worked?' she asked.

'Of course,' Valerie said slowly.

'You told me. Not Dad, not Biddy – you. Why?'

'I – I don't understand.'

'Neither did I,' Amy replied, 'not at the time. You were so calm about it, so mechanical. You brought me in here, do you remember?'

'I could hardly forget,' Valerie answered.

'No, of course not. Because you were protecting him, weren't you? Protecting how I'd remember him. He never really talked about the cancer with me. It was always you.'

'That wasn't deliberate.'

'Everything's deliberate when it comes to you,' Amy argued. 'Admit it, you were trying to protect me.'

Valerie leaned back until the chair shrieked. 'You're my daughter, I love you.'

'You see, it never felt much like that. Maybe it was just because you weren't being honest with me about my dad. Then you started to let me in last year. You were open with me.'

A shiver overtook Valerie then her shoulders crumpled. She pressed a palm against her eyes, but the tears seeped out between her fingers. Amy rounded the desk and knelt beside her.

'Mum . . .'

'I'll be fine. If you just –'

'No, you won't. Stop pretending you're okay. I know you're hurting, I know why. The only thing I don't understand is why you're putting yourself through this. Mum, he's . . . Well, he'd have to be something pretty special and he's not. He's the worst man you could possibly pick. It wouldn't be as bad if you loved him, but you don't.'

Valerie's hand drooped from her face and Amy clasped it between her own. More tears began streaming along Valerie's cheeks, bringing mascara streaks with them.

'You love Max,' Amy said as she held her gaze. 'Any idiot can see that.'

'Yes . . .' Valerie sniffed then shook her head. 'She doesn't love me – not anymore. How could she? I behaved abominably.'

Amy sighed. 'Yeah, you did. You kept her in the dark and you hid her away. You used her friends in a cheap publicity stunt that never even made it to air. God, Mum, you actually let Foster paw at you when you weren't interested, just so you could get elected. Maybe you'd convinced yourself she'd be there waiting for you when it was all done with. And, you know, I think she might have been if it hadn't hit her all in one go like that. I don't blame her for walking away.'

'Neither do I,' Valerie whispered. 'I knew what I was doing, I won't deny it. I was counting on her being too invested in our little f-family to really react to anything.'

Her voice cracked and she averted her gaze. That slight rebuff was enough to propel Amy across the room. She skirted around the desk and ended up staring at the puckered spines of Tim's case law collection. It was the only way she could say what she needed to.

'What you did was cruel and cowardly. You hurt Max, you hurt me. Not that you seemed to care. And I hated you, I hated you for it. I couldn't understand why you were going along with it all. But are you really going to marry that idiot? I've seen you with him, remember. You don't want him anywhere near you. Do you honestly think that's going to change? He's arrogant, he drinks – can you imagine what Dad would say? Not to mention the fact that he treats you like – I mean, have you seen his voting record?'

'You looked up his voting record?'

Amy twisted back towards her. 'Of course I did. If he had his way, you wouldn't even be allowed in the House of Commons. And you know his views on gay rights, don't you?'

'Yes,' Valerie said through gritted teeth.

'Doesn't it bother you?'

She briefly closed her eyes. 'Yes.'

'Then why, Mum? You can't stand him, let alone anything else. Talk to me – explain.'

'I – I can't –'

'You can,' she insisted.

'Amy –'

'Remember when I'd just found out about Max and you tracked me down at the café? You were honest with me, really honest, and I felt like we were close. And, at Christmas, you were the same. Just be like that. Tell me the truth.'

Valerie rested her palms flat on the desk. 'What's the point of trying, hmm? It's better to be married to John than to deal with the aftermath of breaking off the engagement.'

'Is it, though? I don't claim to like your career, Mum, but you love it. I mean, you really do. You're good at it – he's not. He might be a minister now, but I can't see it lasting. He's too abrasive, he doesn't fit in with the new regime. Are you really going to shackle yourself to someone who'll be lower down the food chain than you in a few years?'

'Oh, Amy, you make this sound like a master plan. I don't have one, not anymore.'

Amy studied her for a moment. In front of a packed chamber, she was self-assured and articulate. Whenever she took part in television or radio interviews, she ran rings around political commentators and opposing members alike, barely letting them find solid ground on one point before skewering them on another. This was like another woman, brittle to the touch.

'Answer me two questions,' Amy said finally. 'And be honest with me. I swear, Mum, if you're not . . .'

Valerie raised her chin. 'I will, I'll be honest.'

'Did you cheat on Max at all?'

'Not in the – I flirted with him, yes. And, yes, I made him believe that I might want something more, but I never intended to follow through on any of it. That kiss at the hospital was one of about half a dozen, that's all. I know that doesn't excuse it, but it wasn't cheating. At least, I don't think it was.'

'I think that's between you and Max.' Amy paused and met Valerie's eye. 'Were you really going to do it, though?

After the election, were you really going to stand up and be publicly in a relationship with Max?'

'Yes,' Valerie answered with a limp smile. 'I knew I'd have to in the end. I told myself I'd just get the election out of the way. I didn't think we could break.'

'You never do,' Amy said.

'But I can't fix it, not now. There's nothing I can do.'

Amy squinted at her. 'Seriously, Mum? I mean, you fought with the local party to become the candidate, you overturned a majority, you've made speeches in front of the rowdiest bunch of arseholes in the country, and you're telling me there's nothing you can do to get out of this mess? You're being a coward. If you're saying you're happy here, I'll shut up and we're done. But if you're not . . .'

She allowed the thought to dangle. Valerie pressed the sleeve of her suit to her face and watched as it came back smeared with mascara. She stared at it for a moment then cleared her throat – once, twice.

'I'm not happy,' she said as she straightened her shoulders. 'And I'm sick of being a coward.'

The shouting rattled through the house the next morning. Amy stumbled to the top of the stairs and leaned on the banister, keeping one hand steady against the wall.

'No,' Foster was saying, 'you still haven't told me why.'

'It's the twenty-first century, John, I don't have to explain myself. If you're still curious in thirty years, you can read my memoirs, although I think you'll have it figured out by then.'

Amy stifled her laugh as she teased the sleep from her eyes.

'What does that bloody well mean?' Foster demanded. 'When we went to bed –'

'We didn't, though, did we? You passed out drunk on the sofa.'

'Well, you wouldn't –'

259

'No, I wouldn't, and do you wonder why? I'm sorry, I truly am, but this is over. There's nothing to be gained by prolonging it, and I'm certainly not leaving it open for debate. Please, just get your things together and go.'

'I'm staying the weekend!'

'Not here, you're not. If you refuse to leave, I'll call the police and that'll look good on the front pages of the Sunday tabloids, won't it? I can keep quiet, John, about all of it. The drink problem, the arrogance, the things you've said behind peoples' backs – that can all be kept strictly between us, as long as you go peacefully. I'll dribble the news into a press release or something. It'll just fizzle out and neither of us is to blame. You don't love me any more than I love you. It's not an engagement, it's a transaction. I'm sure you've had your fair share of those in the past, but I've seen the light and I'm not prepared to be one of them.'

Amy smile grew as she imagined the look on Valerie's face right now. She only wished she could see the expression on Foster's.

'Are you screwing someone else, is that it?' he queried.

'No, but I'd like to.'

He sniggered. 'Whoring your way to the top? You're all the same. Get out of my way.'

The hall table clattered as he walked into it. Amy heard the wood screech just before he stepped into her line of sight. He yanked the front door open and let in a gust of summer air that rippled up the stairs and curled around her shoulders.

'John?' Valerie called after him. 'Your wallet and keys are on the kitchen table. Remember to move the seat back. I had to drive home if you recall because you were unable to walk in a straight line when we left the meeting.'

He swore and stomped back into the house. It took him thirty seconds to retrieve his things then he made sure to slam the door until the house reverberated. The car squealing away outside probably brought half the neighbours to their windows.

Amy padded down the stairs to find Valerie in the hallway. She was immaculately groomed, dressed for business in one of her pinstriped suits with make-up flawlessly applied. Her eyes were brighter than Amy had seen them in months.

'So, that went well,' Amy commented as she rounded the banister.

Valerie broke out into a laugh, a genuine laugh that echoed around the hallway. She stretched a hand out then faltered and allowed it to flutter back to her side. Amy swept forward to gather her into a hug, resting her chin on her shoulder.

'I'm proud of you,' she said. 'Whatever happens next, I'm proud of you.'

# Chapter 39

'What's up with you lately? I'm the one not sleeping and you're the one in a strop.'

Max chucked her pen onto the desk. 'Leave it, Drew.'

'I'm just saying.'

'Yeah, every bloody day,' she snapped. 'I'm off out in the cab.'

'Hold up, I thought you were doing the accounts.'

'Changed my mind,' she answered on her way to the door.

His arguments followed her out onto the street. At least when the door swung shut, she had a bit of peace. This part of town shut down on Sundays, so even the paper shop was closed. The most noise she could hear was their swing sign clanking in the breeze.

She leaned back against the brick wall and closed her eyes for a minute. Then something blocked her light and she opened them again. She'd expected Drew to have followed her out, not to have Valerie standing there with her arms curled around her stomach.

'Hi,' Valerie said.

Max pushed off from the wall, knotting her hands behind her back. 'What are you doing here? Is Amy okay?'

'She's fine, but you see more of her than me so . . .'

'Not for a few days. We've been missing each other.'

'She's enjoying it, you know,' Valerie replied with a smile. 'It was good of you to give her the job. I'm sure it would've been easier not to under the circumstances.'

'There's no reason I wouldn't.'

'No, I – I know that, I didn't mean to . . .' Valerie sighed, scrubbing her forehead with her palm. 'Here I go, making a mess of this again. I'm sorry. What I'm trying to say is that it's good you two are friends. You're good for her. She's been lucky in that respect. I mean, her father might have been completely useless, but she had Tim before and she's got you now. I didn't do too badly on that score.'

Max swallowed. She could count on one hand the number of times Valerie had voluntarily mentioned Amy's real father. Even though she still didn't know his name, she knew enough about what had happened to realise it'd left Valerie with a few scars. Here she was, freely opening up those old wounds in the middle of the town. Something wasn't right.

'Amy's always got me,' Max said finally when the silence stretched a bit.

'Does it hurt?' Valerie asked. 'Having her around. Whenever I'm with her, it feels –'

'What do you want?' Max interrupted.

Valerie tugged at her sleeves. 'Can we go somewhere private? I really need to talk to you.'

Max hesitated, just long enough for the confidence to drain out of Valerie's eyes. That was aggravated by Drew suddenly bursting out of the office and pulling up short at the sight of the pair of them. Valerie's sincerity vanished behind the stony stare she usually reserved for people she didn't want to waste a smile on.

'What are you doing here?' Drew questioned.

'This is really nothing to do with you,' Valerie answered. 'I'm here to see Max.'

'Yeah, go find another street corner to hang out on.'

'That's a little rude, isn't it?'

Drew growled. 'Oh, piss off back to your fiancé.'

'The engagement's off, actually.'

It was said so casually that Max reckoned she'd misheard at first. She lowered her eyes towards the pavement ridges, trying to get rid of that buoyant flicker in her chest. It faded into an ache, but she still didn't trust herself to say anything.

'Dump you, did he?' Drew asked.

Valerie coughed. 'As I said, this is none of your business, so, if you don't mind . . .'

'Bugger off and leave us alone. Or maybe I'll go to the papers, tell them exactly why you're sniffing round here and why that Foster's dumped you.'

Max looked up, seeing Valerie's hackles rise. 'Oi, give it a rest, the pair of you.'

'Get inside,' Drew muttered as he reached for her arm.

'I can walk,' Max insisted.

He still kicked the door open and guided her through it. One glance over her shoulder was all she managed before he slammed the door. The switchboard was blaring, but he slapped her arm away when she went to answer it.

'Was that planned? You and her – out there. Had you planned to meet her?'

Max kicked her heel back into the sofa. 'Not that it's anything to do with you, but no. What about you? What were you doing following me?'

'You never got into the cab,' he said with a shrug. 'I was worried. Seems I had right.'

'I don't need a bloody bodyguard, Drew. And I can't stay cooped up in here all day either.'

She pushed past, dodging well out of the way of his hands this time.

'Don't follow her,' he shouted as she left. 'Don't be an idiot, Max.'

## Chapter 40

Amy had been watching the door for twenty minutes. The moment the bell jingled and she caught sight of the expression on Valerie's face, her stomach dropped. She signalled to Ed and he had a filter coffee in front of Valerie before she'd even taken her jacket off.

'Thank you, Ed,' she said, attempting a smile.

He nodded then made his escape back to the counter. Amy turned her attention to Valerie, noticing how her thumbs were knocking against her cup unconsciously. She suddenly pulled her shoulders back and took a sip of coffee.

'A resounding victory by the Opposition,' she said.

Amy sighed. 'I'm sorry.'

'I can't say I blame her, sweetheart. I know how much trust it took for her to let me in at all. I'd be a fool to think I can talk my way out of this one.'

'She does love you,' Amy said.

'It'd be nice if that was the panacea it professes to be.' Valerie paused and inched her fingers across the clefts in the wood. 'If it were, perhaps I could make up for all I've done to hurt you over the years. I'd hoped that if I could get Max back, I may get you as well.'

A lump had formed in Amy's throat that she couldn't get rid of.

'Stupid, I know,' Valerie added abruptly.

'No, it's not,' Amy said, grabbing her hand before it disappeared from the table. 'But, Mum, there's something I need to . . .'

Valerie squeezed her fingers. 'What do you need, darling? I'll do anything, I promise.'

'It's me, it's about – I've got to tell you the truth. I've screwed up really badly and I've been hoping it'll go away, but it won't.'

'Are you pregnant?' Valerie asked, casting a glance towards the counter.

'No,' she replied.

'Well, then, everything else is completely manageable. I may like Ed, but I'm not sure either of you are ready for parenthood. I know I wasn't, as do you.'

'I'm not sure that's fair.'

Valerie picked up her coffee with her free hand. 'I would've thought you'd be the first to agree. I was hardly a model mother.'

'You know, I wanted to believe that,' Amy said with a grimace. 'I think I fooled myself into just remembering all the times you'd told me off or we'd argued. I mean, you were always the one to tell me off for everything.'

'Well, your father was a peacemaker, that's all. He worked a lot, there was no need for the pair of you to be upset with each other on an evening.'

'So, you deliberately took on the role of the bad guy?'

'I've always been rather good at it,' Valerie said.

'Don't be blasé,' Amy warned.

'I apologise. I only meant that your father deserved a strong relationship with you.'

'And you thought you didn't?'

'Amy . . .' Valerie extracted her fingers and wound them around the hem of her jacket. 'In the spirit of honesty, can I tell you something that I've never told anyone? Not your father, not Max.'

'Okay,' she murmured.

Valerie's chin trembled. She took another sip of coffee then let out a long breath.

'I booked in for an abortion, darling. The only thing your biological father did for you was pay for it and, as far as he knows, I went through with the procedure. My mother had completely disowned me by that point and I was on my own in that waiting room, just thinking and wondering. The best thing to do would've been to close my mind to it, but I was young. I couldn't help picturing you – a girl, I wanted a girl – and I couldn't go through with it. So, I walked straight out of there with a goal to

266

find you a father, and I did. Sure, I saved myself from ritual humiliation and a life on benefits, but it was never just about that. I grew up in a squalid flat with a pair of alcoholics who cared more about themselves than their kids. I watched how they lived. I always wanted more for me, and I would've been damned before I let you anywhere near that environment. You deserved everything I could give you.'

Tears were glistening in her eyes by the time she concluded. Amy stretched across the table to rub her arm, unable to speak again. It took a few moments for her to find her voice and then she turned the subject back full-circle.

'I didn't apply to Durham, Mum. The college wouldn't let me go for Law and I failed the LNAT too.'

Valerie's lips parted, but she was out of her chair in an instant. Amy recoiled as she swept around the table then she found herself cocooned in her warm arms. She let out a shuddering sob and burrowed in further.

'Oh, sweetheart, I'm so sorry,' Valerie whispered. 'I won't let you down again, I promise.'

# Chapter 41

The bar wasn't heaving, but it was busy enough for the middle of the day.

Max got herself a beer first off, numbing her brain against the thumping of some dance track she'd never heard before. It'd been a few years since she'd been in here, not that the place had changed much. The grimy back corner where the pool table was had fresh stains across the walls and the ruts in the floor had deepened. She took up root over there, sticking a 50p piece next to the chalk. It wasn't long before a woman wandered over and took her up on the offer. She wasn't a blonde, thank God.

'What's your name?' Max asked as she racked up.

'Louise. How about you?'

She handed her a cue. 'Doesn't matter. You break.'

It was foreplay, the way Louise played pool. Every angle, every moan when she missed a pot had been dragged out of some cheap manual on how to pull someone. She strutted around the table as if she was thinking of hopping up onto the felt and opening her legs. Max didn't rise to the bait, not at first. She saw the game through then excused herself to go to the loo.

Louise followed her in, unfastening her belt before they'd even got into the cubicle. She tried to lose herself in the sensation of a hand slipping into her underwear, but the frigid finger was too unfamiliar. Max yanked the hand out and shoved her away.

'Thought you might want to be in control,' Louise said with a smirk. She raised her skirt above her hips, showing off the black lace underneath. 'Come on, then. Make it hurt.'

The instruction stuck in the air until Louise flushed. She let her skirt fall and barged past her on her way out of the door.

'You're a freak,' she snapped. 'It's your loss.'

There wasn't enough alcohol in the world to keep Max's brain from turning over what Valerie had said about the engagement being off. She left the cab outside the bar and walked back through the town, trying to get her head straight.

Her feet took her in the direction of the café, while she wondered if Amy would be there on her day off and whether she knew about the engagement being cancelled. It wasn't guaranteed that Valerie would tell her about that, considering she hadn't told her she was engaged to Foster in the first place.

No one wanted to stay in the town centre once the shops were shut, especially with all the scuzzy bars opening up down the bottom of the town. Good for business, bad for everything else, so Max had commented to the lads last week. She dodged around the clumps of smokers on the pavements, earning a few elbows in the ribs for not looking where she was going.

The café lights were on. It was only when Max got closer that she realised something was bothering her. A swish of a head enlightened her as to what it was then she stopped, stubbing her toe on a paving slab. Ed was passing Valerie a cup and the pair of them talked for a second before going over to join Amy by the window.

Max squinted until her eyes smarted. Then she turned around and walked back up the way she'd come. The only way she could think to get rid of the foul taste in her mouth was to veer straight into the first bar she passed.

# Chapter 42

Staying with a repentant Valerie was better than staying with a grouchy Biddy. It gave Amy time to clear her head and work out how she was going to approach the future. It also allowed her to keep an eye on Valerie, who'd been increasingly erratic since Monday. She'd gone completely AWOL on Thursday and Amy had vaguely heard her tumble in after midnight.

The house was quiet again on Friday morning.

On her way downstairs, Amy glanced through Valerie's open door and grimaced. The bed sheets had been dragged onto the floor and there was a distinctive leg cavity where she'd obviously extracted a trapped limb. Both wardrobe doors were flung open, with several blouses pooling on to the shoes below. Items had been pulled loose and thrown haphazardly onto hangers, including her favourite suit jacket that hung limply against the door.

Amy frowned and took the stairs two at a time. She hoped to find Valerie in the kitchen nursing a hangover, but no such luck. Now her stomach was beginning to churn. She started to go back upstairs to get her phone, then she caught sight of the newspaper poking through the letterbox. Even though it was curled over, a flash of blonde hair was unmistakable. She ripped it out of the bristles and stared at the headline: *Local MP in Lesbian Sex Shocker.*

Black spots swam in front of her eyes, blurring the words together. She stuffed the paper underneath her arm and bolted back up to her bedroom. Her phone was on the bedside table, night mode still activated. It was brimming with messages and missed calls from nearly everyone in her phonebook, including Drew and Elena. When she skimmed through the list, though, she couldn't find anything from Valerie, Biddy, or Max.

Even as she stood there staring, another call buzzed through.

'Elena?' she murmured as she answered it.

'You've seen it already. I'm sorry, I thought I could get to you first.'

'I – I don't understand. I didn't – I couldn't read it. And I don't know where Mum is. Her room looks like – Was it Max?'

Silence stretched over the line until it snagged in Amy's throat.

'You think it was,' she said.

'Amy, honestly, I don't know. She's hardly been at work since that episode on Monday. And, when she's there, she's in a foul mood and she's got a hangover. Maybe she could've called the papers when she was out of it or told someone else who did.'

'I can't imagine her even doing that,' Amy admitted.

'Then what about Foster?' Elena asked after a moment. 'With the engagement off, he's got motive. It makes him look like the injured party.'

'No, she didn't tell him about Max. She just sent him off with a flea in his ear.'

'A man like that could get information.'

'Not in a week, not that much.'

Elena paused. 'Has your gran seen it, do you think?'

'I've had no missed calls or messages from her.' Amy squeezed her eyes shut, picturing the house on a typical morning. 'But it could've given her a heart attack, couldn't it? I should check, I should –'

'I'll take care of that,' Elena interrupted. 'I'll go around there and keep things calm while you try to find your mum. I know she pretends she's tough, but everything's just blown apart for her. She must be feeling that, and I know you care.'

Amy took a long breath and opened her eyes. 'She might have gone to Max. She might be there. I'll – I'll get a taxi.'

'Don't worry about that. Drew's already on his way.'

It wasn't often that Drew was quiet, at least not in Amy's experience. He was usually complaining about something, often through a mouthful of biscuits or Yorkshire Tea. To sit beside him mute in the driver's seat was the surest sign that something had gone badly wrong.

'I don't like your mum, you know that,' he said suddenly when they were a mile from Max's.

'I know,' Amy muttered.

'She's messed Max around something chronic and she's not been the mum to you she should've been.'

Amy tapped her thumb on the side window. 'You know, she's not as bad as I've made her out to be.'

'I wasn't saying –'

'It's not that she's like Elena's parents. If I needed her, she wouldn't abandon me. That's what her mum did to her the moment she got in trouble.'

Drew swallowed. 'Right.'

'Do you get it now?' Amy pressed.

'I didn't –'

'She's not evil, she's not. She's done some stupid stuff, but she still my mum, okay?'

'Okay,' he echoed, shooting her a sideways glance. 'Amy, you know it wasn't me, yeah?'

'Of course I do,' she replied with a snort. 'You're too scared of Elena to risk it.'

Three minutes of persistent knocking hadn't achieved anything.

Every second that they stood there tightened the knot in Amy's stomach. A closed door was indicative of Max's guilt, even if she didn't want to believe it. She was about to pull Drew away when the door was yanked open and Max squinted at them.

'What the hell's all the banging about?'

Amy opened her mouth, but the words died in her throat. She looked to Drew and he handed over the newspaper he'd been tapping against his leg before stepping back a few paces. Amy didn't follow suit. She wanted to see Max's face while she read the article. The flash of horror was brief, but it was enough.

'Where is she?' Max questioned. 'Is she all right?'

'I don't know,' Amy replied. 'I'm worried for her. Since Monday, she's been all over the place.'

Even if they didn't mention exactly what had occurred on Monday, they all knew what she was referring to. Max bit into her lip until it whitened and Drew scuffed his sleeve against the wall. Amy sighed, taking the paper back from Max and folding it into quarters.

'Max, when she broke up with Foster, she lit a stick of dynamite. If he did this to her because she wanted to get away from him and try to do the right thing finally . . . Well, I don't care if other people think she deserves it. I know she doesn't. She's my mum and we're in this together.'

'That's good,' Max murmured, running a hand through her hair.

'And what about you?'

'What do you mean?'

'Are you in it too?' Amy asked.

Max shot a glance at Drew then cleared her throat. 'I need to know she's all right. I owe you that, even if I don't owe her.'

## Chapter 43

Thank God for social media.

That wasn't something Max had ever thought before, but, since Valerie had turned both her mobiles off, that was the way they found her. There was a post on Twitter about the local MP getting drunk in a cocktail bar in the town centre. Max hadn't even heard of the place, neither had Drew. He drove them over without so much as a sarcastic comment and parked up around the corner, promising to wait. Whatever was going on in his head at the minute, Max was just grateful he wasn't kicking off.

The bar was above an estate agent's, up a dank stairwell that rivalled some of the grimiest clubs she'd ever been in. Then, suddenly, they were in a massive room, full of glistening glass and panoramic views over the town. From here, the hospital was the focal point, glittering in the afternoon sunlight while apartment blocks and office buildings loomed around it. Jazz music was echoing around the bar, coming from a proper piano in the corner.

'Whoa . . .' Amy murmured.

'Yeah,' Max agreed.

She was looking around for a flash of blonde hair, but there was nothing yet. A large window separated the bar into two halves, offering a bit of privacy without blocking the views. Max motioned Amy through the gap and there was Valerie, perched on a stool at the bar chatting to a bemused barman while a cocktail glass wobbled in her hand. She might've been oblivious to everything outside her bubble, but the other customers were blatantly staring.

Amy nudged Max. 'That one's filming it.'

Heat raced through her body. She didn't know what she was doing until she snatched the phone out of the guy's hand and squeezed it in her fist.

'Oi, what are you doing?' he demanded.

She fended him off with one hand while trying to work out how to delete the video with the other. Amy grabbed it

274

and pressed a few buttons before slamming it down on the table. The man glanced between them then shrank back into his seat.

'Max,' Amy hissed with another elbow into her stomach.

Except for the music, everything else in the bar was quiet. Max twisted around to find Valerie slipping off her stool like a cat, staring at her the whole time.

'Max,' she whispered.

She risked a step forwards. 'Hiya.'

Valerie hesitated then closed the distance between them, padding over the floor in her tights. She stretched out a hand and took Max's into her own, all the while nibbling on her lip. In the past, she'd taken what she wanted, but this was an outright question.

Max's breath hitched as she lifted her free hand up and trailed it through Valerie's hair. She felt the little buzz of desire against her wrist and couldn't help leaning forward to kiss her until Valerie's fingers had hooked inside her belt and brought them within millimetres of each other. They mutually brought the kiss to an end and rested their foreheads together.

'My knight in shining armour,' Valerie said.

'Habit,' Max replied.

'Can I buy a drink to say thank you?'

She shook her head. 'Just cook me dinner sometime.'

'You've got a deal,' Valerie returned then she kissed her again. 'I love you. And I love Amy – where's Amy?'

They looked sideways at the same time. Amy was watching them with one eyebrow raised and her arms crossed. If Max hadn't seen this a hundred times – from both of them – she might've been worried. As it was, she reached out an arm to Amy and the three of them ended up in a lopsided hug right in the middle of the bar. It was only the click of another phone camera that snapped Max out of the moment, but Valerie grasped her hand.

'Max, it's okay,' she said. 'Let them.'

She frowned, but she didn't have a chance to speak before Amy butted in.

'It was you, wasn't it? You talked to the paper. You leaked your own story.'

Max almost laughed at how stupid the idea was just as the truth of it hit her. Valerie's brand of silence was as good as a confession, snuggling into Max's shoulder like it was her own personal cocoon. All Max could do was manoeuvre her over to the nearest table, a high-backed circular booth slanting towards the grand windows.

'Three Americanos with milk, fast as you can,' she called to the barman.

Judging by the look on Amy's face as she settled into the booth, he'd taken his cue. The three of them sat in silence until the coffees appeared, though Valerie was still curled into Max's side. She made to reach for her cup then Amy caught hold of her hand, forcing her to look up.

'Why didn't you tell me this is what you were planning?' she asked.

Valerie shuffled closer to Max. 'I should've told you. I was scared.'

'Scared of what?'

'Changing my mind,' she answered with a wispy smile. 'I knew it, I knew what I had to do. On Monday, when I realised how alone you'd felt – because you didn't trust me – I knew what I was up against. But I still thought I might bottle out and I didn't want you to think less of me than you already do.'

Amy exhaled. 'Mum, I don't know if you're brave or crazy. Why do it so publicly?'

'I thought it was my only chance. Grand gestures, deeds instead of words. You told me that on election night, do you remember?'

'I remember,' she said.

Valerie turned her face towards Max. 'I hoped if you saw I was serious that . . . Oh, Max, I need a drink for this, a proper drink.'

'Just talk to me for a minute. You look like you've had enough.'

'I'm not drunk,' she insisted.

'You're well on the way. Keep going, come on. You're doing fine.'

'What am I doing?' Valerie asked with a frown.

Max pressed a kiss to her forehead. 'Talking. You're good at it, remember? Carry on. What happened with Foster?'

'Nothing happened. Not when we were together, I promise.'

'Keep talking,' Max instructed, stroking her cheek.

Valerie nodded and kissed her fingers. 'Once you'd – once we'd . . . I thought, why not? It was logical, it made sense. It didn't matter to me whether I was with him or somebody else. It wasn't you, it didn't matter. I just needed to get through the election, deal with it after. But when I lost you, I lost Amy. I lost us – me. And John's useful, he's there. So, why not marry him? What harm could it do? It's the best thing, it is. The best thing for me and my career, and it doesn't do John any harm either. It's right, it's the right thing.'

'Go on,' Max prompted when she stopped.

'Amy had it right, she could see it. She's always been more intelligent than me. I hated John, every little thing he did just grated. Some people you can learn to live with – he's not one of them. I had the job I wanted and that was fantastic, but nothing else was close. Nothing else was right. And, in the end, the job wasn't enough.'

A tear ran down her cheek and Max scooped it up.

'It was perfect,' Valerie continued as she dabbed at her eyes. 'The three of us, it was perfect. But I just had to push and push. I thought it'd ping back into place, all of it. I knew I had to take responsibility – that's what the newspaper article was about. I don't care what the consequences are for my career, I honestly don't. I just need you – both of you.'

When her chin lifted, it was as if she was doubtful what the response was going to be. Max didn't prolong the suspense, kissing her until the answer sunk in. Then, when they broke apart for air, Amy shuffled round the booth and gave Valerie a hug too.

'I'm proud of you,' she said.

Valerie rubbed her arm. 'Not nearly as proud as I am of you. Whatever you choose to do with your life, we're going to be there cheering you on.'

'You bet,' Max added.

Amy straightened her spine, reaching out for her coffee. 'Then we need to talk to Biddy.'

# Chapter 44

The closer they got to Biddy's, the more nauseous Amy felt.

Drew drove them, saying nothing to Valerie during the journey. If that was their idea of a truce, Amy could cope with it. She was far more concerned about what awaited them at Biddy's. To keep herself busy, she messaged Ed with a long thread about everything that had happened so far.

Elena's car was still in the drive when they pulled up. Drew muttered something about staying well out of the way, leaving the three of them to walk across to the door like a troupe of condemned prisoners. Valerie tried the handle and it gave, though the buzzer warned Biddy they were coming. Amy reached out and clutched Max's arm as they went straight through into the conservatory.

Biddy was in her chair with Hannah asleep in her arms. Elena was standing beside the door, gnawing on the inside of her cheek. She glanced over as they came in and Amy knew at once how painful this was going to be.

'Clarice,' Valerie said.

'You're not welcome in my home,' she answered, keeping her gaze fixed on Hannah. 'Amy can stay, of course, but I'd rather she had nothing more to do with you. You're poisonous, absolutely abhorrent.'

Amy's snicker slipped out before she could help it. That brought all eyes over to her, including Biddy's. She quivered at the sight of her next to Max and Hannah began squirming around at the movement. Elena stepped forward to take her then, without hesitation, put her straight into Max's arms. A couple of soothing words and Hannah settled against Max's chest. Meanwhile, the expression on Biddy's face had morphed into something indecipherable.

'Listen, Clarice,' Valerie said after a prolonged silence, 'I refuse to ask for permission. Contrary to what you may believe, my relationship with Max is nothing to do with you. It concerns the two of us and Amy – that's all. I would appreciate your blessing, but, since I already know I have Tim's, I won't beg for it.'

'Timothy wouldn't approve of this,' Biddy snapped.

'Oh, but he would. He was the most generous, openhearted man I've ever met. You know his last wishes, you were there. He wanted Amy to live her life and for me to live mine. I'm only doing what he wanted.'

'You're twisting something noble into something sordid.'

'It has never been sordid. I've been a coward, but I've never been ashamed of Max. Now, I don't want to argue with you. However, there is something else we need to tell you while we're here.'

Amy stiffened until she realised Valerie was referred to the Durham situation rather anything else. Brushing that mess under the carpet while the spotlight was on her relationship with Max was so motherly that it brought a weak smile to Amy's face.

'Okay,' she said.

Biddy's forehead creased as she levered herself from her chair. 'What's this now, hmm? Don't tell me she's marring the gorilla. That'd be the final straw.'

'Ed's a good man,' Valerie answered. 'He owns a business that Tim invested in and he's been nothing but a gentleman all the time I've known him. It's not about him, though.'

'Go on,' Biddy muttered and Valerie crossed her arms.

'Amy isn't going to Durham. She doesn't enjoy Law and, as a result, her tutors refused to let her apply. She'll be taking a bit of time out and seeing what she wants to do with her life.'

Nothing happened. At first, Amy wondered whether Biddy had heard or understood, then she saw her nails working against the fabric of her trousers. She shrank closer to Valerie while Max shushed Hannah behind them. A glance at Elena suggested she wished she was anywhere

280

else, but she stayed still and let Biddy's silent fury ripple through the room. Biddy eventually fixed her attention back on Amy.

'Is this true?' she queried.

'Yes,' she said as Valerie slotted an arm around her waist. 'Please, please, don't be mad. I tried so hard to do everything you wanted me to, but I couldn't. And I thought that – that Dad wanted me to do it as well until I realised that he loved me anyway, whatever I did. It didn't matter – it doesn't matter – it still doesn't. He chose Law because he loved it, didn't he? You wanted him to be a doctor. If I suddenly decide I want to be a doctor, does that mean I'm doing what you wanted him to do?'

Biddy frowned. 'Do you want to be a doctor?'

'No. Maybe. I don't know. I haven't been able to think of anything except Law since he died. But, the point is, he didn't follow the path you wanted for him, but you still wanted me to follow him down that path. And I know why.'

'You know everything,' Biddy replied.

'You miss him,' Amy said, feeling the crack in her voice before she heard it. 'The same way I do. The same way Mum does. You think that me going into Law is him living on or something. I don't need to do that to make him live on in my head or Mum's. Why would he want me to do something I don't love just to stay close to him? He wouldn't, Biddy. You know that as well as I do.'

'But it's your future!'

'I'll find another, I just don't know what it is yet.'

'At your age, that's the death knell for any career. You mark my words –'

'Biddy, please, it isn't. I haven't been able to think logically in the last few years, not really. You know, I don't think I grieved properly. I got so caught up in being angry and trying to be this person I wasn't that I didn't let myself grieve. I think I need to do that, maybe you do too.'

281

'She doesn't need to,' Biddy said, jabbing a finger towards Valerie. 'She's already moved on to this degenerate new –'

'Please, don't,' Amy interrupted.

'How on earth can you condone it?'

'Dad would've loved to see us happy again.'

'You can't seriously tell me you approve of it.'

Amy let out a chuckle. 'Approve of it? Biddy, I love Max. She's already like a second mum to be, things are better when she's around. That's the way it's meant to be and – and, if you can't accept that, we've got a problem.'

Horror crept over Biddy's face as all the colour drained out of it. Amy saw the attack looming and darted forward to catch her before she fell.

'Where's her spray?' Valerie asked.

'Handbag,' Amy said.

Biddy struggled away, trying to steady herself. 'I don't need it.'

'Well, do you want to end up in hospital or worse? You need the spray.'

'Fine,' she muttered.

Once they'd settled her back into her chair, it took a few minutes for the spray to take effect. Elena discreetly excused herself with Hannah, leaving Max and Valerie hovering by the door. Amy had started off by Biddy's side, but she'd edged away as the danger faded. She ended up between Valerie and Max, something that immediately caught Biddy's attention when she came back into her herself.

'You can't expect me to simply accept this,' she said.

Max coughed and took a step forward. 'Can I say something?'

That surprised all of them. Amy exchanged a glance with Valerie then they both raised an eyebrow when Biddy assented in a murmur. Max scuffed her hand through her hair and spoke directly to Biddy.

'You're within your rights to think whatever you want about me. I can't change it so I've learned not to care. But I know something about pushing away your family and not treating them right. That's what Elena's parents did and all that happened was it pushed her closer to Drew.'

'She told me,' Biddy said.

'Yeah, and my parents wanted me to be something I'm not. So, I decided to carry on being me and stuff them. They'd have to crawl back on their hands and knees for me to listen to anything they had to say now. Elena's parents would have to do the same, I reckon, and they're missing out on Hannah – their granddaughter. But Amy's here and she's asking you to just – I don't know – suspend your disbelief. Maybe that's it. Suspend your disbelief for a bit and let it play out. No snap decisions, no words you can't take back.'

Biddy tapped her fingers together. 'Suspend my disbelief, you say?'

'I can tell you what'll happen if you don't,' Max replied.

'I'd rather you didn't, thank you.'

'Right, so what's it to be?' Max questioned. 'Keep your granddaughter or push her away? Because that's what it comes down to.'

Biddy clenched her jaw and closed her eyes. Amy held her breath for a second, wondering what the response would be, but the expression on her face when she opened her eyes again was more like resignation than anything else. She exhaled and met Biddy's gaze.

'Thank you,' she said.

'I still don't like it,' Biddy warned. 'Any of it. And I want to see progress, young lady. You can't sit about doing nothing all day.'

'I won't,' she promised. 'But it's going to be the right kind of progress this time.'

# Chapter 45

'Honestly, when was the last time you opened a window?'

Max ignored both Valerie's comment and Amy's snort, though she found identical looks of disdain on their faces when she flicked the light on. She watched Amy nudge the door shut then the three of them stood motionless in the hallway.

'All right, it smells,' she conceded.

'I thought I'd housetrained you,' Valerie said. 'Now, you get the bleach and I'm opening every window in the place. Just be grateful it's summer and not the dead of winter.'

'We could just go to a hotel,' Max suggested.

Valerie slipped her coat off. 'At a hotel, we'll be easily exposed. If you don't mind, I want an evening where I don't have to think about politics or the mess that my career's in. I'd like to savour the moment, preferably without the stench of decaying pizza in the air, so, if you don't mind . . .'

'Fine, all right,' Max said. 'Get on with it then.'

She watched Valerie's little smirk as she swept through into the living room before turning back to Amy. It looked as if she was still shivering a bit, the way she had been when they'd left Clarice's, and she wrapped an arm round her shoulders.

'How you doing?' she asked.

'Okay, I think,' Amy answered.

'I think we got as far with her today as we could've hoped, you know.'

'No, I know that, I do. I just wish . . . Well, there's more, isn't there? Maybe I should've told her everything and got it all out in the open.'

Max shook her head. 'Come on, you know that would've been the tipping point. Look, you did great. We got her from homophobia to tolerating me in half an hour – that's a bloody miracle. She's accepted that you're not doing Law and that you need time to get your head straight. Much more than that –'

'Much more than that and we might've killed her,' Valerie interjected.

They both looked sideways. Valerie had crept back in without them noticing and was leaning against the wall with a serious expression on her face. She trained her gaze on Amy.

'This was never your mess to deal with, darling. In all the ways that count, Tim was – is – your father. Telling Clarice now would be a way of absolving your conscience, I understand that. But what good would it do you or her? Forget me – I can weather most storms one way or another. You don't deserve to have to do it though. Of course, if you want to tell her, I'll support you. It isn't necessary, that's all. Your dad adored you and you're Clarice's only grandchild, blood or no.'

Amy wiped her eyes with the back of her hand. 'You're right.'

'Thank you,' Valerie said instantly and all three of them laughed. 'So, why don't you order Chinese while we clean up? Did you say Ed was on his way over? Order enough for him.'

The switch in tone was enough to send Amy off to the living room. Max lingered long enough to kiss Valerie then they both followed her through.

They'd just about managed to get the flat smelling right when the buzzer went. It was Ed, breathless and sounding a bit on the crazy side. Once Max'd let him in, she called Valerie and Amy into the hallway. Ed steamed through the door with a wide grin on his face.

'You landed well on your feet,' he said.

'What do you mean?' Max asked.

He pulled out his phone and turned to Valerie. 'This morning, you were public enemy number one, getting it from all sides. The far-right voters were throwing that traditional families crap at you and calling you a cheat, the rest of them were saying you hadn't got the guts to be yourself. A couple of hours later . . .'

After clicking a few buttons, he held up a video on his phone. Max squinted at it then let out a growl. From the angle, it was that little toerag who she'd taken the phone from. He'd gone and taken another video then uploaded it onto Twitter.

'That little git,' she muttered.

'No, you don't get,' Ed replied, throwing a smile at Valerie. 'Everyone's gone crazy over it. Being yourself, being open. You couldn't have planned it better if you'd tried. Apart from the usual arseholes, everyone reckons you've redeemed yourself.'

Valerie's eyes flickered as he pressed the phone into her hands.

'I can assure you, it wasn't planned,' she said.

'Scroll through that though,' he answered. 'You've probably done more for LGBT rep in one day than the rest of your party's done in years.'

Her hand was trembling as she looked at the Twitter feed. Max and Amy read most of it over her shoulder and, for the most part, it was all positive stuff. Yeah, there was the odd comment from a homophobe, but that was shut down by a dozen voices one after the other.

'Mum, this is brilliant,' Amy said.

Valerie just pressed her lips together and Max cleared her throat.

'Why don't you two go find us something to watch?' she suggested.

Although Amy opened her mouth to argue, Ed yanked her away before she got the chance. Max steered Valerie into the bedroom and sat her down on the edge of the bed. By the time she'd shut the door and turned back, tears were streaming along her cheeks.

Max knelt in front of her. 'It's all right.'

'No, it isn't.'

'It is,' Max insisted, but Valerie just shook her head.

'I was meant to lose. If I win – if I come out of this with no consequences – then I've failed.'

'How have you failed?'

'I deserve consequences, I deserve some punishment for what I've done to you and Amy. If I get to keep my job without a fight then I've basically got away scot-free. At least if I'd had to fight –'

'You did fight,' Max interrupted, rubbing circles into her knee. 'You leaked your own story to the papers, you risked your career and everything else when you didn't know what would come out of it. If that's not fighting, I don't know what is. What good would being punished do?'

'I'd feel as though I deserved you and Amy,' Valerie said.

Max exhaled and moved to sit beside her on the bed, keeping one hand fixed on her leg. She felt the quivering that Valerie was trying to keep control of, so she twisted sideways and rested a hand on her cheek. She'd missed looking into these eyes that she couldn't get to calling just blue, however long she thought about it. They were sapphire, sparkling sapphire.

'It's not for you to decide what you deserve,' she said after a moment. 'We're here because we want to be, because you've shown us what we needed you to. That's all it was about. Through the election, I didn't care that you were keeping quiet about us so long as it wasn't permanent and you weren't being a hypocrite. What you did to Drew was the icing on the cake then seeing you with that prat . . . You deserved me walking away, I couldn't have done anything else.'

Valerie licked her lips and nodded. 'I know.'

'But what you've done this last week to try and atone for it, that's what matters. That's why I'm here, that's why Amy's here. You've still got bridges to build with Drew, but he looks like he's willing to listen. That's all because you put yourself at risk. I didn't think you'd do it, neither did Amy.'

'I had to,' Valerie murmured.

287

'There you go, then,' replied Max with a smile. 'So, you put yourself out there and you risked losing. There's plenty of stuff we still need to talk about, but there aren't any secrets anymore. As long as we're honest with each other, we'll be right.'

Valerie sniffed then rested their foreheads together. 'For someone who doesn't do relationships, you're very good at this, you know.'

'It's not easy,' she admitted. 'I've still got this impulse to run every now and then.'

'But you won't,' Valerie answered.

'I won't,' Max promised. 'If you won't, that is.'

A soft laugh gurgled up in Valerie's throat. There were no mascara streaks down her cheeks this time, but she still had that open expression on her face that Max remembered from the nature reserve car park all that time ago. She couldn't help kissing her, wrapping two arms around her waist and pulling her as close as the laws of physics would let her.

They were both smiling when they separated and Max's body was still tingling.

'I won't run,' Valerie said finally. 'If you won't, of course.'

Max pressed another kiss to her swollen lips. 'Deal.'

## Author Bio

Kit Eyre lives in Wakefield, West Yorkshire, with her long-suffering fiancé.

Her first novel *But By Degrees* was published in 2016, garnering a positive reception from readers both in the UK and beyond.

For more information about Kit, visit her website at www.kiteyre.co.uk. You can also find her on Facebook, Twitter, Instagram, Pinterest and YouTube.

Printed in Great Britain
by Amazon